Crush

by

Christina Strigas

This is a work of fiction. Names, characters, places, and incidents are either the product of the author's imagination or are used fictitiously, and any resemblance to actual persons living or dead, business establishments, events, or locales, is entirely coincidental.

Crush

Contact Information: info@thewildrosepress.com

Cover Art by *Diana Carlile*

The Wild Rose Press, Inc.
PO Box 708
Adams Basin, NY 14410-0708
Visit us at www.thewildrosepress.com

Publishing History
First Edition, 2021
Trade Paperback ISBN 978-1-5092-3894-1
Digital ISBN 978-1-5092-3895-8

Previously Published Muse It Up Publishing 2015
Published in the United States of America

I was running through the dark forest, breathless and thirsty. Blood trickled down from my open wounds. Not that there were many, but enough to not think straight.

Dizzy and weak, it was not surprising that being abandoned was a recurring theme in my life.

I thought we were supposed to be immortal, but apparently no one is. Everyone can die. Everything Hunter had shown me had been a riddle. I was figuring it out now as the night whispered to run as fast as my legs could carry me.

This power frightened me. It'd been only a few days since I'd been born again, and now I wished I was dead.

Not undead.

I stopped running and waited—my eyes shut tightly.

No vision.

Nothing.

I tried again, and then I saw him. His nose was pressed up against the tree trunks, following my trail. He knew my scent. They'd bottled my DNA in a tube and placed it in their vault, I guess in case of AWOL. But what did I know?

Hunter knew exactly what he and his gang were doing when they made me one of them. All I knew was that I hated Hunter. I wished he would die, but he was already undead, and the only way to kill him once and for all was to have him follow my path leading us both to Dr. Pappas, who had the answers I searched for.

I felt petrified and alone. How will I ever escape Hunter?

I closed my eyes and sprang into the air like a cat. Thoughts of Jack raised my spirit and gave me the kick-start to fly faster than the wind itself.

I will find you, Jack, and I will bring you back.

Praise for Christina Strigas

"For lovers of romance, the paranormal, fantasy and even disbelieving, non-followers of these genres, there is substance, values, and dreams to be explored in beautifully written, descriptive, action-packed storytelling that will capture the reader's attention, and provide entertainment and surprise until the very end in wonderfully artistic prose that will remain in your heart long after the final page has been turned."

~Deborah Bownman, author of Living In A Shadow

"This book grabbed me from the start! It's chock full of vivid detail and emotional oomph, putting the reader smack dab in the thick of the story as it unfolds. The paranormal elements have enormous appeal and are highly authentic."

~S.A Healey, author of Empty Me Out

Dedication

To all the soulmates out there still searching for each other.

Part One: Maria

"Don't forget to count the ways you love me."

Prologue
2009

I was running through the dark forest, breathless and thirsty. Blood trickled down from my open wounds. Not that there were many, but enough to not think straight.

Dizzy and weak, it was not surprising that being abandoned was a recurring theme in my life.

I thought we were supposed to be immortal, but apparently no one is. Everyone can die. Everything Hunter had shown me had been a riddle. I was figuring it out now as the night whispered to run as fast as my legs could carry me.

This power frightened me. It'd been only a few days since I'd been born again, and now I wished I was dead.

Not *undead.*

I stopped running and waited—my eyes shut tightly.

No vision.

Nothing.

I tried again, and then I saw him. His nose was pressed up against the tree trunks, following my trail. He knew my scent. They'd bottled my DNA in a tube and placed it in their vault, I guess in case of AWOL. But what did I know?

Hunter knew exactly what he and his gang were doing when they made me one of them. All I knew was that I hated Hunter. I wished he would die, but he was already undead, and the only way to kill him once and for all was to have him follow my path leading us both to Dr. Pappas, who had the answers I searched for.

I felt petrified and alone. *How will I ever escape Hunter?*

I closed my eyes and sprang into the air like a cat. Thoughts of Jack raised my spirit and gave me the kick-start to fly faster than the wind itself.

I will find you, Jack, and I will bring you back to me and count all the ways you loved me on your fingertips, on your toes, and all along your beautiful body.

Chapter One
Let me count the ways
1989

I was twenty-two years old when Jack came into my life like a breeze. I think I fell in love with him in a split second. Okay, it was love at first sight. No matter how corny that sounds, it was true.

I had finally finished university and decided to go to Europe. Some of my friends met up with me for a few weeks in Greece and Italy, but in France I was on my own. I think I preferred it that way, because quite honestly, my friends were driving me nuts. I had wanted to go sightseeing, and all they wanted to do was get drunk every night. I was all for drinking and partying, but I also wished to walk around and visit the land. I had slept all through the island of Paros. We'd wake up at two o'clock in the afternoon, eat, sunbathe, eat, nap, then party till six in the morning. It had been exhausting. My skin looked horrible from all the drinking and smoking.

By contrast, France was a dream. I was by myself, discovering every nook and cranny, side street, café, museum, and shop, as well as the landscape. And what incredible landscape it was! Now I fully comprehended why artists congregated here. Between the landscape of Saint-Tropez and the architecture, there was no way to escape the vortex of France. I was falling into it like a child discovering water and its wonder.

My camera swung around my neck permanently. I

was inspired by my surroundings. My intention had been to stay a few months—until that day on the beach.

I had been taking pictures of the rocks, the sand—whatever caught my eye—at la baie de Pampelonne.

He was far off in the distance, playing the guitar. I saw him through my lens as I turned my head to get a different perspective of the beach.

Bam.

There he was. I snapped the picture immediately. He looked toward my direction, and spoke to me without moving his lips. His presence intrigued me like a mystery novel I'd never read. I continued on my path with my Minolta strap wrapped snugly around my neck, snapping incessantly, my mind preoccupied by his wind and song following my footsteps.

I stopped clicking and looked at him through the lens again. I was a little closer now. His eyes looked right up at mine again, and he smiled, as if posing for me. I'm sure my pupils dilated, but who knows, really, because I was staring at the most beautiful man in my world. My gaze never left his as I let the camera swing down to my chest.

And then he did something that changed my path, made it crooked for a while, made it mine. He waved straight at me like an old friend, and gestured for me to walk toward him. I did just that and observed his beauty from up close. He had brown hair, shaggy, down to his midneck; wild strands fell into his eyes. He swept it back at my approach, and I focused on his light brown eyes, which reminded me of hazelnuts. His skin was another story altogether: dark, sun-kissed, and glowing. He had a nose sculpted by the gods; seriously, it was perfect. His white open shirt hung loosely on him, and his jeans were faded, cut at the seams. I noticed a few rings and bracelets, but I didn't ogle too long. I was only a feet away, and then he started to strum his guitar again. I don't know when he stopped and started again. I felt a little lost. He strummed a pleasant melody, opened his mouth, and sang in a deep, gentle voice. I swear, it was earth-shattering.

"You have a sexy walk.
I can't wait to hear you talk.
Come here and sit by me,
So you can see what I can see.
The ocean vast and blue,
Meant for me and you.
I sit here every day and wait,
But I didn't know my fate
Till I saw your red hair blow
And felt myself aglow."

He sang in a low voice dripping with harmony. I smiled and felt my face flush. No one had ever sung a song for me before. I thought I was going to wake up soon and feel Butchie's tongue—my dog from way back, when I was a kid—licking my face good morning, but nothing like that happened. I was still standing. I wonder if I even blinked.

"That's all I have for now. You understand English?" he asked in a smooth, calming voice that carried a slight English accent.

"Yes, I do. That was beautiful." I'd have bet he sang this over and over again, all the while changing the girl's hair colour. He was definitely a player or a Casanova, as my *yiayia* used to say.

"I just made it up as you were walking and snapping pictures."

"Yeah? Really?" I didn't believe it for a second. He was too good-looking. I'd been warned about men like this.

"Okay, then while you were walking toward me. Do you believe that?"

"No, but keep going. I'm listening."

"Actually, the answer is both."

I didn't reply. My God, he was a specimen. His eyes twinkled like a child's, and his accent was melodic, like a foreign song.

"So, do you want to take another one?"

"Another what?" I asked.

"Picture of me."

I blushed, sure this time I was red like a tomato. I felt my cheeks heat.

"Uh…I wasn't taking a picture of *you.* You just happened to be in the way."

"In the way of what?"

"Uh…the beach." What the hell was I saying? "I mean, the rocks."

He smiled, and I noticed the sweetest dimples. He placed his tanned hand above his eyes to block the sun.

"Which one is it, then? The beach or the rocks?"

"Both, I guess." Now I sounded like him!

"Would you like to sit down?" He gestured for me to sit next to him on a rock.

"I don't know you. For all I know, you could be a…" I had no idea what I was saying.

He prompted me, smiling. "Go on."

"A killer," I blurted out.

"Do I really look like a killer? I'm a lover, not a

fighter," he jested, still showing me the rock as if it were an empty chair.

"I don't know." I remained standing, sweating a little at this twisted conversation that, of course, I had started.

"Try something else." His smile was contagious. I laughed.

"A rapist?"

"Now you're getting crazy." He laughed loud, and I felt as tiny as one of the grains of sand at my feet.

"I'm not crazy, just careful."

"Well, you did come over here."

"And now I'm leaving." I turned to go and took a few steps away.

"Wait up!" he cried. "I'm just teasing you. You seemed like an easy target. Sorry about that. Let's start over. So, are you going to tell me your name?"

I stayed where I was, and said, "You never asked." I was flustered by his physique as he stood up, walked toward me, and towered over me by a foot. It was like a favourite billboard of a male model coming to life before my very eyes.

"What's your name?" he asked me gently.

"Maria." I extended my hand.

"Maria, it is exciting to meet you. My name is Jack." He shook my hand, and I burst out laughing.

"What's so funny? You find my name funny?"

"You're really good, you know."

"At what?"

"At playing the game."

"What game? I hadn't realized we were playing a game. If I knew that, I would have put on my game face."

The conversation was knotting me up inside. I really

had to be on my toes with this man. He looked me up and down, and I felt his gaze linger for a few seconds too long on my chest. Feeling slightly self-conscious, I squirmed, but then his eyes rested on my face, and I tried to imagine what he was thinking. I was wearing jeans, a bejeweled turquoise shirt, and sandals. My red hair was long and straight, down to my butt, and it kept blowing around in the wicked wind; it seemed to have a life of its own.

I had to snap out of it and continue with what I was doing. But I'd forgotten what I was doing. His eyes were locked with mine while his guitar hung on the side of his left arm like a best friend. I didn't know what to say next…so I ran off at the mouth. "Well, it was nice meeting you…Uh…I have to go, Jack. Take care."

"Nice? That's a horrible word. We use that word too often."

Of course, he was right; I gave him that. I tried again. "It was interesting meeting you."

"Interesting? I don't know which is worse, nice or interesting. I find it exciting to meet you, and you find me nice and interesting to meet me?"

He gave me another smile.

I voiced the next word that entered my head, because I felt cornered by his witticism. "Intriguing!"

"Now we're talking. That's a word to build on."

I burst out laughing again, feeling a little edgy, like a cat on a hot tin roof.

"What's so funny this time?" he asked, smiling wider.

"You are."

"How so?"

"In many ways."

"Ah, 'How do I love thee? Let me count the ways.'"

"Elizabeth Barrett Browning. Sonnets from the Portuguese," I quickly replied.

"You are a smart cookie, Maria." His eyes glowed. He pronounced my name by rolling the *R*, and my heart skipped a beat.

"Chocolate flavour or oatmeal?" I joked. "That's what my grandmother used to say to me." I looked away, embarrassed.

"Now *I'm* intrigued. You intrigue me as well, Maria."

Fire burned my cheeks and neck.

"Though rosy cheeks within his bending sickles compass come."

"Shakespeare. The Love Sonnets." I laughed hard now. He was testing me. I had had to memorize that particular poem for my creative writing class in college.

"I think, Maria, you are the one I have been waiting for. I was told you were coming, and I have been waiting every day. What guy believes in psychics? Not many, but I surely do."

I started to feel anxious again.

"Come, let's sit down." We took a few steps to the rocks and sat next to each other.

"I have a friend. His name is Hunter. He is kinda special."

"How is he special?"

"He can see the future. Like I said, he's a psychic." He looked so at ease, I didn't know what to think. I was perplexed; that was for certain.

"No, I'm not crazy. I can tell by your expression that you don't know what to think. I'll just tell you a few things about my relationship with the occult. I believe in spirits, ghosts, psychics, and the supernatural world beyond ours."

"Are you in some kind of cult?" Was he trying to brainwash me with his good looks?

"No." He laughed. "You're funny. I am a free thinker. A free spirit, if you like. I could never be part of a cult."

"Phew. You scared me for a second."

"Now, my friend Hunter is a different story. He has followers, but he is not a leader of anything. The lost souls just adore him, place him on a pedestal. He is their so-called 'Master.'"

"That sounds exactly like a cult to me." I got up to go. "I have to leave now."

"Don't let that intimidate you. I'm not part of anything. Let's talk about you. Please, sit." The way his eyes begged me pulled me into his tornado.

"What about me?" I asked defensively.

"Who are you? Tell me everything. I am intrigued." There was that smile again.

I sat back down. It was easy to give in to him.

"I was born and raised in Montreal," I stated, but then stopped.

I wasn't about to reveal my life story to Jack. I had issues—big-time issues. Like firstly, I had been abandoned by my mother, and I never knew my father—not even his name. My mother's parents raised me and loved me like their own. My y*iayia* said my mother was a complete failure in her eyes. From the time she was a baby, she defied my grandmother. As a teenager, she would run away at any argument. My grandparents decided to leave Greece and immigrate to Canada. My mother was only seventeen when she came here and completely disengaged from her parents and family. No one had seen her since my birth. She had me, and the next day, she was gone. Not dead. Just gone.

"What are you doing in Saint-Tropez?" His question flashed me back to reality.

"What are *you* doing in Saint-Tropez? You're not French. Where are you from?"

"You can't answer a question with a question. I asked you first." He had a point.

"Well, I'm taking pictures." I smiled.

"I can see that, smarty-pants," he joked, and smiled back.

"I'm a photographer," I said in a serious tone, and that was all he would get for now. "Your turn."

"I'm playing the guitar." He glared at me now, and I couldn't help but smirk. "Can you take down that wall around you?" he asked, and folded his arms across his chest.

No, I couldn't, because I didn't trust anyone—men, women, mothers, fathers, boyfriends, ex-boyfriends…guys I'd just met at a beach. How could I? Everyone had let me down. The only people I felt safe with were old people.

I thought of my *yiayia* and *pappou*, and I pined for them. They'd died a year ago, within months of each other. I missed them so much, it hurt like hell.

"Not ready quite yet," I bounced back at him. The ball was in his court.

"I am exasperated now." He gazed at me and through me as if I were a crystal ball.

"Are you?" I smirked. "Is it because a woman would be eating out of the palm of your hand by now?"

"Now, what makes you presume that, Maria?"

Again that twinkle was in his eyes.

Because you're fuckin' gorgeous. "I just know."

"You certainly know a lot for your age."

"You don't even know how old I am!" I think I shouted this a little too loudly.

"Love the temper. Yes, I can guess. You're twenty-two."

"Let me guess. Your friend Hunter told you."

"You catch on quick."

It was quiet for a second, but I felt jittery. He looked out to the ocean and, without looking at me, asked if I wanted to go for a cup of coffee.

"Yes." I didn't want our conversation to end.

When we got up and walked away, we both turned around at the same time to glance at the spot we just vacated. I instinctively snapped a picture of the rocks and the empty space.

Click.

"I would like to see your pictures one day," he said with an enchanting smile. "Especially that one."

Chapter Two
Bossa Nova Love
2009

I was trying to remain undetected in this undeniable vastness that confused me. My aura had an invisible trace that was indubitably my DNA function.

It was a recall. They wanted me to be revoked, like an overused and abused car no longer allowed to roam the streets. All that kept me going was the remembrance of things past. The title of one of my books that I'd never finished, being capable of reading it wasn't the problem, what with my abundant knowledge of the French language, it was always the time. It seemed that time sped by so fast. Perhaps that was one advantage of being a vampire; I could finally finish reading Proust. I tried to focus on my immediate plan and get my mind back on track.

It was Jack I'd been searching for since anyone had seen him five years ago. He'd disappeared from my life on my birthday. These past forlorn years had been slowly killing me.

I became obsessed with Hunter in my hunt for Jack. Whenever help was needed, I'd call Hunter. Needed a shoulder to cry on, I'd call Hunter. While Jack had been missing, I'd lost my way and turned to Hunter. He ultimately became my best friend.

Hunter would find me soon; he knew my scent like the aroma of a good meal.

I thought of Jack's eyes and how they'd beamed at me; as well, his compassion and loyalty, and felt sick to my stomach. I wanted to scream out in horror, but the only thing left to do was run—run as far away from my demons as my long legs could carry me. The cold breeze refreshed me, smacked me in the face with the awful truth that Jack had disappeared forever.

Closing my eyes, *let the memories flood me*, my inner voice whispered.

****

It was 1989.

Jack took me to a café by the beach, overlooking the ocean.

We sat down and he ordered. "*Deux cafés au lait froids, s'il vous plaît.*"

"How did you know I'd like that?"

"Because we're soul mates." His eyes sparkled.

"And how can you be so sure?"

"I've never felt this way in my entire life," he said nonchalantly, brushing the comment off, not daring to delve into my feelings.

Changing the subject, "How old are you?"

"Twenty-eight." He pulled out a pack of Gauloises cigarettes, when suddenly Axl Rose's voice dominated the café, and humming along came naturally to me as he started to serenade me.

"She's got eyes of the bluest skies…"

"You really do have an amazing voice."

"Thank you." He offered me a cigarette.

"No, thanks. Too strong. Are you in a band?"

"Kinda." He lit his cigarette, inhaled, and offered me one again.

I couldn't say no to those eyes. "Okay."

I put the cigarette in my mouth and waited for him to light it. Inhaling, I almost spit it out, but didn't want to be rude.

He examined me as if I were a patient he had to cure. He watched every move of mine which made me feel uneasy again.

He continued to sing along to the song, and a few people turned their heads, but nothing could have distracted me from him; he was incredible. I was transfixed by him too. He never took his eyes off mine, not even to flick his ashes.

"What is it?"

"You are exquisite." Again, a slight blush enveloped me.

"Especially when you blush."

His eyes were brilliant; his pupils dilated before me, and I couldn't look anywhere else but his fixed stare.

"Why do you take pictures?" he asked.

"Because I'm a photographer." I knew I sounded arrogant, but honestly, I was feeling a bit defensive.

"You've already told me that. Do you work for anyone?"

"No. I'm a free thinker," I said smugly. "A freelancer."

"I love that." He glanced at my lips for a split second. "We have a lot in common."

The waitress arrived with tall glasses of coffee and blue-and-green-striped straws.

"*Merci*," we said simultaneously, then glanced at each other from across the table.

"Do you find a lot of freelance work?" He had an intense look in his eyes, like he was determined to get to some truth.

"Here and there." I didn't really want to get into the minute, boring details of my life.

He frowned. "Can you be more precise?"

"Actually, a few acquaintances hired me to do some work for their companies. I've done family portraits and a few weddings on the weekend to pay the bills. The truth is, I'm in France to take pictures of whatever captures my attention. I would love to exhibit one day."

"You picked the most incredible country to start from. I've been living here in this city for seven years."

"Where did you grow up?" Feeling somewhat dizzy, I butted out my cigarette in the ashtray.

"The question is, where didn't I grow up? I was born in Paris, so actually I am French, and then my family moved to Germany, England, Canada, and the United States. I've changed schools about ten times in my youth, and now I call Saint-Tropez my home. This is the longest I've lived in one city."

"You speak English so well."

"I went to English school in every country I lived in. My parents wanted me to speak English fluently, and my mother adored the British accent. They were both from France, but they worked for the French government."

"Where did you mostly grow up?"

"England and Washington."

"That's a long way off."

"Yeah, I know." He appeared distracted.

His guitar was on the chair next to me, and I instinctively touched it. "Nice guitar."

"Nice?" He laughed.

"Okay. Um…enigmatic." I laughed too.

"An enigmatic guitar…I like the sound of that." He repeated it again, then said, "That would be a great song." He took out a pen from somewhere and grabbed a napkin that was lying on the table.

"Are you a magician?"

"What?" He peeked up at me, already bent over and about to write on the napkin.

"Where did you have the pen stashed?"

"Do you really want to know?" His eyes glittered. "Actually, nowhere exciting. Just my back pocket."

I thought that was exciting enough. I'd never met anyone like him before. I stared at the top of his head as he hunched over and wrote intently. He gave me the impression of an erudite professor. I lit another cigarette and took a puff, enthralled by the fluidity in his motions. His hand flowed like a pastry chef icing a cake. His hair fell in his face, and he gently turned a strand around his ear like a schoolgirl. Jack was definitely the sexiest man I'd ever met.

I didn't disturb his thoughts.

He suddenly stopped writing and glanced up at me. "You are my muse now," he said.

"I've never been anyone's muse before."

His eyes flickered. "You want to hear my song?"

"Sure," I whispered, dying to hear it. I took a puff then exhaled, sipped some coffee, and waited for the mystery to be unveiled.

"My enigmatic guitar strums for you,
To listen to my every word so true.
Pouring out of me like tears,
Tears of joy at seeing your fears.
You try to hide inside a shell;
I'll bring you to my wishing well.
Enigmatic guitar strums for you.

Your eyes are my sun.
Come along with me for a morning run."

He stared at me. "What do you think?"

"That's incredible," I managed to say, a little shocked at how everything rhymed so well.

"I feel so alive right now. It's like I've been dead inside all these years." He pointed toward his heart.

I loved the way he spoke to me, but I couldn't believe he felt so much so soon, so quickly, so passionately.

"What are you thinking, Maria?"

"Jack, you're killing me."

"Never say that." He smirked.

"I mean, your words are unbelievable to me. How can you feel that way?"

"It's easy. I let myself open up to you. You can do the same." He sipped his coffee, staring at me again, waiting for a response.

"You're different from any man I've ever met."

"And you're different from any woman I've ever met. I think we're getting somewhere."

I laughed, probably because of the seductive way he was looking at me.

"I want to see you again." He held my gaze.

"Okay." I really wanted to jump the table and touch his high cheekbones. Instead, I took a sip of my coffee and butted out my cigarette, long forgotten. I looked over his shoulder, into the wide ocean.

"You need to break free from yourself." He articulated each word.

"I fully agree." Jack was right. I'd known this about myself my whole life. I didn't give every part of me completely. I always held back, fearing that I could lose again. Every relationship I'd had left me empty, restless, feeling abandoned, like forgotten laundry on a clothesline. I'd be hanging out to dry, and no one would care enough to take me in, fold me, hold me, and place me in their love. I was drying up—inside and out.

"I-I think you can help," I stammered in a voice that showed a vulnerability I didn't know I'd possessed up until that moment, looking at Jack and his expressive eyes.

"Maria, where are you staying?"

"I'm subletting."

"Where?"

"Near Place des Lices Market. The apartment is on one of those narrow streets. I can find my way by following the pastel colours of the buildings; don't ask me the street name." I grinned.

"I know the area. Every Tuesday and Saturday, everyone goes to buy fresh vegetables and the catch of the day. It's alive with people. I'm not too far. A couple of blocks and some more narrow streets." He laughed and looked at me for a few seconds without speaking.

"Would you like to come over?" he finally asked.

I couldn't. I shouldn't. I wouldn't. He was a stranger, for God's sake. *Say no, Maria.*

"Okay," I said, disregarding the negative thoughts. I threw them into the vast blue ocean and shooed them out of my head.

He instantly got up and left some money on the table. I picked up my camera, and he intercepted me and said, "I'll get that for you." With one hand he hung his guitar over his shoulder, and with the other he slung my camera around his neck. "I didn't realize it was so heavy."

"I know. Thanks. You're such a gentleman," I said with a smirk.

"I don't know if you would say that if you could read my mind right now."

As I stood, I felt a little light-headed, unsure of the last time I'd eaten. I glanced at my watch. It was five o'clock. I remembered arriving at the beach at three. How had two hours gone by so fast?

As we exited the café, the girl who served us flirted—a little too much at Jack—and said, "*Merci, et a bientôt*." Thank you and see you soon.

"*À bientôt*," Jack said, and I said, "*Merci*."

I followed Jack outside, catching a glimpse of his full upright body, so tall and lean. I quivered a bit at the thought of kissing his lips as he turned to let me go first. "Let's go, Maria."

We walked for a while side by side, each with our own thoughts. It was as if we had invisible membranes connecting our minds; without knowing each other, we somehow knew each other's needs. Our thoughts were racing to connect as we stepped on the cobblestone road and admired the pastel homes and bright flowers.

I didn't know why Saint-Tropez fascinated me. Perhaps it was the movie *And God Created Woman*, or the fact that I'd read once it was discovered by the Greeks. I wanted to explore it and capture its essence in pictures.

"How long have you been here?" Jack asked, sneaking a sideways peek at me.

"About a month."

"The question is not if you like it here, but how much do you like it?"

"Even more than I thought possible."

We walked past small shops, fresh-smelling bakeries, back alleys, and shuttered windows, and then someone caught my eye.

"Hold on a second, Jack." He stopped next to me.

"What?" He looked in the direction I was looking in, then back at me, puzzled.

"Can I have my camera, please?"

"Sure." He passed it to me and watched intently.

An old woman was bending down to pick up her groceries in a brown paper bag. I hurriedly dropped my attached lens case and snapped two shots. She didn't hear me.

"What do you see when you snap that?" Jack asked curiously.

"I see my grandmother, her vulnerability at that age. I see a genuine moment in someone's life that is natural, human. Basically not posed. It's like she's struggling to go about her daily chores, and no one is bothering with her. I feel her burden somehow, and I want to acknowledge how sometimes things are not as easy as they seem. If that makes any sense."

"Perfect sense. I just never thought about it that way." He gazed at me, almost as if in awe.

"There're so many ways to look at moments. I feel like they pass us by, and people just ignore their surroundings, like a pot of flowers discarded in some corner you forgot about. You ever notice how old people always move flowerpots around?"

"What do you mean?"

"They move the flowers as the sun moves. My grandmother did it all the time. My grandfather called it a 'transplant' and would laugh. She always wanted her flowers to be in the sun, and she made sure they wouldn't die." I looked off in the distance, remembering how *yiayia* would bend and adjust her flowers to perfection.

He was silent, but after a moment, he said jokingly, "I don't have a green thumb."

"Me either." I half-grinned.

We stopped in front of a gated door. It was about eleven feet high and sculpted with cherubs.

"Beautiful door." I gazed at it in wonderment, examining all the details.

"I know. That's one of the reasons I rented the apartment." He smirked.

"It's full of history."

"Certainly is. Did you know that in the 1920s, all the international stars from the world of fashion gathered here?"

"No," I replied, clueless about the fashion world.

He pulled out a key from some other pocket and unlocked the door. He did this thing with it, lifting it halfway till it gave.

"An old designer used to rent my apartment. That's what the landlord told me."

I heard a click, and Jack turned the golden doorknob. "These old doors have a special connection to us humans. Over the years, wood changes and distorts." He opened the door completely now. "I think we do the same if left untouched." Inside the building was a wrought-iron staircase and a tiny cubicle with mailboxes and doorbells with addresses below them. "Do you agree, Maria?"

I didn't know what to say. He was having this philosophical conversation with me, and I was too consumed by watching his every movement to concentrate on anything else.

"I fully agree," I said.

"With which part?" He took out a different key, which was attached to the main door key, and unlocked his mailbox. "Empty. Just the way I like it," he said to himself. I started to feel a little strange. "Well?" He continued his conversation with me even though I hadn't.

"Everything you say sounds right," I replied. *What am I doing here? Why am I going to Jack's apartment? I've just met him. Why do I trust him?*

"What's wrong?"

I hadn't realized I was frowning and not walking. "I don't think this is a good idea," I said, reluctant to walk.

"Why not? You still think I'm a killer?" he jested. "Look, if you don't want to come up, you don't have to." He looked at me with sad puppy eyes. "But I would really love to show you my dingy apartment." He laughed. "I promise I'll be on my best behavior."

I wanted to follow him everywhere. I wanted to scream yes. "Just for a little while," I said.

"Phew." He looked pleased. "I was holding my breath." He stepped in front of me and walked up the staircase, and I observed all the décor, tiles, marble floors, apartment numbers—102, 103, 104—shoes of all sizes outside the doors, till we stopped in front of 106.

I added one and six, and since seven was my lucky number, I felt it was a sign to continue this walk into his life.

Jack grabbed another key, this one long and silver and very old, almost antique-like, and twisted left, then right, as if it were a combination on a school lock.

"If you think the doors are old, you should try to

open one of these locks." He grinned and struggled some more.

"Do you mind if I take a picture of it?"

"Go right ahead, but promise me you'll show me all the pictures you've taken today."

"Continue what you're doing," I said, and snapped a picture of the door as his arm turned the handle.

He opened it, and I took a deep breath. It felt like I was walking into an old studio that one would see in magazines or art books. A wall was filled top to bottom with books and albums. "Bohemian" was the word that came to mind.

Jack placed his guitar on a black stand and locked it in securely.

"This is my humble home."

"It's definitely not dingy," I said.

"Does that mean you like it?" He half-grinned.

"Yes, it's very inviting. At least it feels that way to me." I automatically walked toward the massive bookshelf.

"Do you like to read?" he asked, a few paces behind me.

"It's one of my favourite pastimes."

"Come and see this." He headed toward the side of the bookshelf, where I noticed an old chest that looked like a pirate's hand-me-down treasure from another century.

He bent down and squatted. I stood next to him while he undid a latch and opened it up. There was a bunch of old, hardcover books squished together like sardines.

He hunched over the chest and searched for something. "I collect books, especially the ones with handwritten sentiments to a loved one." He opened one up and took a deep breath.

"June 2, 1945. To my darling daughter Beatrice on her eighteenth birthday. May Alice's journey inspire you to do great things and always look for the Rabbit Hole in every path you travel. Love, your father, Edward."

"That's…so beautiful…so poetic," I stammered, feeling pangs of pain from never having received anything from my lost father. Beatrice had been so loved and so lucky.

"Isn't it?" He looked up at me. "It's my favourite one. You can look at the rest while I make us something to eat."

"Eat?" Here I wanted to wallow in self-pity, and he wanted to eat.

"Aren't you hungry? I'm starving." He rubbed his stomach. "It's been growling for a while." Through his crisp white shirt I saw the outline of his stomach and took a deep breath. *Forget about the unwritten sentiments you'll never receive from your father,* I said to myself.

"Don't go out of your way," I said, totally distracted.

"Sit down and relax, and I'll be right back." He headed to the back of the apartment, and I immediately heard some banging. I couldn't see the kitchen, but knew from the noise he was about to start cooking.

I glanced down at the book I was holding and flipped through the pages. The illustrations were marvelous. The pages were bent and worn out, guessing Beatrice must have enjoyed the book. I was envious, so I reread the note over and over again, and felt worse. Closing the book, I picked up another one. A fan switched on in the kitchen, then Jack's footsteps approached and stopped a few feet away, in front of his albums. I peeked at him from the corner of my eye. He rummaged through his albums, searching for one in particular, it seemed. He then tilted an album jacket sideways, and with his fingertips, delicately pulled out a vinyl disc. He didn't know I was watching him. His back was spectacular—broad shoulders and a perfectly shaped ass. He took a few steps toward his record player, placed the album on it, and lifted the needle up then down. I waited. He waited.

He then searched me out and found me staring back at him. He caught me gawking at him with dirty thoughts running through my mind.

I was still sitting on the floor in front of the chest, admiring his collection, and when I grinned at him to erase his naked body from my mind, he smirked right back at me, and my heart skipped beats I long lost count of.

Suddenly, Jim Morrison's voice filled the room. I had this album too.

"I love this record," I said.

"You know why *I* love it?" Jack asked.

"Why?"

"Because you can read the lyrics like a book of poetry."

I agreed. "I think that's how it's meant to be read."

He walked over to me. "What did you think of his grave?"

"How did you know I went?" He scared me sometimes.

"If you know *An American Prayer*, then you are a true fan. And if you went to Paris, you went to Père Lachaise, did you not?" He smirked, and I nodded.

"You?"

"Yes. I started off in Paris, but hated living there. Too cold, rainy, and the people are exactly the same—cold and rainy. I hated the environment. So, I left and came here and fell in love with this town and haven't looked back since."

Jim's voice echoed in the background.

"I've got goosebumps," I murmured.

"I know. He had the best voice I've ever heard. No one can compare." Jack's eyes poured into mine, and I lowered my gaze to his lips, which were beckoning me. Jack did the same and bent down inches away from my face. He touched my cheek with his hand.

"You're so beautiful," he whispered.

"You have a perfect face," I whispered back. He pulled his hand away at the sound of something sizzling in the kitchen.

"Oh my God! The food!" he shouted, and ran into the kitchen. I got up and, in a daze, followed. My insides were all jittery. *Get a grip, Maria!*

Jack's kitchen was tiny. Pots and pans hung from the ceiling like in an old medieval cottage. It fit only two people—literally. My thoughts were preoccupied with wanting to kiss him. *No, too soon.* Way too soon.

I was right behind him, gawking at his lovely back again as he rushed to get his wooden spoon on the counter and stir the vegetables. My senses filled with the scent of garlic.

"Smells delicious," I said as I let my gaze travel up and down his frame.

"I'm making pasta with marinara sauce."

"Mmmm." I didn't move from behind him. I couldn't, and I didn't want to. Kept watching him intently sauté the garlic and onions then grab a bottle of tomato juice. He lowered the heat from high to low. He looked like such a professional.

"Can you stir this for a few seconds so I can open the bottle? It's always hard to open." He peeked at me from over his shoulder and stepped aside so I could take his place. He reached over my shoulder and let go of the wooden spoon, passing it into my hand as gently as a caress. It was extremely tight in the kitchen, and that was about the time I started to feel warm—really warm—and I was sure the heat wasn't coming from the stove.

"Can I have a glass of water after you open that?" I asked, feeling faint. I noticed him struggling with the bottle: turning on the hot water, letting it run over the lid, banging it with the back end of a knife, and muttering under his breath.

He swung around to look at me. "What a horrible host I am!" He put the bottle down and turned slightly; our backs almost touched as he reached over my head for a glass. "Excuse me." His hand touched the top of my head accidentally.

"It's okay." It really was.

Then Jack opened the fridge, and I heard him pour the water. Jim Morrison's voice was nonstop in the other room but difficult to hear with the loudness of the fan. Still, it was in the background. Ambiance.

"It's kind of cramped in the kitchen," Jack mumbled.

"It's European. I kind of like it." I hoped he didn't misinterpret that to mean that I liked him bumping my head or any other part of my body. "I mean the style."

He half-grinned at me. "Either way, I like it too." His gaze scanned over my body, and I squirmed slightly. He handed me the glass of water.

"Thank you."

"You're welcome." He quickly went back to opening the tomato juice and succeeded. He poured in the liquid, and it bubbled immediately. The scent was getting better and better. On top of his stove he had a wide selection of Italian spices, which he added to the pot. I watched his every move.

"Would you like some wine, Maria?" He sneaked a peek at me while swirling the sauce. I drank all the water in one gulp. My throat was as dry as a desert in the sun.

"Wow. You were thirsty!" He laughed. "So, red or white?"

Oh, the wine. "Whatever you have."

"I only drink red."

"That's fine by me," I replied.

Jack reached under the sink and pulled out a bottle. Château Calon-Ségur. I'd never heard of it, not that I knew much about wine.

"You want to reach nirvana?" he jested.

"In vino veritas," I articulated slowly.

"I love it when a woman speaks Latin," he said in a soft voice.

"I studied literature in university."

He opened the wine easily with the bottle opener. "I thought you were a photographer." He gave me a fleeting puzzled look.

I countered with a questioning look of my own and said, "Can't someone be a writer *and* a photographer?" He pondered this while he poured the wine into the wineglasses.

"Well?" I was eager to hear his response.

"Definitely. I'm just more turned on now." He studied me as if this new revelation explained my life story, when in essence, it was just a mere fact. His long-held gaze gave me chills. It felt as if he were flipping through the pages of my life that I was trying desperately to hide—or burn.

"Here you go. Why don't you indulge in some nirvana?" Jack handed me a wineglass. "*Salute*."

"*Salute*."

"What do you think?"

"Let me see." I took another sip and let the wine linger for a few seconds in my mouth. Then I swallowed it. "Jack, I have to say, this is the best-tasting wine I have ever had."

His face beamed with satisfaction. "Let's sit awhile at the table while the sauce simmers."

I sat at the small wooden breakfast table for two and placed my glass on it.

"Tell me more about yourself," he said as he sat down across from me.

"What do you want to know?"

"Everything." He looked serious as he sipped his wine and inspected my glass. *"Drink up"*—Jim Morrison's voice checked up on us every so often. From this vantage point, we could hear his beautiful language flow through the apartment and scrutinize our every word.

"I like pasta and sauce." I caught his eyes twinkling at me and chuckled.

"Me too," Jack said. "What else?"

"Pizza."

"Me too."

"I like the colour blue."

"Me too." He took another sip. Then, out of nowhere, he asked, "Why don't you have a boyfriend?"

He popped the question like a magician pulling a rabbit out from his hat.

"I don't know. Why don't you have a girlfriend?"

"Every girl I've gone out with has never given me what I need, what I want. Now you tell me why, because 'I don't know' means you know and you don't want to tell me."

It was as if Jack could see through my safeguard, my tough exterior. I held my breath, thinking, and then blurted out the truth—or parts of the truth, at least.

"Every guy I've ever dated could never figure me out. They said I was too distant, too preoccupied." I took a sip of the wine and felt the warmth. "I've always felt abandoned. Every time I'd give a part of myself to someone, I would be rejected. It was a cycle. Guys wouldn't call me back when I thought they should have. I don't think I did anything wrong; I think I just picked the wrong guys. I felt lost even when I was around them. The last guy I dated I stayed with for six months because I didn't want to be alone. He was a decent guy, but there was no passion, no tugging at my heart." Through the rim of my glass I watched how Jack listened so attentively to my every word. His hair fell into his eyes, and he left it there. He was godlike; his features were quintessential of one. "I guess I haven't found the right guy yet."

"Until now," he said quietly, and got up to stir the sauce without waiting for my reply.

I didn't have one to give him. Maybe he was right; maybe he was wrong.

I drank some more wine. When Jack came back to sit down, he had two cigarettes in his hand. He lit one and handed it to me, blowing out the smoke. Everything he did uncontrollably pulled me toward him.

Until now.

"Until now" kept playing in my head like a record.

As soon as he lit his cigarette and took a few puffs, he got up to get a pot and filled it with water. He added some salt and oil. His movements were so fluid.

He reached up toward a tiny pantry above his fridge. He didn't even need to go on his tiptoes, he was so tall. As he moved cans and jars around, searching, he asked, "Penne or spaghetti? That's all I have. My stock is low." He'd raised his voice to be heard over the fan.

"Penne is fine," I answered. I wasn't in the mood for a messy spaghetti day.

"You don't want to try for *Lady and the Tramp*?" He threw me a sly glance.

"If you had meatballs, I'd go for it," I hollered back, smiling. His fan was awfully loud and annoying.

Jack snapped his fingers. "Shit."

I flicked my ash in his exotic turquoise ashtray. I felt dizzy from the cigarette—and probably the wine and empty stomach.

"Cool ashtray. Where is it from?" I knew I was inquisitive, but my curiosity was way beyond the curb.

"Morocco."

"Wow. How is Morocco? I love the architecture."

"You took the words right out of my mouth." Jack covered the pot with its lid and returned to his seat. "It is by far the best country I have ever visited. The architecture is stupendous. Unique. The food is incredible. You know, you eat with your hands in their authentic restaurants. They say you taste the food much better. They're right." He gestured with his hands as he spoke about the food, showing me how he ate it, while his cigarette was left to burn in the ashtray.

"Did you go to the desert?"

"Yes. That was also the most incredible experience! I rode a dromedary."

"A what?"

"A one-humped camel. They are everywhere—on the beach, in the desert, in the villages. It's all visually breathtaking!" Jack threw his hands in the air like he couldn't believe it himself.

"I'd love to take pictures there."

"You must." He quickly stood up. "I'd love to go back." He winked at me, and I almost fell off my seat. He sat back down when he saw the water hadn't boiled yet, and he stared at me for a few seconds without speaking.

"Your eyes are so expressive," I blurted.

"Thank you. It's my flaw. You can tell instantly if I'm upset, content, eager, or excited." Jack emphasized the last adjective and inhaled his cigarette, waiting for my reaction.

I didn't say anything because he'd left me speechless. I inhaled my cigarette again and then took a few quick sips of wine. At some point, he had refilled my wineglass without my awareness. God only knew how many glasses I'd had. I felt light-headed as Jack's eyes continued to enchant me.

"Your eyes are bold," Jack stated, looking at me seriously.

"What do you mean?"

"They tell me the truth. You're honest and curious and strong." He folded his arms across his chest. "Well, am I right?"

"Eyes are the window to the soul, right?"

"Yes and no. I think some people try to hide their true soul by putting up a front, and then you never get to know their soul. Your soul is as clear to me as a diamond."

"How can you say that so confidently?" His observations shocked me. How could he know me so well?

"I just know. I can read people well. It's one of my talents."

"You sure know your own flaws and talents." I grinned.

"I love how much you pay attention to every word I say." He butted out his cigarette and walked toward the stove without looking at me. Sometimes he said things to me and didn't want to look me in the eye.

"Can you read my palm too?" I asked jokingly.

"Yeah, actually, I can." He opened the bag of penne and poured it into the boiling water, then stirred it quickly. "Show me your palm." He came back and took my hand, gently flipped it over, and sat across from me, all in one sweeping movement.

"I feel your energy. It's soothing to mine." He traced the lines on my palm with his fingertips, and electricity ruffled me up inside. "This is your life path. You will change your path in midlife. You are so creative, but it's a long and hard road for you. You are alone, and you have no family ties."

I quickly pulled back my hand. "Bullshit," I said harshly.

"I'm sorry if I've upset you." He looked genuinely hurt. "An Indian man showed me how to read palms when I was a young lad. I didn't mean to offend you."

"Show me your hand, Jack," I muttered.

Jack placed his upturned palm onto the table and showed me his life path.

"Mine is cut in half, like yours. I've been told I will change my direction. I will touch many souls because I have the special gift of music. Give me your hand again." He waited for me to put my hand in his open palm.

When I did, he placed it next to his and compared the lines, explaining how similar they were. I got scared. This was too much for me to handle.

"The water!" He jumped up and stirred the pasta, lowering the heat as water trickled down the pot and onto the burner. The room smelled like something had burned. He turned up the fan, which whirred even louder.

"Believe it or not!" Jack shouted at me as he stirred the penne.

"Not!" I cried.

"You want some more wine?" He took the bottle and poured me another glass without waiting for my answer.

"Do I have a choice?" I asked mockingly.

"You always have a choice, Maria," he declared, as if he were presenting a bill of rights to the government.

I thought about that for a while. *I always have a choice.*

Jack got up again, and I felt anxious, faint, and warm, as fuzzy as a peach, trying to understand myself and my motives, but nothing was coming to me. No realization. No epiphanies. He had me. He was right.

I had made all my choices, and here I was in a stranger's apartment, feeling out of control.

What if he rapes me?

He would have done it by now.

How can I be so sure?

Really, Maria, does he look like he needs to rape

women? It's more like women would be raping him!

I stood up. My imagined conversation confused the fuck out of me. "I think I should leeaavvvenow." My words sounded slurred to me.

He turned his head and stared at me. "What are you thinking, Maria?"

"You don't want to know! That maybe you're fucking crazy!" I shouted at him. I was fuckin' drunk. "I don't know you. I've just met you, and I'm in your apartment. I dooon't…uh…feel…uh…toogood." I put my hand to my head to support it.

"You have to eat, Maria. The pasta is ready." I watched Jack remove a silver strainer. Next thing I knew, I'd placed my head on the table.

"Sorry," I mumbled, and I closed my eyes as the room spun around like Dorothy's house in *The Wizard of Oz*.

Did Jack put something in my drink? Ahhh…sleep.

From far away, I heard Jack bang dishes and talk to himself. "Great, Jack. You should have known better. She drank too much. You know how potent that wine is." His voice had lowered by the time he reached the last word.

"Here, drink some water, Maria." He lifted my sleepy head and forced me to drink the water. I couldn't open my eyes, but I drank the water like a fish.

"Shit, you're dehydrated," Jack stated. I had drunk some water when I'd gotten to his apartment, but that had been hours ago, I thought. I had lost track of time.

I slowly opened my eyes, and Jack quickly placed a plate of pasta and sauce before me. "Eat." He nudged me.

I devoured it within a few minutes, and instantly started to feel better. He sat down across from me and ate quietly, peeking at me but not talking. I refused to look at him, being in such a state. I wasn't thinking about my manners or the rules of etiquette—not that I knew any. My grandparents had never shown me anything proper besides not to talk with my mouth full and to always compliment the chef.

"Jack, that was delicious." I finally met his stare, and for a split second, he looked worried.

"I really feel bad for you," Jack said while finishing his bite. "But I can tell you enjoyed it. You haven't said a word since you saw the plate in front of you." He looked relieved.

Wiping his mouth with his napkin, he poured himself another glass of wine. Standing, he said, "I'll get you another glass of water." He handed me the water, and after I drank it, he asked, "Do you feel better, Maria?" He appeared genuinely concerned.

I nodded as my hair danced around my face. "Thanks."

"You're thanking me for making you feel like shit?" He gave me a half grin as he placed a mouthful of pasta in his mouth.

I laughed. "You're funny."

He swallowed his food. "Thank you. I aim to please. By the way, I like to hear you laugh." Jack pulled his hair back and shook his head, then fixed a stare my way that I couldn't look away from. I must have beamed from ear to ear at the compliment.

"Are you still hungry? I have more."

"No. I'm really full."

He had a few bites left. "Me too." Pushing his plate away, he grabbed his cigarettes, and offered me one, but I refused. I didn't feel like smoking. I actually felt like sleeping. He got up and turned off the fan. He had forgotten about it, and suddenly the apartment seemed so quiet. The needle of the record player had reached the end of the album a long time ago, and I got up to take it off.

"I was going to do it," Jack said as he watched me walk over to the stereo and remove the needle.

"I know, but I can't take that noise. Plus, it'll ruin your needle."

He beamed at me from across the room. "Pick an album." I removed the disc from the record player, trotted over to his record collection, and placed *An American Prayer* back into its proper slot. I glanced at all the records quickly, and the names popped out at me: Elvis Costello, R.E.M., The Clash, Bad Company, The Smiths, Van Morrison, Art of Noise, Massive Attack, The Cure. I took out *Kiss Me, Kiss Me, Kiss Me* and placed it on the turntable.

When I was young, I had borrowed an album from this band from my friend's brother, and just couldn't give it back—the ghastliest deed I'd ever done yet. I kept it. I lied about it. I hid it.

"They have a great sound," Jack shouted over the music. "My stereo is possessed. Sometimes I think it has its own personality. Some albums play louder than others."

"Jack, what time is it?"

"Look next to my bed. I have an alarm clock there."

He was sitting down, smoking, moving his foot to the beat, speaking to me as if I had been to his apartment a hundred times before.

"I don't know where that is." I didn't fancy going into his bedroom, especially feeling a bit tipsy.

"Wait up." He stood. "I forgot to give you the grand tour," he said with a laugh.

To the left of his entrance was a closed door, and when he opened it, it revealed a long, narrow hallway, like a secret passage, with a lower ceiling than the rest of his apartment. I saw two doors.

Jack walked ahead of me. "This way." Two people side by side could hardly fit. He opened the first door on the right. "My bathroom. Excuse the mess." I peeked inside and instantly smelled the cologne he wore. The room was all white, with tiny, symmetrical, diamond-shape tiles. It had an old bathtub with a showerhead and a teensy-weensy window above the toilet. The medicine cabinet was half-open, revealing men's products and some prescription drugs. He quickly shut it. "Come." He continued to walk toward the other door, which was open, and he gestured for me to move ahead of him. "Ladies first."

His bed was a massive king-size. It had a lovely detailed wooden frame around the headboard. The walls were reddish burgundy, and on top of the headboard was a painting of a naked man and woman. You couldn't see their faces, just their dark silhouettes painted against a reddish purple background. The sun was setting behind them, giving an allure of love and beauty in its rawest form.

"What a painting!" I exclaimed.

"My friend Hunter painted it. He is so talented."

A night table fit next to his bed, and on it was the alarm clock. This was the reason for my standing in his bedroom, fucked-up, restless, and scared to death. *Awkward.*

Next to me I noticed an armoire that looked about a

hundred years old. I instinctively touched the carved wood. "This is magnificent."

"Thanks. It belonged to my great-grandmother. Circa 1870s." Not many guys in my acquaintance said the word "circa." Real hot flashes surged through my body.

"What an heirloom." Lion faces were on the four ends where the door frames began. "It's incredible how much detail is sculpted into the wood."

"Artistry," he said.

Jack walked to the side of his bed and glanced at the clock. "It's six-twenty, by the way."

I couldn't care less what time it is.

Why did asking him lead me to the bedroom? Shit. Didn't want to be here right now. This was the first time I'd met a guy and gone to his apartment the same day. People did this all the time, right? I could hear my *yiayia*'s voice. Only, the harder I thought, the more it sounded something like this: *"Are you sure your shirt matches your shoes? You look funny in that top. I could tighten it if you want."* Her needle and thread, ready to attack at any moment.

"It's six-twenty," Jack repeated. I must have looked all fucked-up because Jack just stared at me.

"Already?" I hadn't budged from my spot staring at the lions' faces, lost in my volcanic thoughts. "Time passes when you're having fun," was all I could think of saying. How ridiculous! We were unbelievably close. I stepped back and said, "I better be going soon."

Despite declaring my intention to leave, honestly, I wanted to jump on him and land right onto his tan-coloured comforter.

"You have to stay for dessert," Jack said, his

incredible hazel eyes storming into me.

"Not right now."

"Later, then. Would you like some coffee? I make a mean Greek coffee."

"How did you know I was Greek?" I was stunned.

"I didn't know. Now I do." He looked pleased.

"Where did you learn how to make Greek coffee?" I was surprised he even knew what Greek coffee was.

"An old girlfriend taught me."

I should have guessed. "Oh." Of course he had a past and many ex-girlfriends. I felt uncomfortable again, trying not to look around his bedroom, and at the same time, trying to memorize every object in the room. I walked out first, and he followed close behind. The living room was quiet again.

It seemed like I'd just put the album on.

"Why don't you pick another record, and I'll start the coffee," Jack said as he passed by me and caressed my hair for a second. "Soft," he murmured.

I walked with a little tremble in my legs and skimmed the albums. There were many I had never heard of. I liked one cover that was all black and had an orange square design on it.

Getz/Gilberto, I read, and I played it.

I loved it instantly. Jack peeked over at me from the kitchen and called out, "This is my favourite too!" I listened to the music, and it was like nothing I had ever heard before—magical and captivating.

"Music for the soul," he hollered from the kitchen.

"It's breathtaking." I walked closer to him and sat on the kitchen chair. "Who is this?"

"You've never heard them before?" He jerked his head, an incredulous look in his eyes.

"No."

"You have good instincts, then. This record was made in 1964 by some of the most renowned musicians. But wait—why did you pick it?" He looked perplexed.

"I liked the design on the cover, and their names piqued my curiosity. It's like they were saying, 'Listen to me.'"

The sound of the woman singing was outstanding—the sweetest voice.

"You hear that?" Jack was whisking the coffee briskly and waiting for the froth. He glanced back and forth from me to the tiny pot in front of him. "The song was inspired by a young woman who would stroll past the bars and cafés in Rio de Janeiro. She was supposedly so beautiful that everyone would stop and stare at her. Since the song became famous, she also became a celebrity. I think her name is Heloisa."

"What's the title of the song?"

"'The Girl from Ipanema.'"

"You sure know your music."

"Actually, it was Hunter who introduced me to bossa nova. He loves this music."

"What kind of a name is Hunter?" I blurted. I'd heard his name so often today, I had to ask.

"It's a long story that only he can tell. I'd botch it up," he replied with a smirk.

I closed my eyes and heard Jack bang the cups while the music flowed through his apartment. I lost myself, imagining this woman and how she inspired such an extraordinary piece of music. The woman's voice was ethereal. "What's her name?" I asked, my eyes still closed.

"Astrud Gilberto, his wife."

I heard a light tap on the table as my coffee cup was placed in front of me, and I opened my eyes.

"Sorry to disturb you." Jack's gaze penetrated mine. "Go on, close your eyes again. It's an incredible song."

Astrud—what an odd name, and yet lovely, powerful.

"It's okay. It's just so…"

"I know. You looked so peaceful."

"I was," I murmured. "This song can transport you to any place in the world. The saxophone speaks in a phenomenal way that words never could."

"That's Stan Getz. He's American." Jack sat down and took a sip of his coffee. I glanced at my cup and marveled at the remarkable amount of froth.

"Your coffee looks perfect."

"You haven't even tried it yet," Jack said, smiling.

"I could tell by the *caimaki*."

"I know that word. It means the froth on top of the coffee." He looked a little smug.

"Bravo!" I said in Greek.

"You're easy to please."

I never thought I was easy to please. "Maybe, maybe not."

Jack was waiting for something, but I didn't know what; his expression was hard to read.

"Jack," I said suddenly, just to change the subject of whether or not I was easy—to please, that is. "What exactly do you do as a musician?"

"What exactly do I do? Simple. I make music."

Oh, that sounded like such a stupid question. "I mean, do you perform?"

"Every day. You want me to perform now? I can put on quite a show for you."

I was digging a deeper hole than I thought possible. Meanwhile, Jack grinned from ear to ear, and I—once again—flushed red.

"Maria, what do you want to know?" He was straight-faced now.

"Well, can I hear you play?"

"You already have. Shall I get my guitar?" He grinned again and reached for a cigarette instead. I felt sweat trickle between my breasts.

"No, uh… Do you play at any particular bar?" That sounded coherent, I thought.

"Now that's a good question." He lit his cigarette and nodded. "Yep. I play for a living. How else could I afford this luxurious flat? Now I'm going to ask you a question. Maria, would you like to come hear me play tomorrow night?" The sexy way he glanced at me made my knees weak.

"Where?"

"At Bar La Tulipe. Do you know where that is?"

"No, where is it?"

"On the waterfront." Then I remembered passing by it in the daytime when it was closed.

"Oh, I do know it! What time?"

"Come around nine."

"Okay," I agreed, and he seemed content.

"I think I'm going to play some new material and a few covers."

Jack always wore a playful expression. He was witty—I had to give him that. He was also straightforward, smart, and so fuckin' handsome.

"I feel inspired today," he said in a faint voice.

I had completely forgotten about my coffee. I took about four sips, and in ten seconds, finished it. "So, can you read my future from the coffee grounds too?" I asked in jest.

Jack took my cup as soon as I placed it upside down, grabbed a napkin that was next to him and placed it on the saucer, then flipped over the cup—again, like a magician performing a trick.

How did he know how to do all this stuff? Oh yeah, the ex-girlfriends. I felt a pang of jealousy. *I'm in trouble now.* I really liked Jack and couldn't find anything wrong with him.

"We have to wait a bit," he said, examining my face closely, taking a few sips of his coffee. The provocative music still played in the background, and it was hypnotizing. He took his time, drinking and listening to the music, all the while inspecting me like I was an artifact.

"Tell me more about this music." I wanted to learn as much as possible.

"Well, it's bossa nova. It's Brazilian music fused with jazz, to put it in a nutshell."

"What does 'bossa nova' mean?"

"It's Portuguese for 'new trend.'"

"I love the sound of it: bossa nova. It's fun to say."

"It's automatic. You listen to it, and you fall in love." He scanned my face to see if I agreed.

Yes, I was falling in love with the music, but mostly, I was falling in love with Jack.

I looked down at my cup. He picked it up, flipped it over, and scrutinized it for a good thirty seconds. Silence. I waited impatiently, checking out the top of his head and how his hair parted in different sections.

"Well, I see a lot of paths and a pure soul. It's very light; that's all I see."

"You're bullshitting me again."

"Actually, I'm not. You have a really good cup. I'll show you mine in a few minutes." He flipped his over with one hand, still holding my cup and observing it. He continued to speak without looking up. "I know that a light cup means a clean soul, and you have that. Also, I see some letters that look like a *J* and an *M*." He smirked. "Take a look. It's true." He bent over the table, closer to me, and pointed to some lines. I really couldn't make out a thing.

"I don't see it."

"You have to stare at it for a long time. Look here at the lines." I stared at where he pointed and started to notice the outlines of the letters *J* and *M*.

"I think I see it," I said. "But you know, you could make up whatever you like if you stare at the lines long enough."

"Actually"—he put the cup down— "a real teacup fortune-telling can take up to two hours."

"You know a lot about this stuff."

"It fascinates me."

"Do you like to know your future?"

"Yes. How about you?"

"I don't know. I'm kind of skeptical, but maybe I would be open to seeing someone one day," I added as an afterthought.

"I know just the right person for you."

"I know. Hunter."

"Exactly."

"I hope he's better than you." I laughed.

"I know. I don't know what the fuck I'm saying." He laughed too. "I thought it was a good idea at the time." Then he looked at me intently. "But honestly, I did see the letters that I showed you."

"It did look like them," I said, but they could have been whatever he wanted them to be. Sometimes we search for things and make ourselves believe we've found them. I thought it was time for me to get going, though deep inside, I wanted to stay longer.

"Anyway, Jack, I'm going to leave now. Thank you so much for the meal." I stood, and he looked at me, surprised.

"Wait. Don't you want to see my cup before you leave?"

Of course, I did. I wanted to know everything about Jack. I sat back down, laughing. "Okay, let's hear it."

He picked up his cup and didn't speak for a while.

"I don't know if I can read my own cup or not."

"Neither do I!" I blurted out with a laugh.

"But I'll try anyway." After a pause, he said, "This is weird. Usually it's all dark. Today it seems lighter, clearer." He peeked up at me. "It's because of you."

"C'mon Jack, you can't be serious! I've just met you."

"Oh yes, I am serious! Trust me. I'm always confused, pessimistic, down on life, and that usually reflects in my cup. Sof—" He stopped. "My ex-girlfriend would read my cup all the time, and it was always the same."

I guessed that he was about to say the name Sofia, and I instantly imagined this spectacular beauty. I felt nauseated with envy. "Well, this is all very interesting, but I gotta go." I didn't like these feelings erupting inside me because they scared the shit out of me and because I was actually jealous.

Why the fuck am I so jealous?

"Interesting? You know how I feel about that word." He set his cup down, and I stood up, ignoring his last remark. Emotionally drained from trying to keep up with him. I didn't have a comeback. Thank God for the music, or the silence would have been extremely awkward.

Jack sensed my uneasiness; I could tell by his confused look while trying to figure me out.

"So, tomorrow night, will you come to the bar so I can see you again?"

"Oh. Yeah, of course."

"You forgot so soon?" He waited for a reply, and I imagined myself on a tennis court, balls thrown at me and I had to hit each and every one perfectly to score high. I was frustrated. What was wrong with me?

"No, no. Uh…I just wasn't thinking about it." I hated when I babbled and nothing coherent came out of my mouth.

He stood up and strode toward the door, then stopped in front of me and pushed some hair out of my face. "I like your hair. It really is soft." That was the second time he'd said that, but this time I couldn't move. With his other hand, he caressed the other side of my head. He slid his hands down my hair till he reached the curve of my back. I took a few steps away from him to control myself, but his gaze rested gently on my face. If I didn't withdraw farther away, I would walk forward and drop into his arms, and I would have kissed his lips madly. Tilting my head upward, I swayed toward the door. Jack didn't say a word; he moved one inch closer as soon as he felt my tug.

"I, uh, have to…" I couldn't finish my sentence. Jack pulled me closer and, like a gentleman, kissed me on both cheeks.

"It was a great pleasure meeting you, Maria. I have had one of the loveliest afternoons of my entire life." Jack spoke softly and grabbed hold of my camera for me—which I'd almost forgotten about—without waiting for me to put together a crumbled sentence. He realized I was all fucked-up.

Why couldn't I have been more mature and calm like him? *Dumb idiot. Say something to him.*

"Me too," I whispered while Jack was already at the entrance, holding my camera like it was a fur coat.

"Excuse me?" he said loudly.

"I said, me too!" I shouted, realizing my words didn't have any enthusiasm or conviction. I sounded like a fuckin' robot. *Me too.* I seemed angry, when actually, I was a nervous wreck.

"You are definitely adorable." He laughed.

I stepped closer to him and reached for my camera, but he lifted it and placed it around my neck, gently pulling back my hair so it didn't get caught in the strap.

"Is that okay?" he asked, eyeing me intently as he folded his arms across his chest. Even that natural motion made me all bubbly inside.

"Yeah. Thank you." He appeared so composed, and I felt like a volcano about to erupt all over his apartment.

He swung open the door. "See you tomorrow. *À demain,*" Jack said in a cool voice.

"*À demain,*" I repeated like a parrot and a bumbling fool.

You better say something smart now. Appear unruffled, tranquil—think of the ocean. Don't you want him to remember you? Don't you want to be remembered? Here goes nothing.

"Jack." I gazed into his eyes, serene, preparing

myself to say something intelligent, but all that came out was nonsense. "I loved the song you sang on the beach, even if you've sung it before. For me, it was the first time I'd heard it." *That was awful!* It was as if I'd told him it was okay if he'd sung it to other girls and then to me…*Shut up now and leave!* I stepped out of his door.

He leaned against the doorframe, chuckling. "Wait up." With those two words, he soothed my inner turmoil and made all my crazy thoughts run and hide. "It's your song. Don't forget that." He was smiling. "*À demain.*" I could feel his eyes watch me as I turned and left, speechless once again.

I trotted down the stairs and walked out into the street like there was a fire up my butt. I could have sworn I saw a bird perched at his building's front door, eyeing me carefully. I felt an eerie sensation ripple through me, but then nudged it off. *Don't ruin a beautiful moment, Maria. Just enjoy it.* When I looked back, no bird was there.

It had just been my imagination.

Then I hummed that Rolling Stones' song and sang the chorus a little too loud, but I didn't care who looked at me.

I had just experienced the most incredible day of my life. *Why didn't I say* that *to Jack?*

The truth was, I fell in love with Jack that day. Falling for him was like slipping on a favourite dress or buying my favourite lipstick. I didn't want to feel like a yo-yo anymore. I wanted to be loved for all my tumultuous ways.

Chapter Three
The lost city of Atlantis
2009

I knew Dr. Pappas was on the island of Santorini. He had retired. I searched his name on the Internet late one night to find out everything about the vrykolakas. I made some phone calls to different universities, and I finally spoke to another professor who knew him personally. I explained some bullshit story I was doing on the vrykolakas, and he was open to giving me any information I wanted. He told me where to find Dr. Pappas. It never took long to find someone on the Internet; you just needed to have a little patience. And I had all the time in the world now that I wasn't mortal anymore.

He lived in the town of Fira. This was where the vrykolakas supposedly were discovered for the first time. I read all his articles on the Internet, and finally understood that these undead creatures—that I now was a part of—originated from Greek folklore. From the online Wikipedia, I discovered that the term was derived from wolf and vampire, a kind of subspecies of the vampire without any wolf-like features. Confusing me even more, I read that I was neither a vampire nor a werewolf. What the fuck was I? I needed answers from somebody other than Hunter.

I estimated that it would take me about two nights to get to Santorini from Saint-Tropez. I had never been that good with maps on an actual road, let alone running through forests, mountains, and above water. It scared the shit out of me. Every motion was so new to me, I felt like my bones were going to crack in two with every leap.

I knew Hunter wasn't too far behind.

After Hunter crushed me and turned me into one of them, it had taken me three days and nights to open my eyes. When I did, I saw the world slightly differently—unusual, yet the same. Before that, I had been sick for a few days; Hunter took care of me before and after my transformation. He gave me medication, prepared soup, and rubbed my forehead to stop my delirium. He was the perfect caregiver. Through my fever, I vaguely remembered Hunter, but not much else. I felt myself slowly losing touch with reality. After that, he squeezed me to death. I lost consciousness and saw my *yiayia*'s and *pappou*'s faces from a sweet distance. They were smiling, their arms open wide.

Then I fell into a slumber that converted me into this creature I am today.

Throughout my sleep, I heard everything around me. Hunter spoke to his Gang of Cat's Eyes, explaining that I would have one special power when I awoke and that he didn't know which one it would be. They were all familiar with the stages and grunted a lot.

Hunter had been eager to find out. I felt his hand upon mine, and heard him talk to me. Most of the time he was alone. Sometimes he didn't speak out loud, but I could sense his words and feelings.

I remember him saying, *"You will have one of these powers, Maria: hearing, sensing, touching, seeing, tasting, lifting, singing, painting, or writing. Hearing will allow you to listen to people's conversations from miles away, as if they are right in front of you. Sensing will give you the power to pick up on everyone's thoughts and to distinguish faraway senses as if they are close. Touching will allow you to transfer your emotions onto the person you touch. Seeing will give you the power to have visions of your immediate future only. Tasting will give you the power to heal others' wounds through blood transfusions. Lifting will give you the power to pick up any object into the air. Singing will give you the voice of an angel. Painting will furnish you with the eye and the brushstroke of an artist that you could only have dreamed to be. Writing will give you the power to express your thoughts through words you never thought existed inside you."*

Hunter's voice had been melodic, slow. He'd spoken as if he knew I listened attentively to every word. He knew the process well; he had done it so many times before. Everything had been falling into place. He had turned his gang into vrykolakas one by one. I was the thirteenth member—what a horrid number. I had to escape as soon as possible. Hunter was coming after me and this helplessness came over me, leaving me no choice but to do whatever he wanted. My self-control was floating around me; I was afraid of this connection that somehow bonded us together. This is what scared the shit out of me. This undeniable connection.

"Where is Jack?" I moaned in my sleep, unable to move my lips and speak, hoping and craving that Jack could save me, but knowing deep inside that this transformation would push me further and further away from him.

Hunter's voice had echoed. *"You will be as quick as*

lightning in the beginning."

With that memory, I sprang into the air like a wild cat, unable to control my legs, and stopped only to look at my messy map. At one point, I thought I was going to crash into a tree. Hunter knew I would be fast because I was a "fresh one."

"You're the fastest vryko I've ever seen."

His black eyes had held my gaze way too long after I'd slept with him. I had been lonely, and he had been so giving. I thought I was going to die when he crushed my body.

"This won't hurt."

Suddenly, they were all there: Freddy, Gilbert, Benny, Ed, Nick, Don, Cannes, Donnie, William, Charlie, Todd, and Gonzo. They all watched as Hunter squeezed my mortal life right out of me.

"No!" I'd shouted. *"You're hurting me."*

I knew this was the end. I heard growling, louder and louder.

"Do you want to live or die?"

Live, I'd said.

"You will die and become more powerful than anything you have ever imagined. You are sick with a contagious virus. If I don't do this, you will die forever, and I can't live without you."

I heard more growls from the Gang of Cat's Eyes and then a language I'd never before heard escape Hunter's mouth. That was the last sound I remember—gibberish chanting that left me cold.

Jack.

It was pitch dark now, and I tried to concentrate on my surroundings. I saw cypress trees in abundance; I'd passed the river Arno. Up next was Umbria, Abruzzi. I had to reach the Gulf of Taranto off the Ionian Sea and follow the end of it till I reached the last town, Capo Santa Maria di Leuca. That was the edge of Italy. I knew I was on the right track as I studied my map further. The water made me weary, so I would wait for a boat to take me to Kerkyra, and from there, take another boat to the mainland. It would take me a few more days than I'd planned, but I'd had a head start, so I wasn't worried about Hunter. He didn't want to hurt me, anyway; he wanted to love me.

And I didn't know which was scarier: Hunter hating me or loving me.

I had to focus on my path. My destination was Santorini. I wanted to ask Dr. Pappas so many questions that I hoped he would have the answers to.

The last time I visited the island, I had been with my friends, dancing in bars and acting like an annoying tourist. My friend Anna had her *Things to Do in Santorini* travel guide attached to the hip. I remembered the passages she'd read to us about the Greek philosopher Plato describing… *the disappearance of Atlantis, which, according to myth, was a circular island populated by people of high culture, talent, and wealth... The Atlantis myth is linked to the mysterious island of Santorini... According to Plato, it was the lost city of Atlantis... Archeologists have found numerous civilizations that inhabited the island, dating back to ancient times.*

Who would have thought I would be leaping bounds to get to Santorini. I was surprised I remembered everything so clearly. It seemed my memory was sharper than it used to be, and I was thankful for that.

I had to go to the port to buy tickets. From this

vantage point, it appeared to be a long way down, but I was realizing that though everything looked so far away, in a few seconds I would be standing right in front of what I had been looking at. I was afraid to fly over water. I had a fear of heights, something I desperately tried to overcome—I didn't really have a choice. But water was a completely different story. The idea of falling into the ocean made me sick to my stomach. I knew it would slow me down, but I had to get on a boat somehow.

Brushing my hair off my face, it felt like straw. The wind had damaged it; now would be a good time for some conditioner. *What am I thinking?* I thought maybe I needed sleep. Actually, I *didn't* need sleep.

"Day and night, you can go without sleep. Saturday, though, is the day you never come out. You sleep all day and night. A day of rest."

Hunter's voice replayed in my head like a forgotten record—over and over.

Even vrykolakas have a day of rest.

The article I'd read on the Internet came back to me as I slowly entered the port, trying not to leap too high so I wouldn't be seen. There were a few people walking home from clubbing, a few others waiting at the port.

The article went something like this: *Apparently, this creature starts out as a dead human that is known to change form by entering the body of an animal…* I could only guess that this meant some of us were shape-shifters. The article included specific anecdotes from villagers who had witnessed this mysterious transformation. That was kind of cool in a fucked-up way. Everything scared the living daylights out of me, but I was starting to accept—or at least I coaxed myself to accept—what was uncontrollable.

I was near a path leading to the port. I landed real hard and then did a few somersaults to break my fall. Landing was still something for me to master. My running shoes looked like they had been through mudslides.

I stopped a couple who were walking a few meters up ahead and asked them if they knew if any boats were leaving. They looked at me like I had just come out of an asylum. I could just imagine my disheveled appearance after all the running and crash landing. I glanced down at my clothes and noticed all these tiny, random rips. *Yep, I am a fuckin' mess. Definitely not glamorous.*

They sped off. Did I really need this shit in my life?

I unclipped my purse from my belt to count the money remaining. From where I stood, I could read the fare indicated near the dock. I had more than enough. Phew! Delving deeper into my tiny purse and grabbing my hairbrush, I detangled my knots.

Jack was somewhere out there, and I had to find him. Even if Jack didn't want me anymore after seeing the monster I had become, I had to see him. Even if it was just one last time, if only to explain my side of the story. If he was even alive. Deep down I knew he was still breathing the same air I was. I would have felt something if he weren't. Had to hang on to that thought.

Hunter trailed me only to bring me back to his world, to continue our affair.

I never married Jack because I thought marriage was a scam, an institution. Hunter knew I never wanted to get married. He didn't know all of my past as Jack did, but he knew some bits and pieces.

Jack had mysteriously disappeared, and after five years of being my closest confidante, Hunter became my lover. I had felt like a lost soul, waiting for my soul mate to return…waiting for years until I fell into Hunter's hands like jelly. He had been my safety net while I fell out of the blazing building—desperate, lonely, and afraid.

I loved Hunter as a best friend. *"I've been in love with you since the first time I met you at Bar La Tulipe twenty years ago,"* he'd told me a few months ago.

I had been a girl in love with Jack, and now I was a vampire still in love with Jack. I really couldn't think straight anymore. Ever since turning into a vampire, my connection with Jack slowly disintegrated and my connection with Hunter grew stronger. I hated this feeling. I wanted to go back to the way things were.

I hid behind a tree, quickly changed my clothes, and watched as the sky became lighter. I'd have to purchase my ticket before the sun rose. Noticing a ticket booth up ahead, I headed straight for it. Twenty years ago, around the same date, I had been going to see Jack perform for the first time.

Chapter Four
And the love flourishes, and the love awakens us
1989

I wore a simple black V-neck dress and my good luck shoes. They were platforms, so I'd be a head taller than usual. Five feet eight inches—the perfect height, in my opinion. I was short of an inch, but luckily women could wear heels and fake it for a while. Every time I wore those shoes, great things happened. Once, I met this guy, and we talked all night long about marriage—my protestation to not embark and his engagement to a woman he seemed to not love. Another time I found a twenty-dollar bill, and yet another time, I went straight through a mile-long line-up; the bouncer pointed at me and my friends, said, "Nice shoes," and gestured for us to pass.

I was so nervous that I packed on the makeup. I wore my hoop earrings, my purple cross with fake diamonds, and an endless array of bangles. I couldn't do anything to my hair except let it dry naturally, as it was as straight as pins, so what was the point of trying something else?

I examined myself in the mirror one too many times, then grabbed my purse and threw in some cash, lipstick, and my key. I tried to make room for my camera, but to no avail.

Walking toward the bar, I searched out Jack. Our eyes met instantly, for he was sitting at the bar, facing the entrance, waiting. He looked delighted and got up to greet me. He looked like a rock star. He had a bandanna around his head and wore a tight, black T-shirt, leather pants, and cowboy boots. He looked stunning, and a feeling of frenzy rushed through my veins at his confident walk toward me.

"Maria, I'm so glad you came." He opened his arms wide to hug me. He kissed me on both cheeks while hugging me. I smelled his cologne and breathed it in like a fresh summer flower all alone in a forest. Woodsy. Musky.

"Hi, Jack."

"You look amazing," Jack said, and took a step back to look me over. "Wow."

"Thank you," I said faintly. *You look delicious*.

He took my hand and led me to the bar.

"There's someone I want you to meet." I knew who he meant before he told me.

There, at the bar, a man stared right at me. He was beautiful, but in an ethereal way. He looked dreamy, like a faded postcard you didn't want to discard. We walked toward him, and Jack introduced us.

"Hunter, this is Maria. Maria, Hunter." I tried not to stare too closely, but Hunter's black eyes—black as a panther's—brought on a slight shiver.

"I've heard so much about you. It's a pleasure to meet you," he said, and extended his hand, which was cold and enormous. "Sorry if my hands are cold. You know what they say: cold hands, warm heart."

"It's a pleasure to meet you too." I beamed back politely. When he stood and gestured for me to sit on the barstool next to him, I was taken aback, because he was humongous—broad shouldered like a football player and taller than Jack by a foot. As he turned his head, I noticed his long and black hair. He reminded me of an Indian chief, with his prominent nose and high forehead.

"I think you've put a spell on my friend Jack here." I turned my gaze to Jack and grinned. Jack looked bashful for the first time. "And it's no wonder. You are a beauty," Hunter added in a sturdy tone. I should have thanked him for the compliment, but it took me awhile to compose myself. I couldn't understand why Hunter made me slightly nervous.

"Come sit, and I'll order you a drink." Hunter waved the bartender over without looking at him. "What would you like?" he asked.

I didn't know. *Should I have a beer? Wine?* I thought I needed a stiff drink. I needed something quick; Hunter was waiting for my reply.

Sitting on my barstool, Jack sat next to me on my left side. "I'll have a beer," I replied.

"Which kind?"

"Heineken."

"Make that two," Jack added, and touched my back.

"Charlie. Three Heinekens, bro." Charlie was quick to react and serve.

"Thanks, Charlie," Hunter said, and before Jack could reach into his pocket, Hunter added, "Put it on my tab." He winked at Jack.

"Thanks," I said, beginning to feel more at ease.

"Where are you from?" Hunter asked as soon as the beers were opened and placed in front of us.

"Montreal."

"Never been there, but I hear the French women are to die for. The best ones left!" He laughed to himself and said, "Cheers." I supposed he referred to the prostitutes, so I didn't know what to say. He had a Southern drawl I couldn't quite place, probably because I didn't know the actual geographical location of each state. After all, I was Canadian. We knocked our beers together and took a sip at the same time.

"I'm from Louisville, Kentucky," Hunter said as he stood and curtsied. "Grew up in the Cherokee Triangle." Like I knew what that meant. Hunter's voice sounded misplaced, from another decade or century. I had never been down South, so I guessed that was how they sounded, live and in person. He looked Indian, so when he said Cherokee, I kind of nodded as if I knew what he was talking about. *He'd better not quiz me now, or I'll look like a complete buffoon.*

I turned to Jack, who listened while drinking his beer.

"So what time do you go on stage, Jack?"

He looked at his watch. "Whenever I feel like it." His half-smirk lit up the room. "Actually, around ten or so."

Hunter turned around to talk to someone who'd greeted him, then completely turned his back on us for a while.

"So what do you think of Hunter?" Jack asked.

"I don't know. He's kind of scary, intimidating."

Jack laughed. "That's just his way. He's a teddy bear on the inside." The music seemed to suddenly get louder. I recognized the melody immediately.

"*I want to feel sunlight on my face,*" Jack sang along to Bono's voice.

"I love this song," I shouted and sang along with him. "*Where the streets have no name.*" Then Hunter turned and joined us.

We sang loudly now, somehow bonding in the

process. I'd always thought that when people sang together it was as if they cried together too. Emotional connections were being formed.

We all giggled.

"'*With or Without You*' is next," Jack said.

"'*I Still Haven't Found What I'm Looking For*,'" Hunter corrected him. "Wait for it. One, two…" Then I heard the strumming guitar echo through the bar.

"The owner, Don, loves U2. He plays the first two songs of the album every night," Hunter informed us, and Jack nodded. We sang a few bars together again.

"Hey, Don," Hunter called out to a man dressed in black across the room. "Have you met our friend Maria from Montreal?" In a split second, Don was in front of me.

Why did he have to interrupt the singing? I had been so enjoying it.

Don was a Spanish-speaking Frenchman. "We call him Don Juan." Hunter winked. "I think you can imagine why."

Don took my hand and kissed it like I was some kind of duchess.

"*Mademoiselle, enchantée*." Then Don went to the back of the bar and sat alone at a long table.

As soon as Don sat down, suddenly I noticed a group of men who stood out from anything I'd ever seen walk into the bar. They wore black from head to toe, as if they were in mourning. They looked like a gang of some kind, and they all walked toward me. Then they nodded toward Jack and approached Hunter. One by one, they each shook Hunter's hand and said, "Hey, Master." It was like watching Marlon Brando in *The Godfather*, minus the kissing of the hand.

Then I remembered what Jack had told me: Hunter was some kind of leader. I considered Hunter, watching him carefully. He met their gazes and nodded in acknowledgment, and each time one passed me, Hunter spoke his name. I counted eleven. I was sure Don was part of this mysterious group; with his clothes and attitude, he fit right in with this tight-knit operation. They were up to something—maybe selling drugs, but it could have been anything. How on earth would I know? They walked toward Don and nodded.

Jack was talking to someone, and every so often, he glanced at me, but I was too enthralled by Hunter's gang and trying to decipher their movements.

Their eyes were light—almost yellow-green like a cat's.

That was when I named them the "Gang of Cat's Eyes."

Hunter turned to me as soon I thought of it. "Maria, what do you think of my friends?"

"I don't know. I wasn't introduced." I was curious to see what would happen.

"I'm so rude!" With one glance in their direction, they came right back and passed us single file, like I was a bride at a wedding.

It was as if they knew exactly what he wanted from them with one look. It was eerie, and I enjoyed every minute of it. I had never seen anything like it.

One at a time, each member of the Gang of Cat's Eyes greeted me. "Freddy, Gilbert, Benny, Ed, Nick, Cannes, Donnie, William, Todd, and Gonzo. You've already met Don." I shook each cold hand and tried to be polite, but they looked at me with half-grins, then, like robots, immediately went back to their places. They seemed preoccupied, uninterested in meeting me.

"And now?" Hunter asked me again.

I looked down at my beer bottle and took a quick slug before I spoke. "They seem pretty cool." That was all I could think of saying without offending him. Honestly, I wanted to say, *They look like real bad asses,* but I held my tongue. "Are they in a rock band?" I asked, trying to lighten up the atmosphere. His gaze made me unsteady. Jack had mentioned Hunter was a psychic. *Is he reading my mind?* It felt like he was.

Hunter burst out laughing, banging his hand really loud on the bar. "No, they're definitely not. Jack is our only rock star, but he has a mind of his own."

Who cares what I think of your friends, anyway?

I felt a tap on my shoulder. "Maria." Jack turned to me and pointed to a man standing in front of him. "I want you to meet Pierre." Pierre was about two heads shorter than Jack, and he looked at me with refreshingly kind brown eyes.

"Nice to meet you," he said with a French accent.

"Nice to meet you too," I replied politely.

"Pierre plays with me sometimes. He plays the drums or piano—whatever I ask him to."

"Are you playing tonight?" I asked Pierre.

"If Jack wants. That's what I'm here discussing. Jack's the main man; he decides."

Jack had the most perfect teeth I'd ever seen. "I'm still thinking about it," he said jokingly, looking at Pierre. "No, seriously. Not tonight, Pierre. I already told you that on the phone," Jack continued.

"I didn't get the message," he replied, and walked away.

"You're just hoping I'll change my mind," Jack

shouted at his back.

"*Oui*," Pierre shouted back, not turning around.

Jack swirled my stool to face him. "Tonight, I have a special show planned." And he placed both his hands on the edge of the stool, tenderly touching my hips. "One song in particular I'll be playing for the first time."

"I can't wait to hear it."

I felt trapped between his arms, and a fleeting look passed between us.

At that instant, Don approached Jack from behind and told him it was time to go on stage.

"It's showtime," Jack said and pulled away from me very slowly. He finished his drink—to prepare himself, I guessed—and rubbed my back.

"It's for you," he whispered in my ear before stepping away.

I felt nervous, and knew exactly why—eager to hear the song he had written for me. Goosebumps traveled along my back, and my nipples popped forward. I folded my arms across my chest to hide them from onlookers.

I watched Jack walk onto the stage with confidence, pick up his guitar, and sit on a stool. He adjusted the microphone and placed one foot on the first ring of the barstool to lean his guitar on his leg. He removed the pick tucked in his guitar strings and bent his head slightly to one side as he leaned toward the microphone and said, "*Bonsoir*." Everyone hushed, and he started to strum his guitar. He looked over at me and began to sing in a clear, beautiful voice. He was serious and intense.

"That's beautiful," Hunter said next to me.

I nodded, refusing to turn my head, wanting to memorize each word as it was sung. From the beginning, it went like this:

"You were taking a picture of a rock,
I couldn't wait to hear you talk.
Come here and sit by me,
So, you can see what I can see.
The ocean vast and blue,
Meant for me and you.
I sit here every day and wait,
But I didn't know my fate
Till I saw your red hair blow
And felt myself aglow.

My enigmatic guitar strums for you,
To listen to my every word so true.
Pouring out of me like tears,
Tears of joy at seeing your fears

You try to hide inside a shell;
I'll pick you up and
Bring you to my wishing well.
Your eyes are my sun.
Come along with me for a morning run.
I met you and my life is complete.
You are my missing musical beat.
We talked for hours on end,
And I made a new friend.
And I made a new friend.
And I made a new friend."

He sang the chorus again and ended with

"Do you want to be more than friends?
Do you want to be more than friends?"

It was the most incredible song, at least to me, only

because it was *our* song. During the last part, Jack hadn't taken his eyes off me. When he finished, everyone clapped and whistled, including me. Hunter put his fingers between his lips and whistled as loud as he could.

"Amazing," Hunter shouted, and looked at me. "That was fuckin' beautiful."

"I-I know." Jack had left me speechless. The melody and the song weren't like anything I'd ever heard before—so pure and raw and folksy.

And vulnerable.

Then he sang some Van Morrison, and he called his friend Pierre over, who had been waiting like a dog panting for food. Pierre went to the piano, and they played great together. So much for Jack not needing him tonight. Pierre had known, though.

Hunter sat back down. I wanted to learn everything about Jack's world, and Hunter was a good start.

"So how long have you known Jack?"

"Since he moved here." Hunter spoke slowly, eyeing me closely, and then shifted in his seat. "You certainly are inspirational to him. I've never heard him sing a song with so much passion."

"Really?" I quickly asked.

"Yes, doll, you have definitely swept him off his feet. I've never seen him like this, except…" He paused and swept back his hair.

"What?" I was a curious cat now.

"Well, he should tell you," Hunter said dryly, and folded his large arms across his chest.

I glanced at Jack on stage; he was singing another song. I let it go and watched Jack intently, lost in thought.

"Sofia," Hunter said softly, and looked around.

Oh. Her.

"He's mentioned her," I lied. Well, it was a half lie; he'd almost mentioned her.

"Then you know he fell for her blindly. Oh, was she god-awfully bad, as my mama used to say." His Southern accent thickened.

I didn't reply. Maybe Jack should have been the one to tell me about Sofia. It seemed Hunter realized he'd said too much because he changed the subject immediately at my silence.

"Maria, what brings you to Saint-Tropez?" he asked, flipping his hair back again.

"I'm a photographer." My mouth was getting dry, so I reached over for my beer, touching his hand by accident. He moved it right away, but not until I felt the cold again. I drank my last sip.

"Cool." He sipped his beer, pretending nothing had happened. Nothing *did* happen, I guessed. "I dabble in some painting myself." Hunter glanced at my empty bottle. "Would you like another?"

"Sure." I tipped the bottle over to get the last drop and then turned to Hunter. Jack was singing so lovely in the background. "I saw the painting above Jack's bed. It's beautiful." Then I felt embarrassed.

"His bed, huh?"

I turned and looked at Jack, feeling a tingling redness.

"It's all cool." Hunter grinned..

"It's not like that," I said abruptly. "Anyway, your painting was really unique."

"Thanks."

The beers landed in front of us, and we both immediately picked them up and drank, probably just to do something after my awkward statement. *Why did I have to say "bed"? Oh, who cares what Hunter thinks, anyway?*

Hunter quickly took a few more sips. We watched Jack sing; he was so talented. Watching him perform excited me somehow, and I knew precisely why: it was most definitely the guitar and his voice. It was sexy all the way—sizzling hot.

Hunter glanced at me without saying a word. It suddenly felt sweltering hot in the bar. His forehead had a shine to it, and that was when I noticed he wore eyeliner. *Could he be gay?*

Nah. Impossible. He was very masculine-looking, but then again, how would I know?

"Can I ask you a question?"

"Shoot." He looked at me, and his gaze lingered slightly too long on my lips. He was most definitely not gay.

"Why did your parents name you Hunter?" I remembered Jack saying it was a story that only Hunter could relate. I hoped he didn't find my question prying, but he smirked broadly, and the muscles on his face relaxed instantly.

"You really wanna know?" He laughed, and I noticed the lines around the corners of his eyes, and it suddenly occurred to me he was older than what I first thought—about forty. He certainly looked great for his age.

"I do," I replied.

"Well, my papa loved to hunt, and when I was born"—he counted on his fingers—"the sixth son, he was away on a hunting trip. It was the first time he'd missed the birth of one of his children. My papa and my mama had a real, true love—they were soul mates." He was sincere now, looking off into the distance, seemingly trying to capture some long-forgotten moment. I turned to look at Jack, trying to watch both at the same time.

"He came back the next day, and I had already been born. My mama was so angry with him that she wouldn't talk to him for days. He brought back five rabbits and a deer. She cried and cried and didn't wanna see him. He was goin' crazy with heartache, so he decided to prepare a meal for her. And he put so much love into that rabbit stew—blended with onions, tomatoes, and garlic—that when he brought her the dish, she didn't say one word to him; she just ate it ravenously. She finally said, 'Jack'—that was his name—'this is the most delicious meal I've ever had,' and she cried. He hugged her and told her he loved her. 'What will we name our son?' she asked him. You see, she had hoped so much that I would be a girl, she'd never thought of any boys' names. Suddenly she said, 'Hunter. I like the sound of that.'"

The whole time Hunter spoke, I couldn't take my eyes off him; his story had me enthralled. Then he looked at me. "And that's the whole story, cross my heart and hope to die, stick a needle in my eye." He pointed to his eye and winked.

I hadn't heard that since grade school.

"Wow. Now that's a story!" I exclaimed, smiling.

"Yep, that's my life," he said, and I detected some sorrow in his voice.

Now I understood why Jack had said it would be better if Hunter told the story. If I tried to repeat it, I was sure I'd botch it up.

Jack had just finished his set, and we clapped along with the crowd. He walked off the stage, and Don took the microphone. "Everyone, a round of applause for Jack

Woods."

Jack Woods. I liked the sound of that. I realized I had never told him my last name either. Jack came over to us, looking serious.

"That was amazing."

"I'm glad you liked it." He looked delighted.

"So your last name is Woods? You should know how the forest is one of my favourite places."

"Not surprised." His eyes twinkled. "Oh my God, what's your last name? Should've already asked you!"

"Asteris," I replied. I didn't translate it for him like I usually did for strangers. It meant a star in Greek.

"Asteris," he repeated and grinned again. "That's lovely."

"Thank you." I smirked back.

"Star," Hunter said and winked at me. "Very apropos." He turned to Jack. "Your original was awesome, bro!" Hunter slapped Jack on the back enthusiastically, breaking our tranquil moment. Jack flinched; the smack must have been a little too hard.

"Thanks," he said humbly.

"What did you think of the song?" Jack asked me, taking his place next to me.

I couldn't believe Hunter knew the meaning of my name.

"I loved it tremendously," I answered, though I was slightly preoccupied with Hunter's comment.

Jack broke out his grin once more, but I guessed he was probably nervous.

"So what were you and Hunter talking about?" he asked.

"He told me how he got his name."

"Oh, great story."

Hunter asked Jack if he wanted a drink, and Jack nodded.

"You have a lovely voice. It's so touching…so unique," I said.

"You think so? No one has called my voice touching before." Jack reached for a cigarette, then offered me one first. "But I'll take any compliment you give." He smirked, and I shifted in my seat, crossing my legs the other way. Jack offered Hunter a cigarette, and he took one.

Somehow, I banged my foot into Jack's by mistake. "Sorry," I mumbled.

"Anytime." Jack glanced down. "I love your shoes. Very sexy." His gaze lingered on my legs. "Great legs too." Then his gaze traveled up to my neckline. "And your dress is fabulous." He looked up to my face. "Beautiful and exotic." He looked around dramatically, then lowered his voice so only I could hear his last line. "Maria, I like you a lot."

His whole discourse left me feeling dreamy. The way his eyes and mouth moved in harmony made me want him even more. I couldn't respond, still holding the unlit cigarette in my hand. Hunter had his back turned to us and talking to someone.

I looked at Jack closely. He had charisma and talent, and I felt like I was going to fuck it up somehow—like I always did.

It all came down to the fact that I had never trusted men. Why would he be any different?

My grandfather had loved me completely and done his best to be a father to me, but the generation gap was extreme. While in elementary school, I had to write a Father's Day card every year, I felt sick to my stomach.

Other girls would make hearts and draw pictures of their dads and write "I love you" all over the card. I sat there and wanted to barf. An ache would build inside from the sadness. Once, I said my dad was dead, and my friend Jessica, who sat next to me, started to cry. I was in grade two. I really wanted to hit her and ask, "Why are you crying? Your daddy is alive." I was jealous, and I excused myself and went to the bathroom to puke my pain out, but I didn't feel any better after; I just had the worst breath of my life. To my mind, my dad was dead, because he never called me on my birthday. Sometimes I wondered if he thought I never existed. Did he even know about me? I don't know which was worse—Father's Day or Mother's Day. They were both equally traumatic for me.

When I asked *yiayia* and *pappou* about my parents, they each told me a different story, never considering how contrary their versions were. My y*iayia*'s story went like this: *"Well, your mom never told us who your father was, koukla. We don't know. For all we know, he could be dead."* When I heard that, I cried in my room for hours, thinking about my dead father.

Then *pappou* Alex came to tell me his version: *"Maria,"* his lecture began, *"your father loved your mother, and your mother loved your father, even if it was for a brief time. I know this because you are a flower full of love."* He had such a way with words. I listened attentively, my eyes full of tears, urging him to continue his story. *"It wasn't meant to be. Something stopped them from loving each other forever. We will never know. Your mother has left and will never come back. Your father does not want to be your father, but I am your grandfather, and my blood runs in your blood, and*

I love you like my own daughter. You are our second chance."

Although I was only eight, I understood at that moment that *Pappou* Alex was all I had as a father figure, and luckily he was a man who kept his word and taught me many lessons.

In grade three, I made my grandfather a card on Father's Day and wrote him a poem. He was touched and, not understanding English well, read the card slowly. *"God has brought you into our life for a reason," Pappou* said, and hugged me fiercely.

I understood that my father would never come find me and take me for ice cream, read me a bedtime story, teach me to ride my bike, or just love me. But I had my grandfather, who replaced him like one does a bulb, whose light was sharper, more intense, and who was meant to have a second chance.

As for my mother, I learned to let go of the hope of ever meeting her. My *yiayia* had been my mother from the day I was born.

There were worse things in life. I could have been an orphan without any nurturing love, like Angela, an old classmate of mine. I wasn't that fucked-up; at least, I didn't think so. My ex-boyfriends would profoundly object.

Okay, I was slightly fucked-up.

I didn't trust men, but so far Jack had given me no reason not to trust him.

At the back of my mind, a little voice spoke to me: *What if he's like your father?*

And this scared the living crap out of me. Honestly, I didn't know the answer to that question. I didn't know my father—not even his name. I'd made up all kinds of names for him. He would be Gabriel, Jonathan, or Ewan. I'd come up with distinguished names just to fill up the emptiness. Now I referred to him as Dirt. Dirt was a perfect name for a fuckin' lowlife, scumbag, prick, asshole, deserter, and loser like my father. I sometimes called him a cunt just to really get the anger out.

Maybe he was a musician too; maybe he wasn't. Not knowing had driven me crazy.

"Maria. Did you hear me?"

Jack was looking at me, waiting for a reply, while I'd been off in the faraway land of My Pathetic Life. "Sorry." I couldn't say anything else to him.

He was waiting for me to tell him I liked him too. It wasn't going to happen—not yet, at least.

"Are you okay?" Jack looked puzzled. Here he was, laying it all on the table, and I was acting like a scatterbrain.

"Yeah, I'm fine. I'd like another drink, please." Make it quick, I wanted to holler.

Jack came closer to me and touched my hair. "Anything you say." He motioned to Charlie to bring another round but didn't remove his gaze from mine. He was studying me.

"Tell me what's bothering you. You look preoccupied." He lowered his hand to my back.

"Jack, it's not that I don't like you." *That sounded awful.* "I mean, I do like you." He beamed then. "I don't trust men easily."

There. I was honest.

"And I don't trust women easily," he replied, and continued to rub my back.

I melted a bit, like an ice cube on a hot day. I was a piece of melted butter sliding around in a frying pan, waiting for the egg to fall and cook. I was… My mind continued with analogies, till I realized he waited impatiently for a reply.

We were both scared.

"Look, Maria." Jack put both his hands over mine. "I want to be with you."

I didn't reply. I was a fuckin' idiot. The words couldn't come out. Before I knew it, it was time for his second set, and he was off. I watched him stride onto the stage like a star. And just like that, I admitted to myself I was falling for him. I wanted to fall on top of him, under him, next to him—anywhere close to him. I knew I would follow him out of that bar that night, and not stop following him till he disappeared from my thirty-sixth birthday party in 2004.

Part Two: Jack

You have to die a few times before you live.
~Charles Bukowski

Chapter Five

Wind song and words pouring out of me like a thunderstorm

1989

There was something to be said about redheads. I didn't know what exactly that was, because I'd never felt there was anything special about them. I placed my guitar on the stand and wiped my brow so the sweat didn't get into my eyes. Maybe it was the shade of her red hair.

Or maybe it had nothing at all to do with her hair colour, but her actual hair. I always wanted to fuckin' touch it. What had gotten into me? I felt like a fifteen-year-old with raging hormones.

Get a grip, Jack. Be cool.

I was pretty much always in control of my feelings. Even when I was drunk, I still knew what the fuck I was doing—or at least, I made myself believe I did.

The funny thing was, I could make myself believe pretty much anything I wanted.

As I walked over to her, Hunter clapped and yelled out, "Bravo, Jack!"

I took my time. I wasn't in a rush, but I tingled inside.

"Your second set was amazing, bro," Hunter said with another slap on my back with his strong hand, moving me slightly. I had never gotten used to his insane size. Hunter's slap could probably knock me over if I didn't brace myself for it.

"Thanks." I grinned at him.

"It was fantastic," Maria added, staring at me, distracting me, catching me off guard.

In this light, her hair looked copper, like my eighth-grade high jump award. I would stare for hours at that award—a young man jumping high in the air. Probably because the sculpture freaked me out, and I kept thinking it must have been me or some other fucked-up concoction in my head. Or it was the drugs that did it. Way too many drugs.

"Why, thank you, guys," I said to them both, and looked from one to the other.

They were getting along great. Thank God. Most of the girls I introduced to Hunter didn't warm up to him, and vice versa. Girls were slightly standoffish with him, partly due to his size, partly to his attitude. If Hunter didn't like someone, that someone definitely would not like him. He didn't give a fuck about social etiquette or being polite for politeness's sake. If he liked someone though, that person was *in*. He'd treat them like they'd always wanted to be treated.

And he was one of the smartest and funniest guys I'd ever met. He'd have me in stitches half the time, and the other half, contemplating life and its essence.

"Get me another beer for Jack!" Hunter shouted out at Charlie, who placed the beer bottle in front of me before Hunter could finish saying my name.

I turned to Maria, lifted my beer, and tapped it lightly to her bottle. She lifted hers and met mine halfway for the second tap. I watched her keenly as she drank. The way she tilted her head back, leaving her neck exposed, made her hair pass the seat of the barstool—it was so utterly long and inviting, I had to stop myself from reaching for it again. Fuck. She was burning a hole called desire in my heart. Her dress was snug in all the right places. Her bosom peeked out at me, and her sleek, long legs were crossed. And those shoes. They were fuckin' gorgeous on her. I'd already told her that; I couldn't repeat myself—at least not yet.

"I have to go to the bathroom." She stood and reached for her purse on the bar top. "Which way?" She looked from the back of the bar to the front, then to the side, and then saw the WC sign as I pointed to the back.

"To the right of the stage in the back," I said.

"Oh, I see it." She was inches away from me as I sat obsessing over her every movement.

I watched Maria walk away and felt a surge of desire as her ass swayed. She was going to drive me wild with a lovely ass like that.

The lust number was number one.

"She's a beautiful girl." I turned to glance at Hunter and caught him looking at her thoughtfully.

"Yep," I agreed as she walked into the bathroom and we lost sight of her.

"You could lose yourself in a girl like that," Hunter said, expressionless.

"I aim to," I said smugly.

"You're a lucky guy. She's a jewel." The compliments were gushing out—not typical of Hunter.

"I like that. A jewel." It was so true.

"Jack, I really loved that song and melody. It was very catchy, man," Hunter said passionately, and he sprang up, extending his large arms and throwing them about. He came closer to me. "We have to put that on the radio somehow. I know a DJ."

"You know everyone, Hunter." How many times had he told me this? Hundreds. I knew he meant well, but he'd never made that call. "Hunter, you know how hard it is," I said, leaning closer as well.

"I know, bro." He patted my back. "This time I'm serious." He looked away, lost in thought, planning some Hunter scheme. "I'm going to call him tomorrow. His name is DJ Antoine."

"I know." He'd spoken about him so often. It was like he had memory loss sometimes.

"We'll make a demo tape and give it to him." Then he banged on the bar. "Let's go this Friday!"

"We'll see."

"No, Jackie, we won't see. There's nothing to see but the bright future ahead. You have talent. Why waste it?" His voice was excitable, and his hand almost hit me in the face as he started his speech.

"I'm not wasting it. I'm doing what I love."

"Yes, but why not share your music? There's absolutely nothing wrong with that."

"So why don't you exhibit?" I retorted, knowing bloody well what his answer was going to be.

Hunter spit out in anger, "Because I hate art critics!"

"And I hate music critics."

Hunter nodded. "Critics are wannabe artists who don't have enough talent to do it themselves."

"Hallelujah, you said it." This was the way this conversation always twisted and turned, and we'd never go see that DJ.

"Fuck it, man." Hunter turned to me and folded his arms. "You're right. Who needs anyone's criticism? It'll only bring you down. Then you'll start doubting your art, your integrity, your flow." Hunter wasn't going to stop now. I checked to see if Maria was coming, but she wasn't.

I nodded in agreement. What else was there to do? He was on a roll.

"You see"—Hunter leaned even closer—"what you have is yours, belongs to you, and no one can take it away."

From the corner of my eye, I saw Maria walk toward us. Hunter continued. "No money, no words, nothing can be taken away from you, if you don't let it." His eyes were focused, and he emphasized the last five words. Maria sat down quietly on her stool and glanced at Hunter.

"If you lose your gift"—Hunter lifted two fingers on each hand to mimic quotation signs—"you misplace it, like your keys. Don't you get it?" He stared at me, wrapped up in his words, waving his arms about him. "The critics want to make you sweat for it. They want to kill your creativity to have an article to write about something they know absolutely nothing about." Hunter glanced at Maria. "What do you think?" She seemed surprised at his question, but she seemed pleased.

"I think that if you have a gift, you're lucky to know what it is. I think half the world is lost," she answered with self-assurance.

Hunter stared at her, absorbing what she'd said. Oh boy. We were in for a doozy of a discussion.

I reached for the cigarettes. Maria took one first, then Hunter.

"You know," I said, placing a cigarette between my lips, "when you are an artist, you can still be lost—"

"Isn't that the truth?" Hunter interjected. "But you know, at least you can take out all the confusion and anger on your subject matter."

I reached over and lit Hunter's cigarette first, then Maria's, then mine.

"What's your subject matter?" Maria asked, exhaling the first puff and looking at her cigarette to make sure it was lit.

"I'm influenced more by feelings than actual subjects, like, say, Monet, who was so into nature and water lilies." Hunter rolled his eyes as if he was bored. "I love all art—don't get me wrong—but the Impressionist movement…that trend is overrated. It was those fuckin' art critics who made it popular for the masses." Hunter nervously took a puff and continued. "Those art critics were all buddies with the artists. They were followers and wanted their mugs to be in the paintings. Fuckin' dicks. They think they created the movement because they wrote about it. A big ego is a fucked-up ego." Hunter knew all about that.

"I never looked at it that way," Maria said, looking thoughtful. "But I do think Monet's earliest work is his best."

Hunter eyed Maria closely. "That's what I'm getting at. He painted his family life at Argenteuil, and those works were magnificent, not those fuckin' floating water lilies. Water lilies are not my idea of a masterpiece. Does absolutely nothing for me. Again, it was the art critics who jumped on board the rave and claimed the water lilies had some kind of following, just as they did with Campbell Soup, for Christ's sake!" Hunter smashed his hand on the bar and blew out smoke like a madman.

"Too much analysis of art is not a good thing," I said. "I think art is subjective. Hunter, if you like water lilies and cans of soup, well then, why the fuck not?"

"Because it's hammered into you that you should like it!" Hunter shouted. "And people follow whatever those dumb-ass critics write, as if it's God's words, when it's a bunch of wannabes who don't know their asses from their elbows," he hollered, and crushed his cigarette out halfway through.

"I don't really read what the critics write," Maria said reflectively.

"You don't have to read it; it's out there. The media has a powerful way of getting through to us without our conscious awareness. Look at those fuckin' commercials." Hunter glanced back and forth from me to Maria, and Charlie winked at me from behind the bar, giving me a "there he goes again" look while Hunter went on. "Whether or not you like it, most people don't have an opinion, so they listen to any Dick and Harry boast about the relevance of pointillism—which is a scientific, methodological way of painting—like it's the best art movement. It's bullshit."

"Hunter, it's all good," I said so he wouldn't get even more excited and break something. I knew how out-of-control he could get. I'd seen it a million times.

Maria listened and looked at Hunter pensively. "Maybe you have a point," she said, blowing out smoke and watching it whirl around her. Her brown eyes looked off into space, and I wondered what she was thinking about.

Who really gave a fuck about what Hunter babbled on about? God, she was gorgeous, and from where I sat, hard to reach.

"Do you know Ansel Adams?" Maria peered at Hunter, awaiting a reply.

He didn't answer, but his facial muscles twitched.

Who the fuck was Ansel Adams? I pretended to go along like I knew, though she wasn't talking to me.

"He takes pictures of landscapes, rocks—basically nature," she explained. Hunter nodded. He knew exactly who she referred to. "Well, I never saw the big stink about it, whereas Robert Doisneau, who took that picture of 'The Kiss in Paris,' captured the essence of photography." Her eyes lit up like a little girl who spoke about her favourite pet. "It's like you're a voyeur, watching an intimate moment between two lovers."

She was lovely—and smart. Maria was lost in thought. She was right too. I knew that picture very well. In Paris, that picture was everywhere.

"You're absolutely right, Maria," I said, and leaned in closer to her. "Photography as an art captures a moment and freezes it in time. Wouldn't it be great to be able to do that with life?" I asked jokingly, trying to ease the tension. Her eyes widened, and she beamed.

"It sure would," she said.

"And on and on life goes, without stopping, without the hands of time freezing it, although that would make a great painting," Hunter said, coming down from his high on words and with less of an air of authority.

"Didn't Salvador Dali do that already?" Maria asked, sounding sure of herself.

"I like a girl who knows her art." Hunter's dark eyes glistened. Sometimes he was so fuckin' creepy. "This one is definitely a keeper." Hunter turned to me and winked.

Yep, she was. I smirked. "I know."

Maria glanced back and forth. "So, do I pass?" she asked in a melodic voice.

"With flying colours!" Hunter exclaimed.

"I didn't know there was a test," I said, half joking.

"There's always a test, bro!" Hunter's arm landed across my back. "You never know the mark you're gettin'," he continued, emphasizing his Southern drawl. Hunter stood and bowed in front of Maria. "I gotta go, *chérie*. I have a date." His eyes sparkled like a child's who was up to no good. "Can't leave a lady waiting too long. And I'm sure you two wanna be alone." Hunter straightened up tall and then bent down again to kiss Maria on both cheeks. "Enjoy your night," he said, and ran off.

"You too. Bye, Hunter," I replied.

"Bye," Maria chirped after me, but he was already at the door. Fuck, he moved fast.

She turned to me with her doe-like eyes and grinned.

"Did you have a good time?" I asked, stroking her hair lightly. She didn't seem to mind.

"Absolutely."

I glanced around the bar and noticed that not many people were left. The music was winding down, and Charlie was cleaning up.

"You want to get out of here?" I wanted to be completely and utterly alone with her…all to myself.

"Yes. Where to now?"

"Anywhere you want to go."

"Do you want to come to my place? I don't know if I have any Greek coffee, but I can make a mean English one."

"Anything you make, I'm drinking. Anything you want, I'm doing," I said, still stroking her soft hair. I looked at her lips. Man, I wanted to kiss her succulent mouth so badly. I felt pangs of lust in the very core of my body.

Maria got up and reached for her purse. Her slender arm touched mine, and I felt another tingle. Then she gazed at me, and I could tell she felt it too. She showed me a hint of her desire, and I wanted to plunge right into her.

I got up and touched her back. “Let’s go. Lead the way.”

“Have a good night,” Charlie hollered after us. We waved good-bye and walked out, down the street. I didn’t want to remove my hand from her curvy back.

“I love to walk in Saint-Tropez. This city is meant for walking,” she said excitedly, and looked up at me.

“With you, it’s like I’m walking on this street for the first time,” I said, and I meant it. She laughed.

“Is something funny?” I sneered at her.

“You are.” She became a little hesitant, and I felt her back tighten up. What had I said wrong?

“All guys have only one thing on their minds.”

“What I said was a compliment, and now I’m embarrassed I even said it.” I removed my hand from her back. Of course it was true that all guys had only one thing on their minds. Could you blame us?

“No, no, Jack.” She stopped. “It’s really not you. It’s me.”

I knew then that I had to take it slow with her. She was scared.

She looked at me, then continued to walk, her head tilted to the side.

“I’m afraid,” she whispered, “I don’t like men all that much, unless they’re over sixty-five.” She raised her voice slightly. “Honestly, you should run from me. I’m going to hurt you, because I don’t know how to love a man. Every guy runs far away. Most of them don’t want to talk to me when they run into me again." She didn't look at me now, but straight ahead.

I took a chance and put my arm across her shoulders. She relaxed. We were a perfect fit. "I'll take my chances," I whispered in her ear.

Maria didn't say anything else. Her gaze was fixed on her feet and the sidewalk, but she seemed to feel more and more comfortable with my arm around her.

"Also," I added as an afterthought, since she was pensive, "I'm not like any man you've ever met."

I sounded smug, but I didn't give a fuck. I ran my fingers through my hair and removed my arm from her shoulders to reach for my pack of smokes. I walked slowly, and Maria slowed her pace too.

I felt her scrutinize me, studying my every move. I inhaled and blew out the smoke. I offered her one, but she didn't want it, so we continued to walk side by side.

"This way," Maria said, gesturing with her arm, and I followed. I'd follow her anywhere. She was striking under the light of the moon.

"Stop. Hold on," I said, and stood a little closer to her while she took a step back. Just my luck.

"What is it?"

"Nothing. I just want to see your face in the moonlight." She left me breathless; her eyes shimmered, and I lost my train of thought. I stepped closer still, inches away from her face. I examined every pore on her skin. She had a soft complexion, olive skin, and brilliant red hair that looked dark auburn under the moon. I touched her cheek gently, then bent down to kiss the spot I'd laid my hand on. She didn't move.

"I couldn't resist," I whispered.

"I liked it," she whispered back.

I wanted to take it slow so badly. *Don't rush, Jack. She's delicate*, I told myself.

Maria took another step back. "Come, we're almost there."

I smoked my cigarette; I had almost forgotten about.

She turned down an alley, and then a narrow staircase suddenly appeared. I followed close behind like a hound. I could smell her perfume slightly as she walked up the stairs, her cute bum an arm's length away.

"Look at these beautiful flowers," she said, pointing to purple hyacinths growing along a peach wall.

"Lovely." I meant her ass.

Maria turned right, then left, and then stopped. It was easy to remember. "We're here." She searched for her key, placed it into the lock, and swung open the door. No jamming or huffing and puffing. "Welcome," she said as I followed her inside.

It was one of the tiniest places I'd ever seen—tiny but adorable. I walked into the living room in one step, and then two steps led me into the kitchen. I looked beyond the kitchen and saw one small door with a step down. I peeked inside it and noticed a pink-flowered comforter with hues of green on an unmade bed. I beamed. A girl who didn't make her bed…

Now we're talking. I felt like grabbing her and throwing her onto the bed in one movement.

I heard Maria cling and clack. Her shoes were off, left at the doorstep, her purse thrown on the couch, her hair up in a bun, and her jewelry off.

"I'm going to make some coffee," she said. "Make yourself comfortable."

From where I stood, I could see every room except the bathroom, which I actually had to use right then.

"Where's your bathroom?" I asked.

"Next to my bedroom." She pointed. "Through there. You can't miss it." I walked into her bedroom and passed her bed, glancing at her clothes leisurely lying around in different piles on a wooden rocking chair. On the dresser were some earrings, sunscreen, and loose-leaf paper with scribbled handwriting.

I shouldn't snoop.

I did.

Trying to make out the handwriting, I quickly read the words: *Fathers leaving and never arriving, for any event*, read one line.

I continued on toward the bathroom and closed the door, thinking about that line. On top of her tiny sink were a lipstick case and a white perfume bottle with flowers. I picked it up—Anaïs Anaïs. I smelled it. Ah, it was so sweet. *What am I doing?*

I pulled down my pants, lifted the toilet seat, leaned one arm against the wall in front of me, and let my mind go.

It was Sofia who had fucked me up so much. She had lied, cheated, and stolen. She had left me empty. That had been four years ago.

Fuck it. I didn't want to think about it right now. *Get those thoughts out of your head, Jack.*

Maria excited me. She had that allure I craved. From the moment I saw her on the beach, I was hooked, just like a fish caught on a lure it couldn't wriggle free from.

The words had come to me easily as I'd watched her approach. She inspired me. Fuck. I was falling for her. I flushed the toilet and placed the seat down as it had been. Glancing at myself in the mirror, my hair was all over the place. I patted it down with some water, being extra careful not to tip the perfume bottle as I closed the faucet. Okay, I was nervous. Maria made me feel like a fuckin' teenager. I slapped my face a few times to snap out of it.

Then I heard music. My senses awakened; I was alert. It was Edith Piaf. What a storyteller; I adored her. My mom would play Edith Piaf every time she was mad at my dad. Even though it wasn't that often, I had listened too because I didn't have a choice. The thing was, if you had no alternative, you gave in to whatever was around you.

I opened the bathroom door and walked past Maria's bedroom, which invited me in like an old friend. I had memorized the patterns and pieces of furniture already. Listening to the notes, I hummed along as I entered the kitchen in a few quick steps. Maria watched the coffee brew, holding two mugs, her back to me.

As soon as she heard my humming and footsteps, she turned to face me. "I found this collection here. It's mostly French music. I had never listened to Edith Piaf before I'd come here. Isn't she incredible?" It was more of a statement than a question.

I nodded. "My mom played Edith Piaf in times of distress," I said, half-grinning, reaching into my pocket for my pack of cigarettes. It was squished. I hoped none of the cigarettes were broken, as was usually the case. I opened it up, and so far so good. I counted: three left and intact.

At the thought of my mom, I needed to smoke badly. I hadn't spoken to her in months.

"Your mom has good taste."

"She sure does. She taught me a lot about music without realizing it." I lit my cigarette. "Do you have an ashtray?" While Maria searched for one, I continued,

"She could never actually play a musical instrument, but she loved to collect them. She liked antiques, especially antique musical instruments. Every time she left the house, I would jam on them." I sat on her chair, and she finally found an ashtray. It had glass bubbles around it and looked like it'd been around since the 1950s. "The instruments would call my name—'Jack, please play me.'" Maria lifted the pot of coffee and poured two cups. She then opened the fridge, pulled out the milk, and grabbed the sugar jar on the counter, smiling the entire time.

"I wish I played an instrument. I had no one to show me anything like that. I was just grateful to be fed and clothed, only because my grandparents kept rehashing the war and how they'd starved when they were my age. Now it's drilled in my head how grateful I should be." Maria brought the cups over, but she was expressionless. As she spoke, her grin faded, and she hadn't been talking to me directly.

"Thank you," I said, and looked delighted as she placed a Mickey Mouse mug in front of me. "Nice mug."

"The lady I'm renting the place from has quite a selection of Disney mugs." Maria cracked a smirk once again and went back to the kitchen to bring over the milk and sugar.

"Let's get back to your mother. Do you know anything at all about her?" I was intrigued, eager to find out anything I could about her.

"If I could tell you something about her, I would. But no mother, no father. Like I told you, my grandparents raised me. I loved them so much. They were all I had, and now I have nobody." She stirred some milk and sugar into her coffee, watching the colour lighten. "Can I have a cigarette?" She looked up with a serious expression.

"Certainly. Help yourself." I had placed them on the table before I sat down so as not to break the last two.

She opened the pack. "Oh, it's okay. You only have two left."

"Take one." I reached inside the pack and gave her one. "I insist."

She took the cigarette. I flicked the lighter and held it for her, and enjoyed it tremendously when she came in close to me.

"Thanks," she said in a forlorn voice.

"You know, at least you had your grandparents, who were your flesh and blood. They must have done something right, because you are a smart, strong girl." I touched her hand gently as it held the mug.

Maria looked at me, seeming heavy-hearted, melancholic; her eyes were watery. "Jack, you have no idea how much I miss them. Miss their craziness, their bickering and thoughtfulness. They raised me like the daughter they'd wished they'd had. My mom was such a disappointment to them."

"What was her name?"

"Irini," she whispered. "I try not to think about her name," she said abruptly, taking two quick puffs back to back. She was sure getting used to the cigarettes in France.

"It's her loss that she never got to know you," I said sincerely. "You are worth knowing." I blew out the smoke. "And I really want to know you so much better."

Maria took a sip of her coffee, reflecting on my words. She was so long gone from this conversation. The hurt in her eyes was unbearable. I saw it clear as day.

"I pushed everyone away," Maria said in the same monotone. "Till I was alone again—comfortable again." She kept her gaze from mine.

"I like your happiness better than your sadness."

"Sadness?"

"Yes, while you were talking about your mother, you looked so sad. I can't imagine what it could have been like." It was so fucked-up.

"I hated her for years. I hated my father even more. I don't even know his name. You can't imagine what that's like. It's horrible." She had almost finished her cigarette; one more drag, and it would be time to butt it out. Maria had put up her wall again. It was closing in around her. I was determined to break through and get to her other side. I pulled my chair closer to hers.

"I feel for you." And I genuinely did.

Finally, she gazed into my eyes. "You're sweet."

"As sugar," I added, and she giggled.

"I love your giggle."

"This anger has left me empty."

Her honesty brought out a tenderness in me. Cigarettes were dead and forgotten in the ashtray.

"One second I'm melancholic, the next I'm giggling."

I moved forward and placed my hands on my chin, positioning my elbows on the table. She appeared edgy, not wanting to look into my eyes, fidgeting with the ashtray

Without taking my eyes off her, I confessed my feelings. "Maria, you are a beautiful woman, and I like you." It was so simple to say and so true.

We locked gazes, and she said in a low voice, "Jack, you are beautiful too." She leaned closer to me and caressed my cheek in a smooth motion. I lifted my head and bent closer to kiss her lips.

Maria opened her mouth, and I felt her tongue explore my mouth. I met her tongue with mine, and passion erupted. We slowly got up, and our tongues intertwined even deeper. Slipping my hands around her small waist, she clasped her hands tightly around my neck. She took a step back; I took a step back. I wasn't letting go of that kiss for anything. The urgency was alive in both of us.

I instantly felt her sense of abandonment and need to be loved. She led the way, walking backward to her bedroom, and we kissed as if it were a slow dance; moving my hands quickly toward her hair, still pinned up in a bun, and loosening it to flow down. Her hair fell around her and the scent invaded my senses exciting my arousal; trailing my mouth languidly down her neck, gasping slightly for air after that never-ending kiss. Maria let out a sigh that further increased my desire.

I had felt my hardness grow the minute our lips met, but now it was as if a rush of adrenaline flowed from me to her.

We banged into the side of her bed. "Oops," she muttered, and we opened our eyes to see where our blind kiss has landed us. Her eyes were half open, full of desire and naked sex. She made me so horny, I thought I was going to explode right there. *Hold on; take it slow, Jack.*

She took a step forward, then lay on the bed, pulling me on top of her. I lifted her halfway up and pulled off her dress in one motion as she removed my shirt insanely quick.

Hint: She doesn't want to take it too slow. Her brown eyes were slightly red and smaller than usual. She was hungry for me too and ready.

"You're gorgeous." My voice echoed, murmuring desperately in her hair, burying my face in her neck and kissing her there, feeling her melt in my arms.

"That feels great," she moaned.

I put my arms around her back to remove her beige lace bra, and tried a few times to unsnap it. She giggled, and I kissed her sweet lips again, harder this time. Finally, the bra strap gave, and I threw it across the room. Her breasts were plentiful—white with dark brown nipples erect, saluting me, wanting my lips to taste them. So I lowered my mouth to devour her. *So delicious.* She moaned even louder, and I slid my hands lower down. I lay a hand on her stomach, then reached lower still to stroke her inner thighs. She jumped a little.

"Relax," I whispered in her ear. I felt her, warm and wet, and stroked her gently.

"Jack." She sighed.

At the sound of my name, I lifted her peach lace underwear and peeked inside. Yep, I was right—there was something about a natural redhead. Reddish pubic hair greeted me, and I placed my fingers inside her, rubbing up and down till I felt her clitoris throb. Then I yanked off her underwear, and she gasped even more.

I wanted her so badly, and felt her desire ablaze in every part of her body.

Maria lifted her head and stroked my back. Then she reached down to my belt and unbuckled it. She unzipped my pants easily as I lay motionless for a second. She pulled them off, struggling with them around my hips before I helped her. She tossed them on the floor and giggled some more. Then she bent and, with another giggle, removed my underwear and flung them in the air.

"Something funny?" I mumbled, feeling stoned with desire.

"Nervous giggle," she whispered and, naked and breathless, leaned close to kiss me hard on the lips. Her bare breasts rubbed against my chest, and I reached out to touch them. My cock throbbed, and her kisses were like the best chocolate I had ever tasted. Her hair was in my face, her saliva in my mouth. I pulled back and whispered in her ear while flicking my tongue in and out, "I want to make love to you right now."

"Slow down…" Maria whispered back, and kissed my neck, moving lower and lower every second. She licked my chest, and as she reached for my cock to place in her mouth, I let out an uncontrollable moan. "Ah, Maria." I sighed; it felt heavenly. She sucked so hard and so furiously, I couldn't take it, so I lifted her head with both hands.

"I can't slow down…" I flipped her underneath me. She spread her legs and accepted all of me with one breathless sigh and a thousand moans that made my insides roar.

I was home; our senses joined, and it was only us and our bodies in the universe. I never wanted to leave her body—she was made for me.

"Oh, you're so hot, Maria," I moaned in ecstasy, thrusting into her harder and harder. I couldn't be gentle, I couldn't be slow. I was having sex like I'd never experienced before. I reached a height I never wanted to come down from.

"Stop for a second," Maria whispered, and I unwillingly stopped as she slid from under me, rolled on top, and wrapped her legs around my waist to guide me underneath her. She squirmed, and I cradled her hips, meeting her every step of the way. She cried out within a minute, taking quick, deep breaths, then suddenly let out a loud groan. That was it. I pulled out and exploded all over her sheets and her naked hip. I was slightly embarrassed because I didn't have any condoms on me—I rarely carried them around. Maria lay next to me, spent—exhilarated, given her expression. She was glowing, and she beamed at me.

"That was fuckin' incredible!" I shouted a little too loudly. I wanted to pound on my chest like a fuckin' gorilla.

Maria looked at me as she wiped and cleaned herself with a tissue. "Yes, it was." She was grinning from ear to ear.

I loved how you could lose yourself in the sex act—lose all rationale, civility, logic. It was pure animalism.

Maria jumped on the bed and touched my chest, then stared deep into my eyes. "Jack, I think that was the best sex ever!"

"You think?" I grabbed her long legs with one sweep. "Would you like to have a go at it again to make sure?" I bent to kiss her inner thigh, which was so bloody soft and luscious. Not a single hair on her velvety thighs. She laughed but didn't object. Why would she?

"Ready when you are." She chuckled. Boy, was I ready.

"I've just gotten started," I murmured, kissing her cheek, her neck. And then I made love to her again, but this time I took my sweet time. I heard a romantic love song playing, and I realized Edith Piaf still sang in the background.

The music moved through me, in me, and my senses were alert to the tempo, beat, and pitch. But still, all I could do was concentrate on Maria's supple skin reacting to my sensual touch.

Her half-open eyes glistened with ecstasy, her skin alit with sweat, and she was as delicious as sweet pineapple. I was hard instantly and penetrated her slowly, enjoying the sound of her groans, new to my ears as if I were a hungry wolf.

I wanted to please her, to ease her, to feel every part of her—to take away all her pain.

"Ohhh," she moaned, and I lost myself—in her voice, around her, above her, underneath her; I had all of her, and I felt strong. An urgency surged through me, and once I released it, I was exhausted, filled with her being.

"Amazing!" I was out of breath, and I looked up at her.

Her hair fell into my face, and I brushed it back with my fingertips, holding it to the side of her head while looking deeply into her eyes, so red-hot, filled with passion and lust.

"I agree," she hummed, and lay next to me with a thump—squeaky mattress.

Though I tried my best not to, I closed my eyes, and Maria snuggled next to me like a kitten, and then pulled the sheets over our naked bodies. The peacefulness enveloped us as the music stopped, and we slept till the sun rose. I opened my eyes and turned my head to see Maria's beautiful face in deep slumber, reaching over to stroke her hair and back, her body twitched before she slowly moved her legs on top of mine. My body was ready to love her all over again. Her eyes were still closed, and my lips gently kissed her breasts and caressed her heart-shaped ass, feeling the voluptuous curves.

Heavenly.

She was my heaven.

I slid over her to lie on the other side of the bed, rubbing my hard cock against her ass as she slowly moved around, moaning and groaning.

"Am I dreaming?" she whispered, her eyes still closed.

"No, this is real." I entered her from behind and rocked her gently back and forth till the gentleness became rough and uncontrollable. I lost my self-control as she whimpered and sighed in ecstasy. By the sound of her quick gasps, I knew she was coming, thrusting even harder as she came, clutching the pillow and screaming out. I didn't want to brag—actually, I did. I was an incredible lover.

I was falling down a tunnel with her. That would be a great line for a lyric to remember another time when my sanity was more in control and not in a state of sexual frenzy, pulling out and coming within seconds after her.

"Jack, you're driving me crazy," she mumbled. Her head tilted to me as she rolled from under me and landed on her back, legs wide and arms extended. I rolled off her at the same time.

"I'm starving," I said and popped out of bed.

"I can't move right now." She laughed. "Though I could eat a horse."

"I'm making you breakfast." My underwear was across the room as my eyes searched it out to get to the kitchen before her and impress her with my culinary skills.

"I don't have much," she shouted from the bed, apologetic.

"It's okay. I'll get creative," I shouted back.

“You have many talents,” she yelled even louder, and I heard her get up. A few minutes later, she came into the kitchen, fully dressed.

“Dressed already?” I looked her up and down, admiring her body.

“I’ll help you.” She grinned shyly.

“That sounds good.”

We managed to put together some toast, jam, coffee, and two fried eggs. She was right; she hardly had any food in her fridge. We ate everything on the plate in silence.

I observed Maria from the corner of my eye. She ate without glancing at me. A few *mmms* was all I heard from her.

“How’s the egg?” It appeared she loved it. Noticing it was all gone pleased me.

“Digesting it already. I worked up quite an appetite.” She looked up at me. “Sorry if I’m eating like a pig, but I can’t help it.”

“In case you haven’t noticed, I’m eating too. This is no time to be a lady, anyway. Being a lady is overrated.” She laughed. “And I don’t care what you say; you are quite a lady,” I added, giving her a wanting look.

Maria gazed at me. What was she thinking? I sensed a fortress go up around her.

“I’m sure you’ve had your share of ladies,” she said with a slight smirk.

“The ones before you don’t count,” I said, and I sincerely meant it.

“Oh, stop. What about Sofia?” She looked at me as if she had me cornered. Was she ready for a fight so soon? Why? She’d touched a nerve.

“Who told you about—Wait. Hunter said

something."

"Kind of."

"Well, it's all crap. She was nothing like you."

"How can you be so sure?" I wasn't going to get into that heartache. "Tell me about her. I want to know." She eyed me suspiciously.

I knew what Maria was doing. She was trying to sabotage the moment to protect herself. It wasn't going to work, though.

"There's nothing to say. Just that she was a fuckin' bitch." I reached for my last cigarette. "The truth is, Maria, if somebody loves you, they don't fuck with your head"—I lit my cigarette—"and then rip your heart into tiny pieces for no good reason. She was bad news from the start, and I fell hard. I'm over it now." I exhaled the smoke, angry.

"Why are you peeved?" She acted like her questions were normal.

"Should I ask you about your ex-boyfriends?" I said a little too roughly. I couldn't help it.

"I never loved any of them. I pushed them all away. Some were great too. I was the problem. I have issues." Of course she did. Father issues. Mother issues. Abandonment issues. Fuck, she had me all over again by playing the sympathy card. Plus, she had no idea how vulnerable she seemed right now. I smoked silently, contemplating how she was trying to do to me what she'd done to all the other guys—push me away.

It wasn't going to happen.

"I don't think about her." I had to tell her so Maria would know. "If you really want to know, she was married, and I was her fling, her rebound. She went back to her husband, and I sulked and pouted over it. Over something that I'd made myself believe was real." I played with my cigarette. "But that never was." I leaned back in the chair while Maria watched me like a scientist eyeing her microscope.

"She said she never loved me. She wanted to see how it would be with another man. She realized that she still loved her husband. So she left." I inhaled the smoke, then exhaled. "I'm better off. She wasn't for me." I gazed intently at her. "Now you, on the other hand, fit me like a glove." I stretched out my arm to reach for her. "I really, really like you, Maria."

She listened to every word carefully. I read sympathy in her eyes as she touched my arm. "She doesn't know what she gave up," she said, and beamed brightly at me.

I'm breaking through to her.

I'd just cracked that shell a tiny bit, but I knew I had much more pecking to do. Sometimes what seemed simple was actually the hardest thing to do.

Maria stood. "Jack, I want to see you again, but right now I need to be alone."

I stood in front of her, pulled her close, and kissed her softly on the lips.

"Not for long," I said as I released her. "Let's get dinner later. I also have a few things I have to do today."

She thought about it. "Okay." I saw her struggle, so I bent and whispered in her ear, "I won't hurt you."

"It's not you I'm worried about. My mind is fucked-up. I like you, Jack, but…" She hesitated. Her chocolate-brown eyes gave me such a pained look, I wanted to grab her hard and take away all her anguish. She brushed her hair back and nervously rubbed her hands up and down her jeans.

I coaxed her. "Say it."

"I'd always hoped my father would come back for me. Tell me he made a mistake, love me, and spend time with me. I waited. Every birthday, I thought, this will be the year. I waited for the doorbell to ring, but he never came around. I figured my mother thought I was in good hands with her parents, but my father? Didn't he ever think of me?" Maria's eyes were sorrowful, demanding questions that were unanswerable.

"What if he never even knew you existed?" I was reaching for straws to console her in any way possible.

We were facing each other, and she placed her arms across her chest. "I've thought of that too. I don't know what's worse, knowing or not knowing. Deep inside, I always felt he knew I existed. Maybe he watched me from afar." Her voice choked up, and she stared deeply into my eyes without blinking. "Sometimes when I would go to the park, I would see strange men and think, 'maybe that's my father.' I would study their eyes." Her hands were in her jeans' pockets now. "I would look at their nose, their mouth, and pray for some iota of a resemblance. I never saw one."

Maria glanced at her bare feet, her hair falling along her shoulders and breasts, then rubbed her eyes for a few seconds. I waited, placing all my weight on my right leg. I could tell there was more; she wasn't finished.

"Go on," I said, moving closer and rubbing her shoulders. "Let it out."

Maria peeked up at me, unsure, and then her expression changed.

"One time, I was with a friend, swinging in the park, and I saw a man staring at me. I was around ten. I decided to ask him if he was my father. My friend followed me, and I stopped in front of him. He sneered and reached out his arm. He told me I had beautiful red hair. 'Are you my father?' I asked him, ignoring his statement about my hair and taking a few steps back. Do you know what he said?" Her expression became furious. "He said he would be my father if I let him, and he bent to squeeze my arm. It didn't feel right. His words were all wrong. My friend ran off, and I pulled back and looked at him clearly. There was no resemblance. He had beady eyes and a creepy stare. He said something else to me, and I got so scared that I ran off to look for my friend, who was long gone. He didn't follow me."

"That fuckin' prick." Anger brew inside me.

"Forget that, Jack. What I'm trying to tell you is that after that day, I buried my father. I knew he was never coming for me, and every guy I've ever met, I think I treat awfully." She walked toward the window and scrutinized the view, as if she would discover a glimpse of truth out there. "Because I don't know any better." Despair lingered in her voice.

Her honesty drilled in me a permanent screw with her name on it. I was in fuckin' love. I wanted to protect her; I wanted to love her.

I hugged her, and kissed her neck. "It's going to be all right," I whispered, and felt her body succumb to mine.

She suddenly pulled away. "I gotta go."

Where the fuck did she have to go?

I realized I was still in my underwear, and silently walked back to her room to get dressed.

I heard the water run and concluded she was probably washing the cups and plates. I went to the kitchen, stood right behind her, swept her hair back, and kissed her nape. “I’ll see you later. Is seven okay?” I spoke to her neck, inhaling her skin.

“Yes.” She sighed and turned her face to kiss me.

Something stirred inside me. I had to leave before I jumped her.

“Bye,” she said, and placed the clean mugs on the dish rack, then slipped back into my embrace. “See you later.” She kissed me on the lips. “I’ll walk you to the door.”

And just like that, she stepped out of my arms when I could have stayed there for a while longer.

I didn’t want to leave.

I followed her to the door and kissed her again as she remained there, vulnerable and beautiful, waiting for me to put on my shoes.

As I stepped out into the morning air, I realized what a beautiful day it was.

I knew Maria was someone I could easily fall in love with. Every word, every sentence I said came out effortlessly with her. She was my wind song of every season. I whistled all the way back home. It’d been a long time since I’d whistled.

Chapter Six
I've got the rhythm in me

It was almost five, and I still hadn't finished grocery shopping, probably because going home, I'd crashed out exhausted—a good exhausted, though.

Maria didn't remind me of anyone. That was her allure. She was unique, like we all were, I guessed. When she walked into a room, you couldn't miss her, and she seemed to be unaware of it.

The obstacle in front of me wasn't Maria herself, but the fact that she'd never received the parental love she'd required. I wasn't a psychiatrist, but anyone with common sense could have seen that. I thought of my mom and how she'd encouraged me. *"Follow your heart,"* had been her favourite expression. *"The money will come."* My dad, on the other hand, opposed everything I'd ever done. He was a demanding father. Tough as nails. I was everything he loathed—a musician.

So I'd never finished high school. Who gave a fuck? So I'd never followed in his military-diplomat, fucked-up ways. So what?

My father was scared of the unknown. He wanted me to work in a bank. Did he even know me? Why not? What was wrong with a bank job? Everything, I'd hollered.

I'd done it all by the age of sixteen—and all the drugs imaginable. At eighteen, I'd hitchhiked across the United States till I ran out of money and went back home, where I wasn't wanted. My mom's opinions had started to sway; eventually she had become like my dad. They both wanted me to settle down.

"I have dreams," I'd cried.

"We won't support you," they'd shouted. *"Stop your bohemian ways."*

So I left for good. I came to Europe, and once a year, I'd go back for Christmas. They were still not thrilled with any of it, but they'd given up fighting with me, at least most of the time. My little sister, Katie, got married and had two kids. All their energy flowed into her now, thankfully.

We'd moved so many times, it was a wonder I was still sane. From one school to another, I'd tried to fit in but never found my kind of people—till Saint-Tropez.

Now I had Hunter and friends. They'd come with the package. They were my sanctuary—reliable and crazy. I'd needed to settle in one place to get my shit together.

Staying in Saint-Tropez had helped me—I focused on song writing. It was the weather and the sounds here that had captured my heart. This place had helped my creativity to erupt.

When I was young, outside one of my many homes—Washington, I think—I would lie on the grass, listening to the birds chirp from a distance. I'd started to chirp along, following their rhythm. They sang back. I continued to jam with the birds, back and forth, like a symphony.

Rapture had filled me, and I was relaxed under the clouds, understanding that somehow I was in rhythm, in tune, with the singing birds.

I'd once read, "Without music, life would be a

mistake." I was positive it was Nietzsche who wrote that. Not that I claimed to know my philosophers, but I liked to read here and there, especially since I'd been friends with the constant reader, Hunter.

So when I heard that quote, a bulb lit up in my brain. *Aha. That's it.*

I couldn't live without it. Music, that is. It lured me in, and I made it my lush garden of life.

I was probably your run-of-the-mill musician, but who cared. I didn't care about success. One lump sum at the end of a show was enough to pay the rent and buy food and some other extras.

Luxury was overrated. My dad made a lot of money, and I'd seen how hopeless that could be. Wherever his job took him, we followed. His restless life made me even more restless. He thought I was hopeless for playing in honky-tonk bars, but I could see the horizon. It was broad, endless. And now I could see Maria, lying beside me, calling my name.

Gimme some honeysuckle flowers to inhale, and no amount of money could beat that scent—or the scent of Maria. I knew it now, and I couldn't live without it.

I packed up the last of my groceries and waited in line. A little dazed, finally paying and getting my bill, my money was ready to be handed over, not even double-checking it like my usual drill, a habit my mother had taught me. When something was ingrained in you, it was hard to kick it

Today, I didn't care how much the young cashier fucked up; I was elated.

"*Merci.*" I said with delight. She flirted immediately, a silly grin on her face, probably because I was inebriated with love and most likely a ridiculous smirk plastered on my face. This was being high on love.

I couldn't wait to see Maria's eyes again. At the thought of her, I felt giddy and light-headed as I trotted home quickly.

I needed a cigarette. *Shit, I forgot to buy some.* I turned into the closest corner store and put down my groceries.

"*Gauloises, s'il vous plaît.*"

I paid and threw the pack in with the groceries. Turning the corner to my street, Felix's French song guitar playing could be heard. He was at his favourite spot. A street musician practically on your doorstep every day was unavoidable, and to not state the obvious, a weakness for me. My arms were full, but giving Felix some change, bills, whatever, was a necessity right now as I approached him, set down my bags, and nodded. He gave me a crooked grin, singing loud. His open guitar case held some change, so reaching into my jeans' pocket and adding to the pot made me feel better because he looked like he needed a shower badly. Tonight was not the night to be Mr. Good Samaritan, he'd have to go elsewhere. Hopefully, the change would help him.

Felix looked pleased as my change thumped inside his black, worn-out case. As if a fire were up my butt, I unlocked my front door, picked up my bags again, and quickly went upstairs to put away my food.

I lit a cigarette and crushed it out after a few drags.

Stripping off my clothes, I took a long shower, singing some Led Zeppelin song.

I combed out my tangled hair and debated what to wear. I must have tried on three different shirts till I settled on a familiar red one with white blotches and my acid-washed jeans.

I played *Some Girls* by the Rolling Stones and hummed along to the band that continued to inspire me as a musician.

There were girls I'd met who I just wanted to fuck. I'd see them for a few weeks till I was bored to death. The sex was fine, but there was no connection. I could do that, no problem. I had needs, and once they were met, I didn't give a fuck about what she liked or disliked, how she wore her hair or didn't. Nothing interested me. I could be an asshole to get what I want. Girls threw themselves at me just because I played guitar. Shallow. Most girls never pushed the right buttons. After a few dates, I'd be turned off by little things, like the way Anna ate; or the way Gabrielle laughed like a hyena at every joke I made, as if I were a comedian, or the way Emilie probed me with questions. But mostly, the way none of them made me think twice about them.

Conversations were dull, and I only wanted to fuck. They always wanted more, which was normal, I guessed. Only Hunter had luck finding girls who came with no strings. He knew how to pick them.

I wanted more, but they could never give me what I needed. Then Sofia changed that, because she was unattainable. What I wanted from her she couldn't give me. She was in love with her husband, while I had desperately hoped and prayed she would leave him for me.

Even when she told me she was married, I didn't care. They were separated, she'd said. Even realizing she'd lied didn't stop me from wanting her. She was cheating on him—everyone cheated on everyone in Europe. He was an asshole, she'd said. She wanted to leave him… On and on, the story went. Years flew by, and I waited like a dog in heat—loyal, trustworthy, dependable Jack. I waited, and where did that get me? Fuckin' nowhere. Heartbreak.

"I don't love you. *J'aime* François." She'd said his name with so much sincerity that I told her to get the fuck out of my apartment and that I never wanted to see her again. The pain was excruciating. She'd held my heart in her hands, and her words tore me up, leaving bits of my heart floating around. I couldn't put those pieces together for a long time after.

"I'm sorry," she'd said.

I opened the door for her, watching her closely for any sign of remorse. She wasn't sorry at all.

"Never call me again," I said coldly, trying my best not to rush her and run my fingers through her blonde curls. Sofia stood in front of me, looked at me one last time, and said something like, "Thank you for showing me how much love I have to offer. I thought I was dead inside before I met you."

"I'm glad I was of service to your marriage," I said.

She walked out—hurt, I could tell. I stood there, giving in to my feelings for her.

One last kiss, I told myself.

I stepped out into the corridor and took two quick steps toward her. I turned her around and pinned her against the cold wall next to the stairs and kissed her hard. It was bittersweet, one-sided; she didn't fully reciprocate.

Pulling back, and without a word, I left her there without looking back. I shut my door and headed straight to the bottle of whiskey.

I moved out of that apartment. Everything had reminded me of her, so I started fresh.

I shoved those memories aside. I looked at myself in the full mirror one final time, then glanced at my clock. I was early. Usually I'd be late, but not with Maria; just knowing I was going to see her had made me rush like a lunatic.

Desperate? Maybe a little.

Horny? Maybe a lot.

I sat down to have another cigarette. Instead of calming my nerves, it made them worse, so I played some Van Morrison.

I was over Sofia and ready for Maria.

Ah, Van Morrison spoke to me. I could swear his lyrics were written for me.

I wasn't going to fuck this up. I was going to sweep Maria off her feet. She needed me. Maybe she didn't know how much yet, but all I needed was some time alone with her, and I would show her everything I had inside me.

If it was meant to be, then it would be. Stubbing out my cigarette, I turned off the music and lights, locked up, and stepped out into the night to go to Maria's apartment. I remembered the way as if I followed invisible crumbs. I could feel myself getting closer to her—and more nervous inside—with every step. I felt confident I'd be able to break down her barricade. I was going to get past her protective barrier tonight.

I rang her doorbell, and within seconds, she was at the door.

Fuckin' gorgeous.

"Hi," she said, dressed and ready, her purse and keys in hand.

"Hi back. You look amazing." She wore a black halter top and a denim miniskirt. I glanced down her long legs, and when I saw those fuckin' shoes again, I wanted to push her back into the apartment and fuck her hard right there on the tiny couch in her living room.

"Thanks." She stepped out, and I moved backward instead of forward. We kissed hello simultaneously. It was a little awkward but smooth nonetheless.

"Hmm, strawberry lipstick. Delicious." I crooned.

"Glad you like it." She grinned back. "So, where are we going?"

"To an Italian restaurant. I hope you like Italian food."

"Who doesn't?"

"It's not far from here. Somewhere between my place and yours."

"Perfect." Maria looked at me and pulled her purse close at the same time.

I extended my hand, and she took hold of it. We walked side by side. It was a breezy night, but warm.

I peered down at her. "I had a wonderful time yesterday."

"Wonderful?" She peeked up at me, her dark eye makeup done to perfection. "Is that all? Not earth-shattering?" She smirked.

Fuck, I was such an idiot. Be honest with her, I told myself.

"Maria." I stopped, and then so did she as she turned toward me.

"Yes?" She waited, anticipating my words, a curious look on her face.

"Unforgettable."

"Now that's so much better," she said as we continued to walk.

"And you?" I asked.

"Me what?" She looked delighted, having a ball with the word games.

"Your turn." I gave her hand a slight squeeze.

"Honestly?" she asked shyly.

I nodded, waiting. Maria thought long and hard.

"The best night of my life," she finally said in a low voice, looking down at her feet, swinging my hand. Then she tipped her head up and looked into my eyes.

"I couldn't hear you. Can you repeat that?" I felt a tug in my heart.

"The best night of my life," Maria repeated more loudly, pronouncing each word clearly, not missing my provocative gaze.

"So far," I added with a seductive grin and bent to kiss her.

So far.

We ate well and talked all night long over two bottles of wine. We were tipsy, to say the least. Maria couldn't stop laughing. Her tongue was wicked and witty at every curve of the conversation. She enticed me more with her words than with her body—at least some of the time. That was a rare accomplishment. Even Sofia had never got me a hundred percent.

"Dessert?" I asked, rubbing her arm.

"Where?"

"My place," I answered in a low voice.

"Very seductive," Maria replied. "But I don't know… I'm kind of drunk, and I'm uh…uh…afraid I'll pass out."

"Great. I've always wanted a gorgeous drunk girl in my apartment who I could take advantage of," I said jokingly.

"Well, here I am. Ready and willing."

Despite being tipsy, she was still quick with the comebacks. Not as drunk as the first day I met her, when she'd passed out on my breakfast table.

"Don't forget, I've already seen you drunk."

"And this after I've known you only a couple of days."

"Three, to be exact."

"You're counting?"

"I'm not *that* drunk."

"Or so you say."

Maria reached over and stroked my arm. "I think I need a cup of coffee immediately," she said, her hair falling in her face.

"Coming right up." I raised my hand to get the waiter's attention, which I knew would take awhile, given how slow the service was in this restaurant—not unlike all restaurants in Saint-Tropez.

The waiter finally strolled over. "*Oui*?" he asked with an attitude.

"*Deux cafés*."

"*Dans un bol ou une tasse*?"

"*Tasse s'il vous plait*."

He trotted off.

"In about an hour we should get our coffee, Maria. Hold on, baby, they're going to Brazil to get it." I smirked.

Maria burst out in laughter. Sweet laughter. It was infectious, and I cracked up with her.

"Brazil!" she repeated, holding her stomach. "I think I'm going to piss myself."

"You know there are washrooms here, right?"

She stood up, laughing loud and shouting, "Do I look absolutely drunk?" Some heads turned and stared at her.

"No, you look absolutely beautiful. Who cares, anyway?"

"Why, you do, of course. What kind of an impression am I leaving with you in this state?" She reached for her purse.

"A lasting one." I got her there. She gave me an ear-to-ear grin that left me a little breathless.

Freeze. Stay like that for a while. Please, don't move. I don't want to forget the sexiness pouring out of you right now.

As she walked away, I still couldn't take my eyes off her. I could have stared at her poppy ass forever. Lighting my cigarette, I noticed more heads turn her way.

She's with me. Eat your hearts out.

I had a dirty mind when I was with her. I couldn't help it.

I waited, anticipating her walking toward me. What else did I have to look forward to while smoking my cigarette?

The coffee arrived, surprisingly quick.

"*Merci*," I mumbled, preoccupied. Then I saw her. Yes, she had a great strut. Something inside me stirred for what lay under that miniskirt.

"Whatcha looking at?" she asked, examining me closely as she placed her arms on the edge of the table.

"Your lovely body."

"Oh, is that all?" She chuckled.

I caressed her arm. "I want you to come to my place and stay the night."

Her eyes widened and then glimmered. "Do you, now?"

I felt a boner coming on. Oh God.

"Badly." I bent to kiss her hand.

"How badly?" She touched mine.

"Let's get outta here right now."

"What about our coffee?" She teased, and immediately took a sip.

"Fuck it," I said.

"No, I need this cup." She beamed. "I'll be quick."

"Okay." I pouted as I pulled my hand away to drink my coffee.

"Tell me something." There was a sparkle in her eye. "What do you like about me?"

"Everything."

Maria smirked. "Be specific, and *don't* mention my body."

"Well"—I took a deep breath—"I like the way you talk, walk, think, laugh, and smoke. The way you tease me, kiss me, push me away, and look at me while we're having sex." I took another breath. "I also like the way you take pictures." I thought that was pretty good, so I leaned back and waited for a reply.

"Is that all?"

"No, there's more." It was coming to me now. "The way you push the hair out of your eyes, the way you put on your makeup, the clothes you wear."

"That's all superficial." She tilted her head to one side. "And I told you to not mention my body."

"I really like your mind." I leaned forward. "It captivates me."

Maria examined me closely as if she were studying a textbook.

"I'm finished my coffee now," she said, and lifted the empty cup to show me. "And I liked your last answer"—she pushed her hair back, smiling—"the best."

"What do you like about me?" I probed her now, curious.

"I like your quick talk and talent," she instantly replied.

"Which talent are you referring to?"

Maria threw her head back and let out a loud laugh. "Jack, you are hot. I rest my case. The second I saw you, I fell for you." She giggled. "I don't know what else to say." Maria let out a breath—a slightly nervous one—then looked down.

"You've said enough; let's go before I jump you right here." I looked around for the waiter, but he was nowhere to be found.

I sensed Maria staring at me. "You are probably the most beautiful man I've ever slept with," she said shyly as I tilted my head to listen to her.

"Probably?" I asked, looking every which way for that bonehead of a waiter.

"Definitely." She laughed again. "Don't let it go to your head."

"Which head?" I joked, and she laughed harder.

"Oh, you're good." She eyed me up and down, till her gaze rested on my lips for a few seconds.

"Wait till we get back to my place, and I'll show you how good I am."

There he was. I flagged him down angrily, wanting to get the fuck out of there. All that talk was making me fuckin' delirious with lust. Bonehead looked at me from across the room as if I was bothering him. I made a gesture, and he gave me a look as he nodded.

"He finally saw me," I said impatiently, reaching for

my wallet. I was imagining Maria in all sorts of sexual positions, and I couldn't think straight.

"I'm feeling less drunk," Maria said as she straightened her hair and reached in her purse.

"Good. I don't want you falling asleep on me."

"That's not happening!" She declared with her head bent, still searching for something. A few seconds later, everything was on the table: cards, lipstick, keys, eyeliner, tissues—how the fuck did all that fit in her teensy purse?

The waiter placed the bill on the table, and I quickly looked at it, not reviewing the items—*fuck that*—and left the amount on the table along with a lousy tip.

Maria finally pulled out some francs. "How much?" she asked, oblivious to the fact that I had just paid.

"Already paid for." I stood up. "Let's get the fuck out of here."

She shoved her stuff back into her purse and stood. My hand in hers, she followed close behind me as I zigzagged out of the restaurant, casting a cold look at the bonehead waiter.

"Jack, can I have a smoke?" Maria asked outside.

"Sure, wouldn't mind one myself." I lit a cigarette and gave it to her. There was a slight wind, so it took me a few seconds.

"I'm getting used to the smell now," she said, and inhaled it deeply.

"Everything is a matter of habit." My cigarette was lit just as my emotions were. "I used to smoke Marlboro, and now, won't go near them."

Maria reached back for my hand, and we walked in silence, smoking and feeling the breeze tickle our cheeks.

"Fucking doors again."

I opened the door to my apartment, and once inside, I quickly shut it and kissed her hard against it. Our tongues met with fervor, and I tasted the smorgasbord of cigarette, wine, and coffee on Maria's breath; I sucked it all out of her. Then we crash-landed on my couch, and I lifted her in my arms like a bride to my bedroom as she sighed when my lips pressed against her neck.

We made love, then slept with our legs wrapped around each other like Christmas ribbons on a present. Sleep overcame us swiftly.

****

Buzz.Buzz.Buzz.

Who the fuck is that? I barely opened my eyes, then grudgingly rubbed them, not wanting to move from Maria's warmth. I glanced over at her. She was sound asleep. I stretched my body, hoping the buzzing wouldn't continue. If I didn't answer, they'd soon get the picture.

Buzz. Buzz. Buzz. Buzz. This time the ringing was more insistent.

Maria stretched out and slowly opened her eyes. "Is that your doorbell?" she murmured, half asleep, the slits of her eyes peeking at me.

I kissed her forehead. "Yep. I'll go see who it is and kick them the fuck out." My hand gently tapped her bum and I bend to kiss it. *Ah, lovely.*

Grabbing my underwear off the floor, I put it on, and walked to the front door to press the intercom button. "Yeah?" I hollered.

"It's me, bro. Let me up!" Hunter hollered back, the words muffled, guessing it was either him or Felix wanting a shower or a cup of coffee.

I buzzed him up to tell him to get the fuck out,

because my shitty intercom system was out of sorts again. Hunter's loud footsteps trotted up the stairs as I opened the door, ready to stop him from entering.

"Hey, buddy," he said in a calm voice, as if he didn't just run up a flight of stairs or two. "I'm here for your awesome breakfast," he announced, and slid past me. "Were you still sleeping?" Hunter looked around and saw Maria's shoes. "Sorry, man."

"Look, Hunter, maybe you could come back another time," My hushed tone purposefully low as he glanced from left to right, then stared at my bedroom door.

"Is it okay?" he asked, still staring at the door, deaf to what I'd just said. To make things worse, he planted himself on the couch, like he didn't have a care in the world.

No, it's not okay, I was ready to say, but then he suddenly got up. "I'll make you guys breakfast." And he went into the kitchen. I was just about to follow him and tell him to get the fuck out already, when out of the corner of my eye Maria walked out of the bedroom, fully clothed. She peered at Hunter with a questioning look, shrugging my shoulders, sort of to tell her we had an unexpected visitor.

"Hey," was all I could muster still annoyed with Hunter's complete selfishness.

"Maria," Hunter shouted from the kitchen. "How do you like your eggs?"

"Scrambled." She gave me a cute grin which was infectious with my hands in the air like out of luck to do anything about my home invasion.

"Me too, Hunter. I'll go get dressed."

"I'm going to wash up." Maria headed for the bathroom, my feet taking a few steps toward her and intercepting with a kiss.

"Sorry about the interruption."

"It's cool," she murmured, and kissed me back. She seemed genuinely fine with the whole situation, while hiding my annoyance was fuckin' pissing me off. My pants and shirt were on quickly as my feet took me quickly into the kitchen before Maria came out from the bathroom.

"Hunter, I have company," I whispered the obvious to make my point. Aware that Hunter's keen observational skills noticed her shoes when he barged in earlier.

"I'm cooking breakfast for ya'll lovebirds," Hunter articulated with a drawl and glanced at me while stirring the eggs in the pan with a spatula. "But by the look on your face right now, I'm outta here. Sorry, man." He handed over the spatula but looked a little fucked-up, rubbing his hair in the back.

"Wait up." Now, I had just about given up, he was already cooking. "Forget it."

I heard Maria's footsteps approach.

"Mmmm. It smells great," she said, all refreshed. Her hair was pulled back somehow in a half-bun, and her skin looked flawless even without a hint of makeup. "Leaving so soon?"

Hunter was halfway out the kitchen while she was trotting in. He stopped in front of her, and like a freak, he curtsied.

"Hi, Maria," he said, and she grinned at him.

"Are you always so jolly in the morning?" she asked.

"Only after I've had a good fuck," Hunter said nonchalantly. Then he turned to me and said, "I'll make the coffee."

He was staying after all. Whatever Hunter wanted, he always seemed to get, gesturing to him to go right ahead. Maria was dressed in last night's clothes, which were so out of place this early in the morning, and chuckled to myself.

"What's so funny?" she asked, sitting down at the table.

"Nothing. You look fabulous for breakfast." Stating the obvious and looking at her from top to bottom with a sly grin.

"Slightly overdressed, but fabulous, nonetheless."

Hunter peeked at Maria as he paused while pouring the water into the percolator. "Ah, she blushes," and he had a gleam in his eyes.

"Hunter," Maria said, ignoring his remark, "I hear you're a psychic."

"Among other things." He laughed quietly to himself, carefully examining the coffeepot. *Oh boy. Here we go.*

"Can you read my mind?" Maria inquired.

"I get feelings. Voices in my head. Signals. I'm not telepathic, if that's what you're getting at." He walked toward the table. "Jackie boy, you're okay with making us breaky?" He flipped me a look that suggested his question would be complied with as I was already in the midst of it, my eyes focusing on removing the eggs from the burner as they turned a slight golden brown.

"Of course. My specialty." My long grasp reached for three dishes in the cupboard.

"What feelings do you get from me?" Maria asked as Hunter sat across from her.

"A few years ago, my spirit-guides told me that Jack

would meet someone like you, that you both would love each other madly, and by the look on your faces," his quick eyes darted from her to me, "it is quite possibly true that I do know something about being a psychic." He looked away and forlorn for a split second, "Of course, perhaps I am envious." Then he shrugged and grinned. "But there's this feeling that tells me you are troubled, perhaps nervous and quite possibly always feeling lonely." He thought for a second, scratching his head. "I mean scared—scared fuckin' shitless."

Maria squinted while Hunter spoke, as if she was deeply concentrating on his words. I hadn't seen that look before. She twirled a lock of her hair, then said flatly, "Go on."

"Give me your hand."

Maria laid her hand on the table, palm face up, her demeanour somewhat changed now and thoughtful. Fuck what he said, fucked me up a bit; she must be freaking right now…

"Prepared, are we?" Hunter smirked and bent down as if he were a doctor or something. He was such an asshole sometimes—Mr. Know-It-Fuckin'-All. He lifted his head back up and rubbed his hands together for a few seconds, and when he placed his hand under Maria's, she jumped.

"Sorry." Hunter's hands were always as cold as ice. He stared at her palm, not budging or talking for a good minute, lost in reflection, analyzing—or whatever the fuck he did.

"Your life path is split in two. In your forties, life changes for you. You have a creative mind, and this guides you. You are alone."

Maria hastily yanked her hand away. "Thanks, I've

heard enough," she said gruffly. "I'd rather not know anymore."

She wasn't buying it.

Hunter looked at her for a long, tense moment, then shrugged his shoulders and snapped back, "Listen, you asked."

"Well, it's all a bunch of crap." Maria folded her arms across her chest, waiting for a reply.

"Oh, did I touch a nerve?" Hunter's eyes widened, and by the mad look in his eyes I could tell he had his punching gloves on now; a look that got us kicked out of bars too many times. "You know, we're all alone in this world until we find whatever the fuck we want for that moment that makes us feel like we're not so alone, for what it's worth, your palm is a fucking good one."

"How would you know anything about me?" she asked sharply.

"I don't claim to know anything. It is actually my spirit-guides that show me and guide me. I've been waiting for someone. She's supposed to be in her forties. She's supposed to love me. This feeling of waiting for someone can feel like an eternity." Hunter spoke sincerely as he revealed something he'd never even told me about, and then he looked intently at Maria for a few seconds and then that look was gone. Not ever seeing it in his eyes before, it was hard for me to tell what he was thinking, but it fucked me up, and I glanced back and forth between them, noticing that Maria seemed entranced by Hunter's words. His eyes focused on something behind her.

"Eggs are ready!" I announced, trying to smooth over the fucked-up conversation. "Who's hungry?" My voice was a little high, reaching over to snatch three forks from the drawer. The coffee was still brewing, my hands moving nervously all over the place, setting the plates on the table and distributing the eggs evenly in the dishes. "Dig in!"

They eyed each other without another word, then grabbed their forks, placing myself next to them. The room a bloody library. You could have cut the thoughts in that room with a knife.

We ate in silence for a while, and then Hunter opened his big, fat mouth again. "Sorry for offending you, Maria."

I'd never heard Hunter apologize to anybody. He didn't look up; he stared at his eggs. Maria peered at him and extended her hand.

"Friends?" she said, all cool and calm.

"Friends," Hunter replied, raising his gaze to hers, then shaking her hand.

"Now that we're all friends, who's going to pour the coffee?" The brewing of the coffee machine suddenly stopped.

Maria immediately got up, and then Hunter did too. "Please, sit," he said. "I'll do it, I know where everything is." She sat back down and continued to eat. My attempt at winking at her to break the ice, didn't seem to work. She didn't react.

Hunter poured the coffee into the mugs.

"Thank you," she said politely.

I got up to get the milk and sugar. Hunter liked his coffee black and wasn't very hospitable. He couldn't see beyond his four walls sometimes.

We devoured everything on our plates and rested back to enjoy the coffee.

"I think this is the beginning of a great friendship."

Hunter grinned.

"I think you mean a *beautiful* friendship," Maria corrected him as she bit the edge of her fingernail, thinking.

"I've seen *Casablanca* more times than the lot of you. I'm sure I'm right," Hunter rudely remarked, his dark eyes reflective. He turned to me. "Jack, what do you say?"

Definitely had no clue. I'd seen bits and pieces of *Casablanca*. The same line the rest of the world knew, I knew as well. *"Here's looking at you, kid."*

"I'm stumped." I stared from one to the other. "But I'll go with Maria." Hunter gave me a nasty look.

"Guessing we're going to have to see the movie," Hunter stated matter-of-factly.

"It's the last line of the movie," Maria said with a sigh.

"But we must watch the entire movie, because my good friend Jack here, hasn't seen it from beginning to end."

How the fuck did he know that? I looked at both of them incredulously.

"You're not serious." Of course, I knew he was dead serious. As always, he was up for the draw, the gamble, the chance to prove he was right. Or just for the plain fuck of watching Casablanca again. It was hard to tell what was going on in Hunter's head. I glanced at Maria, and she was playing poker—"all in" was written across her forehead.

"And if you're wrong?" Maria teased. "What's the big deal?"

"I'll buy you supper," Hunter said, a little too brusquely.

How immature could he possibly be?

"You're on." Maria challenged him, and that was that.

"I'll go get the movie." Hunter got up to leave, and his chair squeaked.

"Now?" Maria asked, sounding flabbergasted.

"No time like the present." And off he went.

"He's quite a character."

"Yep, that he is."

We drank our coffee and talked for a while, before we knew it, Hunter was back, buzzing the doorbell over and over.

"I'm back," he shouted as he entered the apartment, not even slightly out of breath.

I rose to set up the VCR, and Hunter threw the tape at me like a football, almost whacking my head.

"Watch it!" His immature behaviour aggravated me.

Maria sat on the couch, looking quite at home and not reacting to any of Hunter's follies.

"I'll never get tired of this movie," she said as she crossed her exposed legs and pulled her skirt down to cover them as much as she could.

"Let's get to it." Hunter sat on the other side of the couch and stretched out his legs on the coffee table. He was so massive that his legs extended all the way past the opposite edge of the table.

"Get comfortable." My VCR was not complying, muttering to myself and fiddling with the buttons to press Play a few times before it worked.

"I already am, bro."

I sat between them.

Hunter didn't shut up throughout the whole movie. But when Sam sang "As Time Goes By," with Rick entering the bar and Ilsa's face filled with memories—Rick's all pissed at life, but then he sees her and he forgets himself—it was such an intense scene, none of us said a word.

I actually loved every scene of the movie. It was a little overacted at times, but that was part of its allure. Finally, we came to the last scene.

"This is it," Hunter kept saying as soon as they were at the airport.

All three of us stared at the screen. Every word Rick and Ilsa spoke was clear, and then Rick let Ilsa go. We waited.

Maria was right.

"The End" appeared on the screen.

"I guess. Brains is owed a supper," Hunter whined.

"It's okay," Maria said with pleasure in her voice.

"No, my word is my honour. What's your fancy?" Hunter's Southern drawl seemed more pronounced. When he was upset, he became a redneck cowboy. He hated to be wrong.

"Italian."

"I hate those fuckin' wops!" He did hate them. He said they were all assholes, yet he never said why and this always perplexed me. He always thought his opinion was a fact—plain and simple—and everyone should just agree with him. He stood and hovered over us like a giant.

"I'll meet you both at Dario's around eight o'clock," he said flatly, then left without a proper good-bye.

"He's such a sore loser," Maria said, still sitting cross-legged on my couch.

"Yes, he is." *And a pain in the ass as well.*

"Where's Dario's?" she asked.

“I’ll ring you, and we’ll walk there together.” Sliding next to her, my hands reached for hers.

She turned to me. “I have to go.”

“What’s the hurry?” I glided my hands under her skirt.

“I need a shower.”

“I have a shower.” My voice came across groggy, kissing her neck and wanting her all over again.

“Seriously, I need to do a few things.” Her voice had changed slightly and feeling her reluctance, I pulled away, slightly pissed.

“Sure.” My mind wandered as my feet stood up, but my hands wanted to be somewhere else than next to me.

I watched as she gathered her purse and shoes, and then she came close to peck me on the lips.

“A penny for your thoughts,” I said.

“You’ll need more than a penny.” She grinned, and then her face took the wind right out of me. “I’m not ready for all of this. It’s too fast.” She eyed me closely. “I need to be alone for a while. It’s not you—it’s me.”

“Okay.” Everything *was* moving fast; it was a whirlwind. I walked her to the door.

“See you later.” A surge ran through me as we kissed, and she wrapped her arms around my neck, kissing me back passionately.

“Don’t leave just yet.” My begging was getting the better of me; this desire for her that pushed me to want more of her.

“Later,” she whispered, then left the space empty between us, her wind leaving me wanting her even more.

I went back to bed and slept, dreaming of Maria walking on a tightrope in a circus. What the fuck did that mean? My eyes were on her, watching her closely, and there was only one other person in the audience.

Hunter.

His eyes were watery.

I woke up, reached for my cigarettes on the night table, and smoked in bed while thinking about *Casablanca* and what a fuckin' great movie it was; forgetting about the dream in order to not think about it. A shower was essential right now and to stop thinking so much. Why did Hunter want to watch *Casablanca* anyway? Just to prove a point? He ended up being wrong. And why the fuck was he crying in my dream? Wanting to find an ashtray led me to get up and search the room aimlessly as heading for the toilet was my closest ashtray. It was just a movie. It was just a dream, my thoughts told me, throwing the cigarette in the toilet bowl and peeing on it, watching it twirl around. My Led Zeppelin albums called out to me to be listened to; nothing like Robert Plant and Jimmy Page to wake you up and help you forget what you were thinking about.

I was already counting beats in my head, turning on the hot water faucet. Playing air guitar was my other escape. Being naked in the shower and singing my ass off. There were many reasons to sing loudly, indulgent in the music in me.

The one thing that remained by my side in the world, was music. At least I had that.

Part Three: Hunter

Yes, I'm one of them.

Chapter Seven
Could she be the one?
1989

I skipped half the steps, leaving Jack's apartment. Really wanting to jump out the window and show off, but instead, opting for the traditional way of exiting, only because Maria was one of my soul mates from a past life. She didn't know it yet, because she wasn't able to see the light shining down on her left shoulder that indicated that she was "my one."

Only my cursed and blessed eyes could see that, being a vrykolaka in *dead* flesh and blood. Okay, call me a vampire if that makes you feel any better, because you don't like Big Words and you don't read Big Books and you sure as hell never heard of my type before.

Or maybe you have.

I hated Italian food, hence hated Italians. They were such fuckin' pricks. That was that. You see, ya'll, I was a hick. A redneck from the South, born in 1920, nine years before the Great Depression.

My mama's name was Jeannine, and my papa's name was John, but everyone called him Jack. That was why my heart had a soft spot for my friend Jack; he was also a heck of a great guy. I'd never convert him because loving him like a brother came easy and I would never want him to suffer like me. He was too much of an artist that had more to give to the world than someone like me.

My mama and papa were pretty smart. Papa was an

engineer, and Mama raised us with a strict hand and an excessive vocabulary. She loved to read.

In the year of our Lord 1960, someone shot me, as in being a nice guy, bad things happened; needless to say my Good Samaritan persona didn't go smoothly that day.

We had a nanny, Betty, whose name was short for a Swahili name no Southerner could pronounce. As a youngster, she took great care of us when we were little and loving her was second nature; she was there for me more than my own Mama most times. In 1960, she was around eighty years old, and she'd certainly seen it all. Her bedtime stories consisted of African slavery ships and runaway slaves—not exactly your typical fairy-tale stories. She opened up my eyes, feeling compassion for her people. It was goddamn crazy how they were treated. There was no Civil Rights Act in 1960; there was only plain old Hate.

Mama and Papa never hated anyone.

Well, one day that year, going to visit Betty at her home with a box of cherry chocolates and a bottle of Coke, something crazy happened. Betty sure loved her Cola that was for sure. When she saw me, she hugged me so hard in her big embrace, for a second it felt like my breathing ceased, she squeezed me so tight. Her dark skin shone in the heat, and her eyes squinted in the sun. It was bloody hot and humid. Betty told me she was being harassed by some young folks. They had broken into her home and stolen all her jewellery.

"Not that there was much," she'd said, "but it was mine." Tears welled in her eyes.

"Did you know the kids?" Her well-being, my main concern.

She nodded and told me their names, and of course,

it being a small little town and all, and knowing their daddy, made me think I could save the day. I'd gone to high school with their daddy, Tommy, and from my recollection he was a fuckin' alcoholic, wife beater, and the lowest of the lowest scum. This made me furious, fucking angry and aggressive.

"I'm gonna pay him a visit." My anger perhaps showing all across my face.

"No, you ain't," Betty cried. "I don't want no trouble at my age, Hunter. You better calm down, right now. I know your temper and it ain't gonna help at all. Leave it be."

"You'll never have any more troubles with these punks again," I said, knowing full well, that letting this go would not happen, my vow to Betty already made and not to be broken. She saw it in my eyes that it was futile to change my mind. Lord knows she should know that. So going over to Tommy's got ugly. Pretty fuckin' ugly. One thing led to another, and all of a sudden, he hollered "nigger lover" and had a barrel shotgun pointed to my head.

I didn't take shit from no one, let alone Tommy. My hand reached for the gun, and he threatened me some more, till my moves were outplayed by him, and he shot me.

He shot me right there and then in his bright, feminine-looking living room. The last thing my eyes witnessed before my unconscious state took over were these fucking pink-flowered curtains, and then everything went black.

As soon as my eyes opened, someone was suffocating me. My breath was caught in my throat, the grass under my limp body was poking at my skin. *What the fuck?* Inside my head, my voice was yelling this mantra, but no sound came out of my mouth. Then my consciousness was lost again, with visions of Mama running after me, holding a corncob in her hand 'cause as usual, my actions called for her actions to overtake mine, being up to no good.

Blackness.

When my eyes fluttered open once again, chattering or laughter could be heard nearby. My body felt cold and dried up like a prune, realizing that the forest surrounded me, not far from Tommy's, I gathered, but this could have been in Timbuktu for all I knew. Then my recollection of being shot made me think if this was my death or not. Everything seemed muddled in my brain.

And then, angels appeared out of nowhere. They looked a little weird and fucked-up for angels.

One of them spoke. "Look, ya'll. Look who's awake." But my eyes couldn't focus, couldn't make out a face. Everything was blurry and fuzzy, but slowly the faces became clearer. None of them seemed familiar, counting five strangers, and trying to figure out if this was heaven or hell, because these angels sure didn't look like what angels should look like. Perhaps, this was hell; after all, I was a selfish motherfucker—most of the time.

"We're the Glass Fairies," the one wearing the blue glass dress said. I was mesmerized by her sparkly blue hair and eyes. "We found you like this."

"What the fuck is going on?" My loud voice shouted at them as my body simultaneously bounced up with such strength, that even scared me. I felt different. Weird. Agile.

"Well, we watched someone turn you into a vrykolaka," Blue Glass Nutjob replied like a television broadcaster. *Fairies, my ass. This must be a dream.*

"What's that?"

"You're a vampire, idiot," Green-eyed Monster explained.

"Yeah, right. Have you ever looked in the mirror?" My roar and my jump seemed uncontrollable. My body was doing strange things now.

"Look, we see this all the time. You were left for dead, and they revived you, and now you're one of them. Usually they don't leave their kind stranded and alone, but Evan was in quite the hurry. He asked me for a favour, and here we are. We're supposed to wait till you awaken, then bring you to Evan."

"You are fuckin' crazy!" My loud yell had no effect on them.

Yellow Canary Fairy spoke. "Follow us," and she leaped into the air.

"I can't fly!" No matter how loud my holler, and my stomach tied up in knots, somewhere deep inside, this felt unreal.

"Try it," Little Red Riding Hood, with permanent red-eye, said. *Poor thing.*

"Just use your legs," Black Witch Fairy shouted from high up, looking down and grinning.

So listening to the lunatic fairies, and then realizing they were the Glass Fairies after all, because they were right and they weren't crazy. I flew in the air, following them as if I'd been doing this for years. It was like driving over potholes, except the potholes were the trees. It was scary as hell and exhilarating at the same time. It was unbelievable that my body had this capability to fly in the air like this. They landed gracefully as my aim was not as perfect as theirs, but after a few somersaults, my back fell against a tree trunk without feeling as much pain as a mortal would have. My body quickly got up as if I'd only stubbed my toe.

They walked ahead, my feet following like a lost puppy, till my eyes spotted the small, fairy-tale cottage in the midst of greenery, the bright moon shining down on it. They opened the door and led me through.

"Evan," Blue One said, "we're here."

I looked around and didn't see anyone.

"Evan!" she shouted a little too loud.

"Coming." A strong masculine voice sounded from the back.

The cottage looked typical country style. I noticed the frilly curtains and handmade pillows, but before further observation of my surroundings, Evan appeared before me, a man that took me aback. He was magnificent-looking—the dark, tall model type with intense black eyes. He sat down on the couch and gestured for me to sit too as he eyed me closely.

"Welcome to our world," he said, as if it were a vacation spot. "What's your name?" He dismissed the fucked-up fairies with a nod of his head and a wave of his hand.

"Hunter." My reply was strong, assessing him closely while sitting down next to him. He looked harmless. "What's happened to me?" The question foremost in my mind popped out of my mouth, but remaining cool was top on my priority.

"I found you in the forest." He leaned closer. "I was hunting, and there was this moan coming from where you were lying down. You were delirious. Someone must have left you for dead. You answered "yes" to my one question, hence, here we are, Hunter. Your answer has led you to my doorstep." His black leather pants were stuck to his legs; how the fuck could he breathe? Did he even need to breathe? Was his breath in me?

"What question?" There was no recollection in me of ever seeing Evan before.

"If you wanted to live or die." He ran his hands up and down his legs nervously, but his words were said in a matter-of-fact tone. My thoughts stormed together, glancing at Evan's upper body, trying to understand, but all my mind was grasping was his physique and how muscular and perfect his body was. Fucking prick. Not that mine wasn't, but he had this otherness to him, this aura. "You said 'live,' so I made you." He smirked.

"What does that mean, 'you made me'?" The anger in me was fermenting again.

"You're a vrykolaka."

"What the fuck is that?" Looking at Evan as if he was crazy, my nerves were completely on edge. If my heart was mortal, it would have been pounding in my chest like a drum.

"Relax, Hunter. This may sound nuts, but you are a subspecies of the vampire." He smirked. "Yep, we do exist. I've been around since the fourteenth century."

That was when my legs got up—then sat back down. My head fuckin' spun.

He continued. "I couldn't let you die. You looked so strong, and there was this fight in your eyes. You wanted to live."

"But I'm dead now." My whispered voice was slightly shocked, talking to myself more than to him.

"No, you're an immortal. If you were dead, you would be six feet under."

My throat felt dry.

"I will teach you." He smirked again. "I'll be your personal trainer." And then he laughed, ignoring my state of shock. His laugh was a little bit eerie. "Three months with me, my boy, and you'll be a newfangled man." Evan's face turned severe. "Whoever you were before this day, disregard that person. You are someone else now."

He spoke for about an hour straight, and trying to concentrate was proving to be quite the task, while my mind was all fucked-up, running up and down the boulevards of my life. He spoke about the nine powers and how my present phase was a so-called 'Fresh One'—I could be very powerful, as my senses were hyper-alert to my surroundings. Suddenly, the fuckin' katydids sounded so close, as if they were singing in my ear. His gaze never left mine. Basically being one of them meant that the Hunter of the past would scarcely be no more.

Yes, being part of them would change my new existence. Who were they? Why was he alone?

That was when a woman walked in from the back room. It was as if he could read my mind. She looked like Morticia Addams, dressed in a tight, black miniskirt, a green halter top with sequins, and platform boots. Everything these two had on seemed painted onto their bodies. She wore full makeup that gave her a dark, seductive look.

"New meat?" she asked, gawking at me.

"My love, this is Hunter. Hunter, this is the enchanting Gabriella."

"Gaby," she added with a slight Irish accent. She came closer and extended her hand, and that was when the smell of Death encompassed me. Rot. It must have shown on my face how close I was to gagging.

"You'll get used to the smell," Evan said. "Some bodies smell more than others. This I'll explain another time." He beamed at Gaby, who stormed out of the room.

"Gaby is my wife," Evan said, narrowing his dark eyes.

She quickly walked back into the room and smirked at me. "Hi," she whispered.

"Hi," was all I could muster, and she licked her lips. Not your typical wife. This was unbelievable.

"You need to rest," Evan said. "I can tell you're not thinking straight." He got up and ushered me to another room that led to a basement with cement walls, lined with about twenty coffins. My body physically jerked at the scene before me.

"You'll get used to it," he said. Needless to say, this was something that never settled with me. He opened one up. "Jump in."

"No." My firm stance expressed my wish to not comply. None of this sat well within me.

"Look, Hunter, whether or not you want to be a part of this, you've become one of us. Three months is the training period. After that, you can do whatever the fuck you want. You can sleep in a normal bed too." How did he know my thoughts?

"I'm a mind reader," he answered. His hand was still on the lid of the coffin. "You have a power too, but you don't know it yet. We have to do some testing to figure it out. That's the pleasant part." He pointed to the coffin. "It's almost dawn, and it's Saturday. Sleep on everything I've told you, and we'll talk tomorrow evening."

My throat was so dry.

"It's not water you want—it's blood. Although we can eat food, it's like drinking coffee when you're hungry—it doesn't satisfy your hunger, only prolongs it." Gaby appeared in a flash from upstairs, holding a cup, which she handed to me.

"Drink," Evan ordered.

I wanted to run, feeling the need to vomit.

"You won't run; you won't vomit." He corrected me. Listening to Evan was easy, doing exactly as he asked, the drinking of the mother-fuckin' blood didn't gross me out. It was like drinking cranberry juice with some copper in it. It was salty, and my throat was no longer dry.

Then Gaby produced a cheese sandwich, as if by magic.

I grabbed it and ate it in one bite. It tasted weird. Yuck. I knew Evan could read my mind, so remaining silent and chewing, my instincts were to wait for further instruction.

"Now lie down."

I did, and for the next three months, I became a model student.

Chapter Eight
I began to lose control
2009

I opened my front door and crashed out. The coolest thing about being a vrykolaka was that we could hang out during the day, except from eleven to two in the afternoon, when the sun was at its strongest. Then being indoors and using a lot of sunscreen was a necessity but knowledge and experience forewarned me that none of that protected me much. Sleep was the only way out of it. Taking long naps.

Evan taught me to live my life like I'd been given a second chance. To do the things that were within my capability now, passionate needs that would fulfill me, and especially to get the fuck out of Kentucky.

I was a missing person, according to the police report. One night, flying into the police station and reading the report should have put my mind at ease. No one had seen me. Tommy's son had confessed to what had happened, and Tommy was arrested. But nobody had been found, so Tommy was released on inconclusive evidence.

He fuckin' shot me in front of his son, and he was released. In small print, my rage surged as the words "nigger lover," flared at me. Man, my fists clenched, but there was nothing to be done. Nostalgically, I flew around my parents' home for a while and then left, never looking back. What's done is done.

Okay, if you want to know the truth, a few tears were shed while watching my mama sitting on the front porch with a heart-rending look in her eyes. My papa was on the rocking chair next to her, chewing tobacco. It was a fact that going back was impossible. Evan had said it and deep down this caused me too much pain to be around on a daily basis.

That afternoon, sleeping well and waking up at dusk, helped my frame of mind. Hopping into the cold shower, I realized that was the only thing left to do, because my morning-afternoon-night wood wasn't going down for anything.

As my thoughts went back to my pre-vampire years, it was Jack Junior that was missing from my life the most. He was my older brother by eleven months. Everyone thought we were twins because we were so close in age and in height. *Those two can read each other's minds,* Mama used to say. *You don't reckon,* Papa would reply in his sarcastic tone.

The three months with Evan were a wild ride. He taught me how to fly like a plane, eat small animals, and to bring out my power of art.

I became a painter; it was something I'd thought of doing, but whenever my papa saw me with crayons and a paper, he'd called me a sissy boy, and that was the end of those dreams. *Real men don't fuss over that crap,* he'd repeat often enough; so trading my crayons for pencils, I'd let that dream go and forgotten about it. The thing was, you never *really* forget about these things. I'd buried it deep inside me till that day when Evan put a canvas and oil paint in front of me and said, "Try painting." It was as natural as a fish takes to water.

"And there you have it, my fellow," Evan said,

eyeing me closely with fascination. "You are an 'artiste' now."

I was always an artist—I'd forgotten that he read minds as he nodded at me.

My hand painted without a thought; it led itself into the colours of jade, turquoise, merlot, magenta, and sienna, creating faces, landscapes, still life, and everything I'd ever wanted to paint but hadn't known how to. Painting made me forget the past and live for the future. Now this fresh new talent made me feel alive for the first time in my life.

Alive yet dead—what an oxymoron that was. Figured I'd be in this predicament, the way my life had been. So what if vampires do exist? This realization made me feel the best I'd ever felt; the strongest and the most creative. Even my body enlarged slightly after my transformation. In those three months, Evan forced me to run obstacle courses in the dark forest, becoming one with the night and opening up to the sounds of the animals and letting go of all my human fears. Killing animals and sucking their blood came to me like second nature. No fangs, though. It would have been cool to have fangs, but Evan explained that we had the strongest teeth of all the vampires, so we didn't need fangs.

"Over the centuries, our kind evolved and transformed," Evan explained. "You are non-human now." His dark eyes beamed like a professor's at a university. "Our history dates back to Greek Asia Minor. Folklore refers to us as devils, but we don't drink human blood. We live by sucking the blood of animals. Many are evil, just as there are many humans who are evil. You have three months to discover your abilities and to come to maturity."

Suddenly, none of this interested me anymore, what with no wife or kids, there was always an abundance of girls to fuck. Even in my hometown, this loneliness never left me.

"You can convert others and have company," Evan said, reading my mind one month into my so-called training. Psychologically it was taking a toll on me. I felt like a manic-depressive—high on my abilities and super non-human strength one day and depressed over my circumstances the next.

Fuck me. I wanted out today.

"You need to mature. Just two more months left, Hunter. Your thoughts are normal." Evan and his psychotic wife talked me through all my turmoil. Gaby proved to be an absolute cock tease. Oddly enough, she was faithful to Evan, and they lived quietly in their gingerbread house. A few times they had visitors.

Evan talked about the philosophy of vrykolaka life and the rules to follow: If ever anyone was dying right before my eyes, I had to ask them if they wanted to live or die. I had the power to turn humans by crushing and suffocating them. I could have all the sex my body craved or wanted; all my parts worked even better now. *Never fall in love with a human.* I had no heart per se beating inside me, but my senses and emotions were highly intensified.

I had followed all of Evan's rules like a model pupil—until now.

****

I dressed quickly, not paying much attention to my ensemble, and combed out my tangled hair. Maria was likeable; she was good for Jack. She had a profound sexual energy about her. She smelled like a favourite dessert, at least to me. Evan had told me the women who smelled like rotting food would not attract me in the least—thus Gaby's stench—and the ones that would smell like a flower in perfect bloom would attract me sexually.

I grabbed my vest and hurried out to go to the restaurant. Hunting last night curbed my appetite. I would eat pasta to be polite, but it would taste like rubber elastics. Once upon a time the taste of pasta was familiar— now I'd forgotten.

My sense of smell was on high alert as soon as my feet entered the restaurant, sensing both Jack and Maria to my right. They were holding hands over the table. *Never fall in love.* Evan's voice echoed in my head. It was easy to resist. I'd always be loyal to Jack; he was like my brother. This was for sure the reason for this certain affinity toward him. He reminded me so much of Jack Junior, he made me feel at home again. Maria was like my new sister-in-law, I said to myself, trying hard to convince myself.

Maybe thinking of Maria like that would force my mind to resist her exotic scent.

"Hi, lovebirds," I said, and they both beamed. "Are you ready for the best meal of your life?"

"I think this is the beginning of a beautiful friendship," Maria said with a grin.

"Yes, it is." The seat looked tiny for my long legs, as the only thing plaguing me were my senses. Out of whack. Completely.

She smelled delicious tonight.

"What are you wearing?" I suddenly asked, ready to kick myself as the question blurted out before my reasoning did.

"Clothes." She laughed. *Ah, a smarty-pants.* My mama's voice came to me from a hidden corner of my mind. Once in a while, her voice felt like it was right next to me.

"I mean your perfume."

"Anaïs Anaïs," she replied.

"Do you like her writing style? Anaïs Nin." My thoughts came at me quickly, alert. "She and Henry Miller had quite the love affair. *Tropic of Cancer* is my favourite book."

"I've never read their works," Maria said reluctantly.

"You still have time. You're too young, anyway."

Jack had not said a word, but upon glancing at him and seeing him roll his eyes at me, I figured perhaps shutting my trap was in order, but it was too late to listen to anyone now, let alone my own logic, which was thrown out the window the minute I smelt Maria's scent.

"Why do you say that?" Jack asked with some annoyance in his voice.

"Because she is."

Maria looked agitated. "Please, like who doesn't know Henry Miller was a pervert and wrote about cocks, pussies, and sex. His writing doesn't interest me." She sounded self-assured.

At the mention of cocks and pussies, my eyes widened.

"Maybe you *are* ready. Maybe you should reread them, Brains. What with the extent of your vocabulary, you should be more open-minded."

Jack grinned at the approaching waiter and waved him over. The waiter nodded, showing some attitude, and gave Jack a "where-else-would-I-be-going?" look.

“Would you like red or white wine?” Jack asked, ignoring the tension between me and Maria.

I was ready to start an argument with her, but decided to tone it down—my impulsive nature was getting the best of me—part of the vampire in me—and most of the time my thoughts were uncontrollable. Maybe it was too late, and she hated me now. I literally had to bite my lips to remind myself to shut the fuck up. I had already started to fantasize about Maria naked and on top of me in a lewd position the second the word “cock” escaped her lips. *Stop that.*

With a curt greeting, the waiter deposited the wine list and three menus on the table.

Luckily, my drinking abilities as a vampire were different from a human, drinking without ever getting drunk. Food had no taste to it; bland, like cotton. Evan explained that eating and drinking were part of the façade, part of pretending to be human.

“Red,” Maria replied to Jack. All eyes were on me now.

“Then red it is. Let me look at the menu and see if they have the bottle that is on my mind.” Picking up the wine list, quickly scanning and finding it, choosing a French Cabernet Sauvignon from the Rhone Valley. “It’s one of my favourites.” From the days when I knew what wine tasted like. Now it tasted like vinegar. My taste buds were all fucked-up.

I picked up my menu, feigning some interest as I glanced at Maria and Jack reading intently, our conversation somehow forgotten but lingering. *Let it go.*

I hated cooked meat, so choosing fettuccine Alfredo seemed like a good choice. Elastic and muck. Whatever. Salads gave me cramps, and vegetables made me vomit.

“So what’s good here?” Maria inquired, looking straight at me.

“I don’t know. This is the first time I’m eating here.” My reply surprised her to say the least and she looked peeved…apparently, my jokes suck.

She looked at me incredulously.

“Just kidding. The ladies like it here. Italian food makes them horny. It must be the garlic that doesn’t sit well in my stomach, but it gets the ladies wet.” Jack laughed, and Maria’s gaze never left mine. She was definitely not impressed with my macho bullshit, but I couldn’t stop my mouth from spewing out nonsense. She made me nervous. This mouth of mine was really fucking me over.

She looked down at her menu and studied it. Jack glanced at his and closed it quickly.

By the time the waiter came back and the wine was ordered, Maria had closed her menu too. He was back in a flash and pouring a glass of wine for me to taste.

Yuck. It was gross.

I nodded to indicate it was tasty as hell. He poured the other two glasses, and my thoughts were on how elegant Maria looked; her hair swept away from her face, and her green shirt was snug across her chest. She wore a Mayan-style sun pendant and a bit of makeup, not overdone like the other night. As soon as she caught me staring, my eyes focused on a painting far behind her on the back wall. Jack was looking around the restaurant. “Nice place. The decor is nice.”

Maria looked around too. “It feels like I’m in Italy.”

“Have you ever been?” I asked.

“No. My intention was to go, but my friends had a limited amount of time, and going by myself wasn’t my idea of a good time."

"Good decision. They're all rapists. The way they gawk and yell at women as if they were pieces of meat, it's obscene. They have no respect," I said matter-of-factly. "And they like to grab." That was my final comment on those pricks.

"Grab?" Maria repeated.

"Asses." It was bloody true. Jack laughed.

"Well, one day, I'll let you know," she said, and then sipped her wine.

"You don't have to actually go there. Look at all the Italian tourists that come here."

"Okay, enough about that," Jack said, and lifted his glass. "Cheers."

"Cheers," we all said together.

"It's about a girl, right?" Maria asked with a smirk. "I get it."

Okay, she was bang on.

"Let's change the subject," Jack said, knowing full well where this conversation was headed.

The "girl" was a total bitch who'd gotten under my skin, but I'd never fallen in love with her. It had only been lust.

"Let's get back to Henry Miller," Maria said with a twinkle in her eye. The girl question wasn't going to be answered, anyway. None of her fuckin' business.

"Well, he was a fuckin' writer who told it as it is. He knew how guys think and wrote like no other writer dared to write."

"Do you have his book *Tropic of Cancer*?" Maria asked.

"Yep. Close by my bed." Couldn't help the wink. "If you want, I'll lend it to you, but you have to promise me you'll give it back."

"You got a deal." She grinned. "Jack, have you read it?"

"If you want to be friends with Hunter, it's a prerequisite," Jack said with a laugh.

"What did you think of it?" she asked Jack, tilting her head and placing her arm on the table.

"I thought it was fantastic. You enter his mind and experience his life. Crazy stuff. A must-read even if you don't like him. You'll appreciate the writing." Jack shook his hair away from his eyes. "Vulgar and philosophical and misogynistic, but brilliant prose."

"When was it written?"

"Nineteen thirty-four. In Paris. He liked to use the word cunt a lot." As if she didn't know that already, but the truth is the truth.

Maria smirked. "I know that already." She looked from Jack to me. "So reading Henry Miller and Anaïs Nin is a must, right?"

"I don't know anything about Anaïs Nin," Jack said, looking at me confused.

"And you, Hunter?" Maria asked. "These are your suggestions."

"What the fuck makes me an expert?" I muttered. "I dropped out of high school way before you were ever born." *I can't believe that just came out of my mouth.*

Maria looked surprised. "How old are you?"

"Take a wild guess?"

"Around forty."

"You nailed it."

"She's good," Jack said, and rubbed Maria's arm.

"Yes, she certainly is," agreeing with every ounce of my being. "She's a keeper." I looked at Jack and winked.

The waiter served our food, leaving me no choice but to eat and moan about how delicious it was, all the while thinking it tasted like leather strips. Maria seemed to enjoy her meal, and Jack munched away contentedly.

I thought of Evan and his fucked-up guidelines. *"You'll soon forget how food used to taste, so when you're with people, think of how good sex is, and throw in some mms and moans. It'll sound realistic."*

We ate and talked all night long, enjoying Maria's company, mostly because she was funny, smart, and sexy. Jack was all over her, and right after coffee and dessert, my head told me to leave them alone, while my gut, well, that was better left unsaid. I picked up the tab, as planned.

"Gotta run," was what I blurted out, when there was nowhere to go.

"Thanks," Maria said. She stood and leaned toward me to kiss me good-bye. Bending down to kiss her on both cheeks and smelling her skin up close, left my senses mouth-watering. She flinched at my cold lips.

"You're welcome. It is refreshing and gratifying when a woman is right." Then, shaking Jack's hand, I muttered, "See ya, bro. Have a great night." Nodding my head good-bye one last time to get out of there so fast, one would think there was a hot date ahead. The only thing waiting for me was loneliness, feeling apprehensive, angry, frustrated, and horny as the fresh air hit me, the only thought going through me, was how the fuck was I supposed to sleep with a boner like this one.

Chapter Nine
Some people have hearts that don't rest
1989

I drove for hours listening to Elvis Presley and John Lee Hooker tapes in my car. Driving until the forest appeared in front of me as the craving to eat consumed me. Parking, I leaped high in the air to stalk the territory. There was nothing in sight, but finding those nocturnal motherfuckers would be easy as pie.

Then in the dead silence, the familiar scent attracted my full attention. I'd be doing the farmers a favour. The thing was to be careful of its tusks and of any family member that might be close by. You rarely saw one alone, and this was a perfect opportunity for yours truly. Slowly creeping closer, I noticed it had light-colour stripes. Great. It was a young one.

Wild boars couldn't see in the dark, but they sure as hell could sense my presence, as its head turned to my direction.

I jumped on its back and bit fiercely. It toppled over, unconscious. Hearing footsteps rapidly approaching—probably its mother—I quickly lifted it high onto a branch, where my mouth bit savagely into its neck, eating ravenously, leaving skin and bones.

Ended up back in my car, content. My hunger pains satisfied, now my boner, that was another story altogether. There had to be more to my lonely existence than just living day by day as a vampire. Condemned to this lonely life forever was hell. How much longer could my soul take this life? How does one just let it be? Where were my answers? Why couldn't Evan have let me die that dreadful day? My body was supposed to be dead. Why was this so-called life of mine going on and on? Love was out of the question. Someone loving me was also impossible; letting anyone get that close would only harm that person. The thing is, being social was always part of my nature, so making friends and turning them one by one helped by taking away part of the loneliness. And they did sometimes; they helped the time go by.

But Maria made me want to die. Stake me in the heart. I'd never had a Yoko Ono by my side. Not that I liked that fuckin' cunt; remembered where I was when John Lennon died, when Martin Luther King died, and especially John F. Kennedy—being in New York then. Evan said that events wouldn't affect me; my bonds that once tied me to mortals—uncaring, a piece of fibreglass, looking through the world and not giving a damn. But my fucked-up self did care. Paul McCartney's voice went through me, recalling how Paul didn't want to sit at home, crying over John Lennon's death. He wanted to listen to his music, so he stayed home and listened to Lennon's songs over and over again.

I had been watching a football game at some bar when Howard Cosell's voice announced John Lennon's death, trying hard not to cry, because blood or mucus would probably come out, but everyone at the bar freaked out, crying and yelling, while my insides were filled with hate and rage, and kept on reminding myself, don't fuckin' cry, you idiot.

I sped faster now, loving the feeling of speeding on the highway; the same way it felt as a human. I'd forgotten how it felt to be human after twenty-nine years, but holding on to some memories was partly normal, while others I'd thrown under the rug to step on them and erase them from my existence.

I reckoned there were some things better to not remember.

"Get on outta here with your foreigners," Papa had said while my leaving home as an adolescent did affect him; not that I travelled long distances, but actually leaving the Cherokee Triangle to go to a community college, well, he was upset, mostly because I'd lied about finishing high school and given them a fake certificate I'd made with some buddies. My knack for writing led me to becoming editor of the college newspaper and then got a part-time job at *The Sun*, our local newspaper. I'd been away from home for two years, but it was only a two-hour drive back. It was like a dream now, remembering less and less as each year passed. The faces of my mama and papa had become blurry, like an old photograph with smudge marks on it. Listening to Evan and not going to see my parents only made me miss them even more—I should have visited them here and there, if only just to see their familiar faces one last time. My stubborn streak never left me. Evan had planted those words "never go back" in my head, and it was as if that fuckin' mantra played over and over like a broken record. As hard-headed a Taurus, my zodiac sign, that is how loyal my nature is as well.

I parked my car and went upstairs to my apartment to paint in order to get the rage out somehow. A blank page used to excite me; now a blank canvas had the same effect.

Painting was exhilarating—demonic at times. It was

perfect for a vryko-vamp like me. Evan called me a VV for short. Vrykolaka is too long and sounds like a disease, he'd noted with a commanding voice one didn't argue with. It was pretty cool-sounding, intellectual-like.

I unlocked my door and went straight for the easel and canvas; grabbing my palette with the leftover paint from earlier, which was half dry, and picked up a long, slim paintbrush that had been soaking in a cup of dirty water. Shaking it out a bit, I patted it dry on the towel hanging from the easel. Looking at the painting that began a few days ago, it was the figure of a woman with long, reddish hair covering her back. Guess who. Yep. It was her out yonder. There was no sunset, no fuckin' romance-glistening nakedness. There must be perfection underneath her clothes, and even if she wasn't, that was cool too. Drawing her had removed the demon lust inside me. This feeling would stay within me; for seeing that alluring, invisible rope pulling me into her, would not make me grab it. No, hurting Jack would kill me. I'd never been that fuckin' kind of guy; even as a vampire, my conscience reigned. Could you fuckin' believe it?

I painted her silhouette against the night sky. The brushstrokes recalled every curve. Realizing that fucking was what would save me from these thoughts, my eyes fell on the clock. It was only three a.m. I'd call Melanie; she was my booty call at the moment. She had that heart-shaped ass that turned every male's head. And she liked it rough; being as that was the only way my membrane worked, roughly, that didn't leave her a choice. The worst part was how I'd try to be gentle, but my libido would get the best of me. Not controlling my libido as humans could was the one thing that I wished was different. Having all this stamina was phenomenal, lasting for well over an hour and fucking till kingdom comes got all my energy out, but a slow love-making was something I missed; that fucked up romantic in me, that was in there somewhere, wanted to take it slow at times.

I placed my paintbrush back in the water, and paced up and down with a hard-on that wouldn't die.

I called Melanie, and she answered in a sleepy, groggy voice.

"Allo?"

"*Allo, chérie,*" I said.

"*Bonjour,* cowboy." That was her nickname for me.

"Voulez-vous coucher avec moi?" I asked in a husky, sexy voice. There was a pause for a few seconds.

"*Oui, viens tout de suite,*" she whispered, and hung up. Yes, she wanted me to come over right away.

I grabbed my keys, put on my shoes, and practically ran out the door. It was a nippy night, but not feeling the cold, only the throbbing of my dick, had me practically flying over to her house. My knuckles rapped on her bedroom window urgently not to wake up her roommate. She pulled aside the curtain and looked delighted to see me, and then pointed to her front door.

Melanie opened the door, and with a *bonjour* and a *bonsoir*, my agile grip lifted her up in one swinging motion, carried her to her bed, and fucked her brains out.

Getting up to leave, my glance noticed her white pajamas ripped on the floor. Shit. Not again.

"I'll buy you a new pair," I said, pulling up my pants, and meeting her gaze.

"Are you mad?" Melanie asked, lying on her bed, still sweaty in the dark, her hair stuck to her head.

"No, just horny."

"You're a real prick, you know," she said, laughing.

“I know.” Her leg reached out to me, my hand caressing it as my lips met her forehead.

“Why don’t you stay a bit?” She looked at me carefully, knowing full well that my motus operandi was bolting out the fucking door; plus, that desperation in her eyes didn’t help my state of mind. It made me want to run away fast.

“I have an early start tomorrow. Someone is coming to purchase one of my masterpieces.” My explanation was truthful, stated without an ounce of guilt.

“Hunter, you’re a prick.” And she rolled over without saying good-bye.

I left and didn’t look back; she knew what to expect from me. “Someone Like You” by Van Morrison popped into my head, and hummed it all the way home. But it sure wasn’t Melanie who was preoccupying my thoughts. It was Maria—the swing of her hair and the sway of her hips.

Chapter Ten
I'm so fucked up

I lay down for a few hours with my eyes wide open. Since it wasn't Saturday, my body didn't crave sleep. Not letting myself get caught up in a hair twist, telling myself that being cool and friendly with Maria and nothing else was the best plan, because I couldn't afford to be anything but that.

Don't be a prick, Hunter. Although Melanie thought that of me—and rightly so—she wanted it too, so who cared?

I got up and took a shower. Smelled like pussy, and although at times that was fantastic, at the moment, it was unbearable. I really needed to paint so all my thoughts would be taken over by being in the zone of painting, rather than pussy. Any one in particular that shouldn't be on my mind. Ever. But the doorbell rang.

Who the fuck was that? Oh, yeah, Mr. What's-His-Name.

I put down my paintbrush and buzzed him up.

I waited at the door. *My gift.*

Evan said it would earn me a living my entire life and that my skill would improve by getting better and better; equally, my eyesight would improve. There was no way down—no losing my eyesight, my bones wouldn't deteriorate, and there would be no fear of getting old.

I had the same face since 1960. Everyone thought

my skin had remained the same and how was it possible? Every twenty years I'd move so that no one would suspect what truly lurked inside of me.

"*Bonjour*." Mr. What's-His-Name popped his head up the stairs and bounced around like a fuckin' kangaroo. He was the nerdy art lover type; his three-piece suit and short-cut *GQ* hair yelled out, I'm Mr. Perfect.

"Mr. Black, nice to meet you." He extended his hand. Nine years ago, when I'd moved to Saint-Tropez, I'd changed my last name. "I'm Mr. Pelletier."

"Come in, Mr. Pelletier," I said. "So how did you hear about my work?" I gestured for him to take a seat on the couch.

"Well, Mr. Scott referred me to you while visiting the United States. He gave me your name and number. He said you have a great talent." *He should know; he created me*. I had to send Evan my address and blood every year for his inventory, bullshit lists, and tracking system. His calls—now that was a whole other story—I avoided. Small talk between vampires could be referred to as insignificant talk. There were no long discussions, just orders.

"Yes, my dear friend Evan." My southern drawl emphasized Evan's name. "Would you like something to drink?" Asking to be polite, but hoping he would refuse.

"No, thank you."

I got the sense that he had his coffee and toast every morning at exactly the same time, at exactly the same location. Dull. A walking zombie, chuckling to myself at my thoughts, while thinking about my vampire traits. I was fuckin' dead. *Or am I?* Not really. Now that was a contradiction. Shut up, I told my fucked-up voices.

"Okay, so let's get to it." He was still standing, and

then I noticed the ugliest brown briefcase I'd ever seen. It was definitely from my time—an antique case with silver metal clasps. Disliking him came naturally. He was a French asshole with a perverse sex life. This flash of him picking up whores and making them do sick things appeared briefly in my mind—a quick vision.

I walked toward the back of my studio. It was one humongous room. My bed was in the middle, and that was my preference. My paintings were lined up against the grand wall under the window sill.

"Take a look." Sitting on my couch and being bored out of my gourd, his nervousness came at me like a slap. He walked toward the paintings, holding onto his briefcase for dear life.

"You could put your briefcase down, if you like," I suggested.

"No, thank you." That appeared to be his favourite reply.

I put my feet on the coffee table and leaned back, rubbing my eyes. Always feeling uncomfortable while my artwork was being scrutinized, and wanting to slap him silly simultaneously left me with the only logical solution: close my eyes. It was pleasant and silent, listening to his footsteps walking by all my paintings. There were approximately thirty or so; some were on top of or overlapping another. There was no fuckin' space in this dump with a superb view.

"Excuse me," he said.

I opened my eyes. "See anything you like?"

"Certainly. How much is this one?" He pointed to a painting of Nikki Beach. My calculation went something like this: seven hundred francs for rent, a hundred for groceries, and one-hundred and sixty for those cool leather pants.

"Nine-hundred and sixty francs," I said, closing my eyes again.

"I'll take it," he quickly replied, placing his briefcase down, then a snap and a creak as he opened it.

I opened my eyes and turned to him. "You're buying it now?" Usually it took a few days for a transaction to be completed.

"Of course." He took out the money and walked toward me. "Here you go, Mr. Black." He handed me the money.

"*Merci.*" I took the money, delighted.

I had to get up now and wrap the painting. Sometimes the paintings were so much part of me that letting them go was difficult. Then I'd drive a tough bargain. Other times, fucking around with someone's head gave me cheap thrills .

Mr. What's-His-Name was annoying the fuck out of me, punching him in the face was my first reaction. Aggression was part of my problem as well. I grabbed some brown rolled-up paper and wrapping the painting quickly. The size of the painting was about ten by ten, so he could easily carry it. Man, watching him leave my apartment would give me pleasure. He smelled up my place with his putrid scent.

I opened the front door.

"Merci beaucoup."

"*Merci,*" he said. "And I-I will be back again," he stammered as he looked up at me. I could squish his geeky face with one hand.

"Looking forward to it," I replied sarcastically.

Boy, did the French know all about sarcasm; they must have invented it. He left in a hurry, trying to balance his briefcase and the painting. I counted the money twice and shoved it in my back jeans pocket.

I was going shopping.

Right now.

Get me those leather pants.

Hee-haw, fuckin' cowboy was right. Shit, my hard-on just wouldn't go away. Throwing my keys in my pocket and running down the stairs, I stopped at my landlord's door and knocked really hard.

Those fuckin' freaks were probably sleeping. They were a couple of wannabe rock stars. Margaret answered the door. Her blonde-dyed hair—in desperate need of a dye job—looked god-awful, as did her horrific streaked makeup. She was holding an eyeliner pencil, and the door was halfway open. She started to fix her shirt, which was as tight as it could possibly get, and just at the sight of her tits popping out of her blouse, my boner went down.

Yep, I'd fucked her once, and she was so smelly, I'd almost barfed afterward. She thought I would come back for a second time, but I'd never be that desperate again.

"*Bonjour, chéri*," she said in a seductive voice. She looked back to see if her lover boy, Jonathan, overheard. He was another loser. Suddenly, like a rat, he popped his head out the side of the door. He was wearing his Pink Floyd T-shirt from high school that had seen better days, and a lopsided grin.

"*Salut, mon ami*," he said. His mohawk was on target today. "You want to listen to my new tune?" He opened the door wide, as if…did he actually think my feet would step in there? *Get the fuck out of here*.

"No." My voice sounded firm as my hand reached into my pocket and counted out seven hundred francs.

"Here's the rent, Margaret." Handing her the money to get the fuck out.

"*Appelez-moi* Margie." She liked to be called Margie while being fucked. She grabbed the money in one swift motion, and feeling their perverse energy coming at me like steam from a kettle, only managed to nauseate me even further.

"*Au revoir*," I said, ignoring their stares as I read how dirty their minds were. The idea of a *ménage a trois* with them almost made me toss my guts right there on the front steps.

Just looking at these two rejects, I'd never feel horny again. At least for a while, my libido was insatiable.

I turned to leave, and they called out to come by anytime. As if that was ever going to happen. If Jonathan knew I'd fucked his Margie, he'd stab me. He looked like the type who'd killed easily. He was a crime-of-passion kind of guy.

I walked into the fresh air and cleared the stench from my nostrils. Those two fucks were rotting inside there. Heading to Boutique Isabelle Dugas, fashion designer *extraordinaire*, changed my spirit. I'd gotten to know her well over the years; she had talent. Too bad she didn't stir me up.

She wanted me, but petite women never did it for me; fucking tiny adolescent bodies wasn't my thing. Some guys would jump on that, but that wasn't my scene. My type of woman was the one that rattled me with just a first look or a glance. My type was the one that made me think, but being a vampire, it was mostly about the lust, sex, the intimacy and wanting took a back seat since I wasn't supposed to fall in love. Locked all that shit up tightly. Everyone has a type heck, who didn't?

I pushed the freshly cleaned glass doors and walked into Isabelle's store. She was sitting behind the cash, hunched over, calculating some figures. She was probably calculating her debt. There were hardly any people in the shop. She had been having a rough time of it lately. As soon as she saw me, her eyes lit up.

"Ah, Unter." Isabelle spoke my name with a typical French accent. "*Bonjour, mon amour*."

"*Bonjour, mon mignon*." She approached me, and bending down to kiss her on both cheeks, my height overwhelmed her again as she glanced up and grinned. She was so tiny.

"*Tu es froid*." You are cold, she told me, her blonde bob hitting me in the face. What else is new?

"I'm always cold, *cherie d'amour*, but inside there's a furnace,"—gesturing toward my heart which was non-existent and all this bull crap was way over her head. Nobody gets the innuendoes and that's my own way of having fun.

We exchanged some small talk.

"I want those leather pants I'd been eyeing for a while."

She ran to the back of the room all excited, glancing up and down at my legs.

"I kept them for you." She handed them to me. "Go try them on."

She led me to the dressing room. The leather felt incredibly soft, and they felt remarkable on me.

"Let me see," Isabelle yelled from outside the door.

"I love them." Before my eyes could even glance at a mirror, her mouth opened in awe.

"*Fantastique*!" she bellowed, staring at my crotch.

I grinned, looking in the mirror and instantly loving them. *Not too shabby.*

"*Tourne-toi,*" she said, turning around at her command.

"*Magnifique.*" She looked at my butt as if it were a piece of juicy licorice or chocolate croissant or something.

I turned back to her. "I'm not taking them off."

"For how many days?" she asked jokingly.

"You know me well." My laugh echoed in the boutique as I went back to the changing room to get my jeans. "How much?"

"*Cent cinquante pour toi.*" She grinned at me, her eyes beaming.

"*Merci, ma belle.*" Paying the bill and stuffing the rest of the cash in my leather pants pocket felt great.

"You look very 'ot." I chuckled at her pronunciation. "You 'ave a big date?"

"No, just have to have these pants."

"You wear them well."

"By the way, your men's clothing line is incredible. Am I repeating myself?"

"Yes, every time you come." She fidgeted with her jacket zipper. "Come back in one month when my new collection is out. I'm still working on them." She took my old jeans and placed them in a silver paper bag with her name on it.

"*Merci.*" She grinned and came close to me for another kiss on the cheek.

"*Bienvenue.*" My urge was to fly with these leather pants on, but couldn't do that in broad daylight. It was a bit of luck that the sun did not kill me and that going about my business in the middle of the day was normal.

Vrykolakas were the best kind of vampire. We didn't have to run away from the sun; limiting our exposure was enough. The sun did make me dizzy, but at least it was bearable.

Any other type of vampire couldn't deal with direct sunlight the same way. It was true they only came out at dusk. Not that I'd ever met one. Evan had told me all about them; they existed, but they were underground.

Vrykolakas were different. We could mingle among humans, and they couldn't tell the difference between us and themselves, except they noticed our body temperature. Our eyes were also more brilliant. It was a necessity to wear sunglasses all day long because the sun bothered my eyes a thousand times more than it bothered humans.

As my feet hit the concrete, it always astounded me how the years had gone by as quickly as they had. Twenty-nine years of this shit already.

I figured I'd go over to Gonzo's place. Everyone would be there. During the day, they all hung around and watched old movies, listened to music, or argued about whatever stupidity they could think of. Gonzo had come into an inheritance and owned a castle. It had fifteen bedrooms, ten bathrooms, a humongous master suite that could fit a porn crew, a courtyard made for dukes and duchesses, and a fuckin' tennis court that we played in at the dead of night. Gonzo's great-grandfather had been a duke of some kind, so we all gathered there and hung out.

I couldn't remember Gonzo's real name, though. He'd told me a few times, but always forgot. Gonzo had the power of listening. He could hear me coming from miles away. He'd prepare my favourite drink—iced tea with three lemon wedges and ice cubes—and as soon as I'd get to his house, the drink would be waiting for me on his gargantuan table, which easily sat a party of twenty.

I climbed the steps, and before my fingers touched the door bell, Gonzo opened the door.

"Hey, what's up?" His dark brows came together.

I walked in and saw Charlie mixing drinks as usual.

"Watcha makin'?" I asked.

"Long Island iced tea. Better than what you usually drink."

"As if tasting is an option. Everything tastes like water." The room was dark as I zeroed in on my drink being made at that moment.

"I'm making yours now," Charlie said, his long, golden locks reminding me of a dark version of Jon Bon Jovi.

"I can see that."

He laughed.

Ed put on a movie. All Ed ever did was watch movies and analyze the direction, editing, and script.

"What are we watching?" My tone was impatient, as he finished up with his shaking and stirring as if he was behind a camera or something.

"*The Terminator*," Ed replied, as if it was the greatest movie ever written.

"Again?" Fuck, I'd had enough of that movie. Ed was in love with Linda Hamilton and anything to do with cyborg killers. His dark hair was braided down to his butt today. *What the fuck?*

"What's with the braid?"

"My heritage, Master." Ed had one-fifth Indian blood, and he took it to the extreme.

"You're nuts, you know that?"

"I know." He chuckled.

I joined them, and talked throughout most of the movie. Everything was boring me lately, my drink empty, my mind wandering where it shouldn't and my legs already up and ready to bolt.

"Master, where're you going?" Gonzo asked.

"You gotta stop calling me that," I said, frustrated and annoyed.

They all turned toward me.

"Since when?" the choir asked.

"Since now." I slammed the door behind me.

Everyone was getting on my nerves lately. It was exasperating, doing nothing relevant for hours—days. At first, looking in the mirror in awe at showing no physical signs of aging, freaked the fuck out of me. Man, you *haven't changed*, everyone would tell me. After a while, having all the power felt meaningless. All right, granted, no heart that actually beat, and some of my emotions were supposedly gone, but still, parts of me thought it was all a hoax. I did feel human emotions—some more than others.

Most of the time and most powerful of emotions was lust. It came in waves—waves of horniness—and then it would go, and then it was okay for a while. Hunger was the strangest one of all; I'd look at a great meal and want to devour it, but it didn't taste the way it used to. Food taste varied between paper clips, elastic, and wood. No fuckin' taste. Insects weren't too bad. I'd pop them in my mouth like Rockets. Fish gave me pain, and sushi rendered me unconscious for hours. I'd never tasted sushi before becoming a vryko; now it was all the rage. It was fuckin' disgusting. Pigs tasted the best—raw, of course.

But back to the emotional part of my transformation. My lack of empathy in this life and my mortal life was more pronounced now. The only human I gave a fuck about was Jack—and now, Maria. Keeping Jack close to me made me feel like there was still something human lurking somewhere deep inside me, wanting and not wanting to come out. The choir just reminded me of who I was.

As for Maria, she was my soul mate. It may sound corny to the dickheads who believe only in pussy and no connection but that light was there. The light I'd seen above her shoulder had shown me the truth, and nothing could be done about it. Other powers pulled the strings. She was meant to be with me—one day. Not knowing how or when, but feeling deep down that it was inevitable. When the light presented itself, you had to follow it. She made me feel comfortable, like being myself was acceptable, whatever the fuck that meant. As every year went by, the parts of me that were once mortal were less and less, but only to a certain extent. Were my emotions getting soft? Fuck, no. And then my thoughts went to fucking, —Jack and Maria fucking to be exact—and my need to fly in the sky became overpowering. These feelings of…Could it be jealousy?

I'd never felt jealousy as a vryko until now. My feelings were just so much more intense, unstoppable at times. It being only Thursday, and needing two more days until deep sleep, didn't put me in a better mood. Needing it to be Saturday to stop the thoughts from consuming me, to stop the feelings from controlling me and to just escape my desolate life, was all that was on my mind. Two more fucking days until total oblivion.

I was a little fucked-up now, my hands reaching deep in my pocket for my keys. No woman was going to do that to me. It had never happened before—not as a human and not now in this state. It wasn't possible, but then again, why had Evan told me not to fall in love if it wasn't possible?

Then it was possible.

Maybe force myself from caring because I wasn't human. The problem was my thoughts were jumbled and my emotions impulsive. Not feeling any better, I'd let these emotions slide off me like I had with all the other women I'd known.

I couldn't reckon that my feelings were that intense.

Yep.

I unlocked my door and walked in, turning on the radio to fill the empty sound of the apartment. "I've Been Waiting for a Girl Like You" was playing on the radio. *What the fuck?* Suddenly, my voice joined in the singing to a song that I never even liked.

I thought I'd better stop myself right then from giving in to any feelings for Maria. *Seriously. Right now.*

Hers was the face that came to mind at singing the word 'girl.' How hard could it be for me to feel less? To desire less? To want less? My emotions were bursting.

Easy, I told myself. Get a grip, acting like a man in love. *I am not in love with Maria.*

Then why the fuck was my instinct to hum along to this obnoxious song and think only of her? Definitely, fucked. That was what I was.

Part Four

Maria in Santorini

Chapter Eleven
I'm senseless
2009

I found him. It appeared to me as if he'd been waiting for me. He seemed like a man who had a lot on his mind. Chairs and pots were scattered across the lawn, and he paid no particular attention to them. He had an overweight body and a slight hunchback. He looked to be about sixty or seventy. It was hard to tell; his hair was all grey and thick as straw. He had kind eyes as he glanced at my approaching step.

"Good evening, Dr. Pappas," I said, extending my hand.

"Good evening…" He waited.

"Maria."

He looked me up and down. My disheveled appearance must have been quite a sight. I'd been running through forests for days, leaping over trees, traveling over waters; I'd actually lost count of how many nights my body hadn't slept on a mattress.

"I'd like to speak with you concerning your research," My voice shook slightly.

"Oh?" He examined me closely. "Are you a student?"

"No. I'm a vrykolaka," I said in a low voice. "And my master needs to be killed."

I thought his eyes would pop out of their sockets. My statement did shock him. It came out of my mouth desperately, this need inside me to confide in someone who would understand, to tell someone my mind, to speak to someone who knew what a vampire was better than me.

"Come in." He nervously led me inside his house and urged me to sit down. "You don't look well." He seemed quite pale to me, and my reaction was to tell him the same thing. Instead, my observation of my surroundings was more acute, detailed, looking around looking around, noticing books on his coffee table, end table, and bookshelves, and the ugliest plaid couch I'd ever seen. His place smelled like a library. Dr. Pappas gestured for me to sit on the couch.

He sat next to me.

"So, tell me, what has happened to you, Maria?" he asked in a calm voice, as if he were speaking to a child. He no longer seemed frantic, and instantly felt at ease. I began to tell him my story.

"I was ill, having some kind of virus, and the man I was sleeping with, Hunter, turned me into one of his kind. My love is Jack, not Hunter." Perhaps my babbling confession was incoherent as tears formed. "He made me love him. He said all the right things. He knows me so well." Rubbing my eyes, my story had him enthralled as he regarded me, waiting for more. "And now Hunter wants me. He'll soon find me, and then what will happen?"

Dr. Pappas stared at me, listening attentively, as if my story were retelling an old fairy tale he'd heard before.

"Listen, my dear. There is only one way to kill a vrykolaka or a vampire." He reached over to his left side and pulled out a worn-out, brown-covered book. "It is with a stake through the heart."

"Then a stake through the heart it is," I said, a little too loudly.

"You have to know that Hunter is stronger and will not be easy to kill." Flipping through the pages of the book, he looked up at me with doubt in his eyes. "You are definitely not as strong as he is." He glanced at my body meekly. "He has been a vampire for many years, no?"

"I don't know how many years, but my strength will get stronger as each day passes." Or so my will hoped to believe.

He held a page open, and glancing, shaking my head, my words caught in my throat. It was a black-and-white sketch of vampires dying, flames escaping their bodies as a stake was placed through each of their hearts by a mortal being. It gave me the creeps.

"What more do you want from me?" Dr. Pappas asked as he showed me the picture up close and pointed to the drawing. "I can only show you this and hope you succeed at whatever you need to do." His gaze darted from the book, to me, to the windows, and then to the door. His anxiety suddenly became apparent. He continued. "You do know that you will be found," he stated as he handed me the book.

He walked to the windows and pulled down all the shades.

I thought about what he said. "They have my blood, and they know my scent, especially the vampire gifted with the power of sensing."

"Exactly. Your master will know your scent; he does not need help from anyone else." He cleared his throat. "What more do you want from me, Maria?" he asked again. Not answering his question, not willing to answer his question, not admitting to any feelings whatsoever, his edginess grew by the second, and his apprehension made me edgy. In my mind, Hunter was going to storm through the door any minute. Dr. Pappas walked toward me and shut the book in my hand. My instinct was to leave, but my logic told me to get as much information as possible.

"Look, this book will show you how to kill a vampire. Take it and follow it." The pictures had looked unreal, like somebody had drawn them for a comic book. I'd heard it all before, and I'd seen all those movies about killing a vampire with a stake, but I'd never thought it was actually true. Not sure what freaked me more: his constant glancing at the windows and doors, or the graphic illustrations from the eighteenth-century world that appeared unreal.

"Are you serious?"

"Very." He pointed to the book. "I've seen how to kill one up close." He sat across from me and shook his right leg up and down as he spoke. "And it is the scariest thing I've ever seen in my life. First of all, they move so quickly. My mind finds it hard to understand how killing them could be done like those images in that book."

"I don't know if killing is in me," I confessed. "Although this is what led me to you, I'm not a killer."

"No one is ever a killer until they are in a life-or-death situation. Why do you want to kill Hunter?" he asked matter-of-factly. "That will not change who you have become." He looked at me with genuine concern now. My loneliness must be so evident, he knew it, and he was lending me an understanding ear when others would have called me insane. Not that there was anybody to confess my story to.

I divulged everything to him; my non-stop confession must have lasted for a good half-hour or so. He studied me closely, listening to every detail and not once glancing at the windows or doors again. Finally, my story led me to the night of my thirty-fourth birthday party.

"Jack had planned a birthday party for me at our place. It was supposed to be a surprise, but he couldn't keep anything from me. He had asked Hunter to bring me to a restaurant, where we would hook up later after Jack's gig. We were wasting time till everyone showed up at the party, and we would walk in and they'd shout surprise. It didn't happen like that at all. When Hunter and I walked into my apartment, everyone—including Jack—shouted surprise, but a few seconds later, Jack realized he'd forgotten to buy ice, so he kissed me on the lips and said he'd be right back. We waited. And waited but he never came back. Hunter went to look for him. Deep down my instincts felt something was definitely wrong and my worry made me sick to my stomach." It must have shown on my face, pausing to catch my breath, reliving that moment in my head again.

"Do you need a glass of water?" Dr. Pappas asked. Why did he offer me water when what my body needed was a glass of blood?

"No, thanks." My only need at that moment was to get the story out of my system. "Hunter came back about two hours later. Hunter said he'd searched everywhere. The cashier at the corner store never saw Jack. Hunter went to all the closest locations and asked if anyone had seen him—you see, everyone knew Jack—but no one had. What could have happened to him? Hunter was so upset and worried; he knew something was amiss."

"Did you ever find him?" Dr. Pappas asked, his warm brown eyes widening.

"No." Recounting that horrible night made my hands tremble and shake. "I went to the police and filled out a missing persons report. There were no clues to anything. Even Hunter did his best to help me find Jack. He loved him too, you see. The police knew nothing. No one saw him. Years went by, and coming out of my depression, the only person there for me during this whole time was Hunter." Anguished, my story continued, looking at the doc's interest in my words, "Then Hunter seduced me. He said all the right words. He was the closest person to Jack and the only one who seemed to understand my pain." Getting up and pacing in the room didn't really calm me down. "I was sad, and he was patient. He somehow turned my tears into laughter; my loneliness into company; falling into his arms and his trap!" My cracked voice couldn't stop, "And he made me into a fuckin' vampire!"

Dr. Pappas stared at me in awe, then finally spoke. "I've heard many stories about vampires, my dear, but this one takes the cake. Do you think Hunter had something to do with Jack's disappearance?"

"Yes. He must have wanted to get him out of the picture." Although the words came out of my mouth, my doubt shouted at me simultaneously.

"Have you ever asked Hunter?"

"No." It was a simple question that infuriated me. "I hate him! He turned me into one of his kind!" I shouted.

"Why do you think he did that?"

"I already told you—because he loves me, because he has been in love with me all along, not knowing until recently."

I stood beside the window and pushed the side of the blind to stare out into the unknown, into the dark sky, and played the scene in my head like so many times before…

It was a fall night in late October 2008, when the weather started to chill you. Not as much as in the winter, but just a hint of cold that reached inside to the very core. We had become the closest of friends, knowing he wanted more from our friendship, but he'd never done anything about it. He knew my inner conflict stopped me.

I finally told him, "It wouldn't be fair to Jack," when he came over one night with take-out food.

"Jack could be dead," Hunter said, placing the food on the table.

"I know, but not knowing what happened to him will always hurt me. My questions, my pleads to God, no one listens." I placed my hands on my head, pulling my hair back in deep anguish. Years of this torment, and still a wreck from unanswered questions. I hadn't been with another man since Jack.

"Maria, you know we've done the best we could to find answers. The police even said that maybe he was hiding from someone or something. We will never know. We just have to let it go—you have to let it go." Hunter sat next to me and caressed the top of my head. "You know I'll do anything for you," he whispered.

I popped my head up, and looked deep into his eyes. It felt like Hunter revealed himself to me for the first time in the four and a half years since Jack had been gone. His dark eyes glistened, and he swept a tendril behind my ear. My gaze never left his, and his eyes conveyed to me, the realization for the first time, that he was in love with me. Before then, pretending there was nothing between us was safer. Tell or convince myself we were only good friends, but at that moment, my body froze as he caressed another loose hair with his other hand. He gazed down at my lips for a few seconds too long, and knowing he wanted to kiss me flooded me with the same violent urge as my eyes fell on his lips, and before I knew it, he was all over me. He was a magician. In a matter of seconds, my clothes were half off, and he was inside me, straddling my hips and squeezing my nipples with his teeth and tongue. It must have been the fastest orgasm in my life and the quickest fuck I'd ever had.

And then it was over.

It couldn't have lasted more than a minute, my orgasm exploded like a wild animal in heat. No matter how corny that sounded, that was exactly how it happened; feelings of shock, embarrassed, and numbness enveloped me.

How did this happen?

Hunter didn't say a word. He pulled up his pants, as I quickly got dressed and ran to the bathroom to lock myself inside was my only thought.

And waited.

I waited for Hunter to leave, but didn't hear anything. Slow minutes passed, and my tears overtook me as my body betrayed me. It had been a big mistake. Then his footsteps approached, and he knocked. "Maria, are you okay?"

"No, I'm not okay. This was a mistake. You should leave," I shouted.

"Please, let's talk about it. Come out."

"No."

I heard his footsteps go toward the front door, and then the door shut.

Slowly, letting myself out, and wiping away the tears, I walked into my living room. There he was, standing against the front door, staring at me as my eyes still teary-eyed looked down and away from him. He didn't move.

"I'm sorry," he said. "I don't know what happened."

"I told you to leave!" I shouted again.

He looked like a sad puppy. "Actually," he continued, "I'm not that sorry. I've wanted you for such a long time." He walked over to me. "Why did you kiss me back?"

"I don't know. Please leave." Need to desperately think about all this without his questioning my motives.

Hunter sat down. "I'm not going anywhere. I want to be here with you."

"Hunter, this was a mistake. It'll never happen again."

"Maria, if that's what you want, then it'll never happen again." He got up and stood in front of me, his lips a few inches away from my face, and feeling a jolt of panic, tilting my head to look up at him, all the thoughts screaming out of me were worrisome. *Have I already fallen for him?*

"I am in love with you, Maria." He bent and kissed my cheek. "Think about that." And then he left.

I stood there, speechless, drained long after the door shut, the sound of his motorcycle riding away…

Dr. Pappas's words brought me back to the present. "You know, Hunter may not even come looking for you," he said in a relaxed tone. "He could possibly be waiting for you to go back home."

"I'll never go back to him after what he's done to me."

"Again, how can you be so sure he wants to find you?"

"Because he loves me."

"And how do you feel about him?"

"I hate him. Jack is the love of my life."

"Jack could be dead."

"Or not," I said.

"Well, not knowing if Jack is dead or alive will never set you free of him, but how can you be so sure Hunter had something to do with it?" He wouldn't let up.

"Why else would he leave me? Someone abducted him."

"And that someone was Hunter? Hunter was with you that night, no?"

"Well, maybe it was his gang. His followers took Jack and did something to him."

I was desperate for answers. Could Jack really be dead? Could he be lying somewhere at the bottom of an ocean?

"He is either dead or living a new life somewhere else," Dr. Pappas said. "If he's dead, you need to face the fact that he's not coming back from the dead. If he's alive and he's not coming back after almost five years, then you must realize that he's never coming back to you."

I had never thought about him leaving me before, pushing back that torturous thought. *Why would he leave me like that?* It didn't make sense. Then again, nothing made sense any longer.

"Maria, there's nothing more for me to help you with, only you have the power to let go of the past and accept your transformation. You are not the first—you won't be the last. You need to know one thing, though." Dr. Pappas lowered his voice and looked around again. "Whoever made you has a deep connection to you. You will eventually seek him out because you need some kind of guidance into this new life of yours."

This truth took me aback, and for a few seconds the realization hitting me like a slap in the face that he was absolutely right.

"You will find him or he will find you, but face it, Hunter is your maker." My head was going to explode.

"I have to leave." I stood up and sped to the door quicker than I'd ever moved before. Dr. Pappas looked up, and before he could respond, my body sprang out the door without a thank-you or a good-bye, leaving the vampire book behind. I'd gotten the picture loud and clear from those illustrations.

Lots of help he turned out to be. He'd made my head spin with more intricate details of this insanity. What was left for me to do?

I leaped to the top of a cliff near Fira and stared at the beautiful, dark ocean, waiting for some kind of epiphany that never came. I didn't know where to go, what to do, what to eat. My throat was dry, knowing full well that my body needed the type of food that left me feeling nauseous.

I heard a ruffling nearby, glancing behind me and seeing nothing, but instinctually and suddenly, fear hit me. Maybe it would be better if Hunter found me and explained what was supposed to happen to me now. This need to cry overwhelmed me, but no tears came. Feeling lost, and hugging myself, I heard another noise, only closer. Daring to not move, I waited for the inevitable to happen.

I heard a thump a few feet behind me. It was him.

And then another moment between us rushed into my memory like a tsunami.

Chapter Twelve
Over a few drinks
1995

I was turning twenty-seven. Without a mother, a father, or grandparents, my life had a permanent gap that constantly left me empty. No family member to probe me about my future: So when are you going to have kids? What are you waiting for? It could have been a good thing. On this particular birthday, the extent of my loneliness consumed me. It would have been so comforting to receive a phone call from my *yiayia* or *pappou*, but they were long gone. Left with only memories and pictures; even the memories were slowly fading with every passing year. Jack's love wasn't enough sometimes. The love never received from my mom or dad would forever hold me back. It was that empty feeling inside me, I never discussed or told Jack about. He may have sensed it from time to time, but knowing my own pain, and not wanting to talk about all the lonely birthdays without my parents, always left some kind of barrier between me and the world. Every picture told a story, and my pictures were filled with no parents.

We were going out for supper and drinks with a few friends. My job as a magazine photographer fulfilled me and brought me some kind of peace.

A few of my co-workers would be at my party as well.

Loving Jack was never the issue, but knowing he wanted more from me upset me. I tried so hard to please him, but there were limitations.

Only the week before he'd asked me that dreaded question again.

"Jack, not yet. I'm not ready."

"We'll wait."

"What if I'm never ready?" I had never admitted it before, but I had to tell him. Even if I might lose him because of it. He had a right to know.

"Maria, you will be an amazing mother."

"You can't know that!"

And this led to an argument about how Jack knew me better than myself. Deep down, my truth remained silent within. It wasn't in me to have children; never wanting anything to do with babies, raising another human being and doing something that would make me feel incompetent.

I ran the bath, angry at Jack for making me feel like there was something wrong with me for not wanting children.

My exact words had been, "Jack, I never want to have kids!"

He looked at me, shocked. "How can you be so sure?" he asked, sounding pained. "Don't you want to have a child with me?"

"It has absolutely nothing to do with you!" Shouting at the top of my lungs, upset at the way it came out, upset by his doe-like eyes with their hurt expression. "It's me. And if you want to be with me, you have to understand me. If not…" I left the sentence to trail off as his eyes widened at my implication.

"No, don't say that. You are the only one for me. I

love you."

"I love you too," My voice calmer now, as his soothed mine.

"Let's get ready for the party," he said, changing the subject.

I let it go, being preoccupied, thinking about all the reasons the idea of having children scared me to death.

I put on my teal dress, pumps, and hoop earrings. My hair was curled, my makeup done, and stepping out into the cool night, the disregarded feelings swept away with the wind.

Jack was a few steps behind, quiet. We walked to the restaurant only a few blocks away.

"Honestly, I don't know if I'm one hundred per cent ready to be a father myself," he suddenly said. "We're good the way we are."

I didn't say anything, but a million thoughts ran through my mind, like why the fuck had he said this now, when he'd just told me earlier that he wanted kids.

"Where's the restaurant?" I didn't answer him, trying to escape my thoughts.

"It's up a few more streets."

As soon as we got there, my co-workers, Catherine and Jean, were sitting at the table. Catherine was a spunky girl who did the entire layout for the magazine. Jean was a column writer on fashion and the latest trends. Next to them were some of Jack's musician friends. Hunter hadn't arrived yet.

I went to greet my guests.

"Ah, *la belle* Maria," Catherine said first.

"*Bonne fête, minion,*" Jean said, and kissed me three times on each cheek. Jack's friends Alex and Jeremy greeted me too. We sat down, and I noticed an empty seat across from me.

"Are you waiting for someone else?" Catherine asked.

"Yes, my friend Hunter," Jack said.

"Ah, *il est beau*," she said.

Yes, she found him good-looking—most women did.

"*Oui, il est très beau*!" Jean repeated, his eyes twinkling.

I smiled at them both, and we ordered drinks and chatted. Jack wasn't so talkative. My mouth was a literal motor mouth—couldn't keep it shut.

"Are you serious?" Jean asked.

"Of course. There was only me and my grandparents."

"I never knew that about you," Catherine said.

I took a sip of my wine and felt the warmth. "It's hard for me to talk about it, but tonight I'm letting it all out!" Noticing everyone looking over my shoulder and behind me, suddenly, Hunter came from behind me and shouted, "Please, let it all out. C'mon, Maria!" And everyone burst out laughing.

I stood up. "Hi, Hunter."

"Happy birthday," he said, and handed me a gift bag. "A year older, a year wiser." He kissed me three times, his cologne travelling strong in my senses.

"Thank you." The taste of his cologne in my mouth reminded me of Old Spice, and then thoughts of my *pappou* grabbed a hold of me and there were the emotions locked up again, ready to break down.

Hunter greeted everyone while keeping one eye on me. Then he sat across from me and looked at me intently.

"You have to smile. It's your birthday. You look like you're about to cry," he said in a low voice so no one could hear.

Jack looked at me, having overheard Hunter. "Are you okay, sweetie?"

Ah, *now* he noticed. "We'll talk later." Not wanting to put a damper on the mood by talking about my dreaded childhood any more than was necessary.

"Cheers," everyone said with glasses raised. Needless to say, that night we drank, and after we left the restaurant, we went to a club. Catherine suggested a new club that had recently opened. The décor was all zebra and leopard patterns. It was awful, but the music was cool. Electronic instrumental dance music that made you want to move your body.

We danced all night, except for Hunter. He stared at us as if we were from another century.

"I need some water!" I yelled out to my friends grinding on the dance floor as they nodded. Hot, sweaty, and thirsty, I went to the bar to get a drink.

Jack was lost in the music, dancing. Music was his escape, his life. Envying that trait about him and realizing that dancing for me was just for the fun while he danced for the love of it. He let himself go to the beat as if he were in a trance.

"Water, please," I shouted to the bartender, and sitting on a stool, my eyes glanced over at Hunter, who was talking to an attractive girl. He noticed me immediately and came over, then took a seat beside me.

"Thirsty, are we?"

"Yes!"

"You can really move. You're so, so…" And he stopped.

"So what?"

He looked into my eyes. "Forget it. Are you enjoying your birthday?"

I nodded as the bartender handed me the bottled water.

"I got it," Hunter said, and paid.

"Thanks." Smiling, then gulping down the water in seconds, I turned to Hunter. "But seriously, Hunter,"—I elbowed him—"What did you want to say?"

I waited for a reply and watched his face. His dark hair was pulled back, and his eyes gleamed. It felt like a magnet was pulling me in; not being able to move my face, waiting for his answer, wanting to hear something. Not knowing what, just something from the way he was looking at me. There was more.

"You're so lonely and…beautiful," he finally said, not moving his gaze from mine.

"Lonely?" I repeated while ignoring the "beautiful" part that pounded in my head.

"Yes."

"I feel so alone sometimes. How is it you can see that?"

"I don't know." He looked away for the first time, like he wanted to hide something from me.

"What?"

"I feel a lot, even though you don't hear it from me. You are the most amazing person I've ever met. You don't know how your loneliness speaks to me. It's something that speaks to me and that is part of my life as well."

Hunter looked down, seemingly somewhat embarrassed. His words echoed in my head. My glass was tilted to take a last sip of my water to compose myself, but realized there was none left.

"You should publish your photographs in a book. You are so talented."

"Hunter, you're crazy!" Elbowing him again, feeling uncomfortable.

He rubbed my forearm. "You're not the first woman to tell me that."

Shuddering slightly at his touch, and pulling my arm back, my thoughts raced. *This was not good. Not good at all.*

He stared at me. There were looks, and then there were looks. This was the look between us that had the power to transcend words. We didn't speak. He told me with his eyes what he wanted to say with his mouth, accepting it and staring back at him.

And then he got up. "I must leave," he said abruptly, glancing around.

"Why?" Looking around too, but no one was there. "I don't want you to leave." The sentence out of my mouth, without thinking how that sounded. "I mean, you're good company."

"That's why I'm leaving. Say good-bye to Jack for me." At the mention of Jack's name, my back straightened and felt my wall come back up.

Phew.

"Okay, sure." I stood, looking for Jack to distract me from Hunter.

"He's over there," Hunter said, as I turned to say good-bye to him. He was already long gone. How did he move so fast?

I went home and opened up my gifts. Catherine and Jean had given me a bottle opener. Jack gave me a shirt. Hunter's gift was left for last. It came in a purple-and-gold gift bag with white tissue paper. There was a card, and my name was written across the envelope.

"Well, are you going to just stare at it? Open it," Jack said impatiently.

I opened the card first. On the cover was a woman on a lake—Ophelia, from the Pre-Raphaelites—one of my favourite paintings. Reading the card, and the simple message would have meant another meaning yesterday, but after tonight, everything had changed.

Hey Brains, ,

Happy birthday. Enjoy the movies. They are a few of my favourites.

Your friend,

Hunter

Three movies were tucked inside the bag: *Casablanca, The Way We Were*, and *An Officer and a Gentlemen.*

Jack kissed my neck abruptly. "Good choices," he said. "He knows your taste. Now, let's go to bed, birthday girl. There's one last gift for you." He teased me by sliding his mouth up and down my neck. Standing up, while Jack walked ahead undressing, he sneered, "I can't believe he got you *Casablanca.* He is a real motherfucker, you know," Jack said as he took off his pants.

I didn't say anything.

Chapter Thirteen
Running breathlessly
2009

I had tucked that memory away somewhere and had left it there, but today it resurfaced.

"You found me," I said, still looking out into the ocean. That was when the realization that his scent was distinct hit me hard.

He came closer. "Maria, I've been where you are right now. It's not easy."

I turned and shouted angrily, "I hate you!"

"I know," Hunter replied, his dark eyes penetrating mine. "But watching over you is what has to be done."

"How could you do this to me?" My voice faltered, and felt my core weaken at his calmness.

"I didn't want you to die." That was all he said, as if that was the only answer that made any sense to him.

"Death is better than this. What am I? A vampire? Did you ask to turn me into one? Did you think this was the answer? You're a selfish prick!" My voice hollering, I wanted to punch him with every ounce of my being. My fists were clenched, my body in attack mode—a feeling that was new to me.

"I know. The question was whether you wanted to live or die. You chose to live, just as the question was asked to me a long time ago, and here we are." Standing a few inches away from me, he looked out into the ocean. "I became one without wanting to."

"What happens now?" My voice was inaudible, a slight whisper.

He looked at me. "I will take you somewhere safe and explain everything to you."

"I want to kill you!" Pushing him away, and crying loudly, all that was left was the desperation inside me taking full control.

"I know." His composure drove me crazy. He hardly budged at my push. "I've been following your scent across the lands to protect you, watching you, Maria. Your desolate feeling is a familiar one to me. Those feelings you're feeling, been there, done that. Just follow me, and we'll talk." He waited, his gaze caressing my face.

"I don't want to go anywhere with you!"

"Please. Just follow me. I'll take care of you."

Perhaps that was the sentence that finally reached my inner being. He waited.

"I need answers." I glanced out, toward the ocean again, thinking of what I'd been through these past few years.

"I miss him too, you know." That was all he needed to say for me to understand that he knew my thoughts.

"I think he's alive."

"I hope he is. How that would be incredible, but deep down, there's this doubt that can't be shaken off. Maria, you have to remember that he loved you too much to not come back to you."

"How will the truth ever be revealed with the little that we know? All these years, his return is what gave me some kind of hope. Now the reality of Jack being alive is further from my mind." Just saying his name kept me closer to him.

"I know," was all Hunter said, and he took my hand. "Let's go."

I pulled my hand away.

He flew up into the air and peered down at me, nodding me on with the tilt of his head and the relaxed motion of his body.

So following him was my choice *for now*. Was there even another decision to be made? There were choices that we had to make regardless if they were good or bad for us. Choices that would lead us to the answers we asked.

He had lit a spark in me in what seemed like eons ago. He'd planted a seed that I'd tried to leave be, but now it had grown. No matter how many times the vision of Jack's return recreated in my mind over the years, at the back of my mind, the questions kept me restless, screamed out at me: Would telling Jack what happened between Hunter and me change everything? What about my feelings right now? I suddenly felt at peace when Hunter appeared. This scared me as well.

"You won't ever feel alone again," Hunter said, while following him my eyes swept over his strong back and height that somehow made me feel secure.

"What?" My loud voice echoed in the air. He slowed down and pulled me up so we were side by side. He took my hand in his.

"I said, you won't ever have to be alone again." I remained silent while he continued. "I've known for years."

Somehow, Hunter had seen the darkness in me, the constant pain, the sadness, and he embraced it. He held onto it. He wanted to be part of it.

"You're my soul mate," he said confidently. "Your

darkness is my light. My light is your darkness. We are one. We are equals." He said this so matter-of-factly that it astounded me. His eyes were fixed ahead of him, like he'd been practicing saying this for years.

"I'm not so sure, Hunter," was what came out of my mouth, and then I added, "I still hate you." His proclamation made me nervous, jittery.

"I've been in love with you since the first time we met at Bar La Tulipe twenty years ago." Okay, now this declaration finally rattled me inside.

"I still need to find Jack." His last statement was left floating in the air while ignoring it was perhaps not having the wanted effect; it was too much truth for me to deal with right now. His gaze penetrated mine deeply, while turning my head away into the far distance still left me vulnerable to his glare.

"I know," he said, and letting go of his hand made me realize that squeezing it hard felt comforting, as if he was understanding my anger. My hand felt empty as the night air caressed it.

Jack would always be the love of my life, and nothing could ever change that. Even if saying it or shouting it loud, or telling Hunter to fuck off, would have eased the pain, then it would have been done already. But, words escaped me. There are words for writing and then there are words for only certain ears.

The reality was that Jack was still missing. Hunter was beside me, guiding me, loving me, caring for me. He understood me better than anyone else. He had a special brand of intuition, but all his talk about soul mates had me whirling in circles.

I flew next to him, trying hard to resist his strong presence, his masculinity, his words of love. It worked for a while because he didn't speak to me or look at me.

After a time, he turned to me, and his physical appearance had an obvious effect on me; a pressure in my body, a stir in my groin, a flush across my face, and my eyes watered. Simultaneously, his eyes glistened and turned red. It was as if we were connected as one. We felt the same way at that instant; it was a connection that binded us somehow; I couldn't turn away.

He grabbed a hold of my hand, and electricity ran through my veins. Lightning struck me as his storm wrapped around me. He looked straight ahead and pulled me down to a nearby tree.

We kissed like teenagers. We kissed so hard, while he filled all my emptiness, all the pain was forgotten…

Then pulling back, I remembered how he'd turned me into a vampire.

And my ability to hate him again for ruining my life consumed me once again.

Hunter flew up immediately after the kiss ended so abruptly. Wanting to hate him more than love him was my priority. But could this be done? The epiphany hit me as the wind did. I loved Hunter. Searching the sky for his form, felt natural. Telling him was another story altogether. Exposing myself, giving in to him, scared me so much. Shaking myself out of the moment, my body soared into the sky to meet him. My concentration was on flying and feeling Hunter's presence next to mine. By doing this, the thought of Jack was being pushed further away from my mind.

I was more comfortable with the idea of hating Hunter for ruining my life than loving him. It felt true that he was my soul mate.

"Maria," he shouted.

"Yes?" I turned to him awkwardly, anticipating his thoughts.

"You are my life now."

I nodded and did not reply.

Concentrate on the wind. Unfortunately, the wind kept whispering to me, *"You are my life now..."*

Chapter Fourteen
Lost in love
Jack: 2004

I should have bought everything yesterday, but it was hectic and being slightly unorganized didn't help my situation. Anyway, ice was always the last item one bought for a party. Having some loose bills in my back jeans pocket, and leaving my wallet on my dresser, I walked over to my closet and chose my jean jacket; my leather would rot in the rain and stink. Putting on a small hat and walking over to Maria in the living room, I gave her a kiss on the cheek.

"Be quick," she said, and turned her head to kiss me on the lips this time, tasting her raspberry lip gloss and licking my lips.

"You're delicious," I whispered close to her ear, and my senses inhaling her mango shampoo. "Just wait till later. I'm going to drive you crazy."

"I can't wait," she murmured. I heard her slight gasp, that familiar sigh that made my loins ache, giving me a slight hard on. She smiled, as my thoughts were on her and the position I would have her in by the time the night was through.

As soon as my feet hit the first puddle, the rain came down hard. Fuck, an umbrella would have been needed right now. Not that using one was part of my rainy-day routine, but tonight would have been a great time to start.

At the corner, there were some guys huddled

together—about four of them, standing and getting soaked in the rain. Were they stupid or what? They glanced at me. They didn't move out of the way. One of them looked at me, and his eyes were dark and fuckin' creepy. He stared at me, and then he said something to his buddies, who turned my way once the distance between us was about ten feet away. They looked to be in their mid-twenties, and they all gave me the creeps. I decided to look down and not make eye contact.

I walked swiftly and had passed them while heading toward the store up ahead and the empty streets. My pants were sopping wet, trying to sidestep puddles.

Fuckin' rain.

That must have been my last thought as something hit the back of my head, and my body collapsed to the ground, unconscious.

Upon waking, my arms were tied to a bedpost in a dark room that looked like a cellar. There was nothing on the walls and no windows, photos, or any furniture near me. Against the door was a small plastic outdoor table with a dingy lamp that looked like it came from a garbage dump.

My head pounded.

I couldn't remember a thing. It was as if my brain was empty. On top of the bed, there was a tiny camera, and that was when the door busted open.

Four hoodlums barged into the room.

"What's your name?" one of them asked in French.

"I don't speak French," I mumbled a reply, playing dumb.

"What's your name?" another one asked me in English. He was the skinny one.

"I don't know. What is this?" I asked.

"Where are you from?"

"I don't know." That was actually true. My memory was blank; and it was the scariest feeling in the world.

I studied these guys and tried to analyze them: They had French accents, which could be from any one of the villages on the outskirts of Saint-Tropez. They weren't Parisians.

"Jack." My name blurted out of my mouth, but anything else about myself was not in my memory bank.

"It's him," the guy with the orange hooded jacket said.

"We know who you are. We work for Evan Scott. He wants to see you," the skinny guy said.

"Wh-who is Evan Scott?" I stammered, feeling out of control.

"He's a friend of Hunter's," Orange Hooded Jacket said.

"A very old friend," Skinny Guy added with a smirk.

"Hunter? Who's Hunter?"

They looked at one other.

"It worked," the long-haired hippy said.

"Evan wants to speak with you, so we have to bring you to him," Skinny Guy said, ignoring my questions. *What worked?* I started to sweat. What was going on? Who was Hunter?

"You won't remember anything about your past," Long Hair Hippy said.

"It's been erased from your memory," Skinny Guy explained.

"What?" I shouted hysterically.

"It's a spell." The silent one spoke now. "We're witches."

"Is this a joke to you? This is my life." *Witches?*

What was he talking about? Witches didn't exist. It couldn't be possible. Could it…? "Can the spell be reversed?" I was desperate for answers.

"Of course, but that won't happen until Evan tells us what he wants us to do with you."

"Enough said." Orange Hooded Jacket lifted his arm.

They all had crazy eyes. This confused me, and my mind felt frazzled. Empty. This scared the shit out of me.

Who was I? Rubbing my temple, trying hard to think of what they had said…They mentioned a name… "Hunter."

I was so tired. My eyes shut unwillingly.

Hands were shaking me. They were waking me up.

I had a memory: Being a young boy listening to music and tapping my knees; counting the beats with my foot. *One, two, three, four.* Musical notes were before me; half notes, whole notes, G minor, C minor—and knowing how to read them all, reached for a guitar and played a song, and my mother and father were clapping. *"Isn't he amazing?"* I heard a voice say. It was my music teacher telling my parents about my talent. *"He's only eight years old, sir, and he can play songs that are difficult for some adult musicians."* Then another familiar voice: *"You hear that, woman? Our son is a musician. Lots of good that'll do'im."*

"We're taking you to Evan."

I opened my eyes and looked at the four witches who looked like vagabonds. They let me loose and led me out. Following them without a struggle, the only thing that appeased me was that answers would be given to be soon enough.

We went for a long drive. The road didn't look at all

familiar. Looking out the window, my instinct guided me to memorize the landscape. Instinctively, I knew this was France, but what was going on was confusing. How was my memory gone? Why France? All these questions…

"How did you become witches?" My question aimed at Orange Hooded Jacket, who was sitting next to me.

"It's easy. Anybody can join. Basically, you learn about spells and magic, and you incorporate what you've learned into the world, onto people, and change paths, directions, and alter stuff." I guessed you didn't have to be too smart either from that explanation.

"It's cool," the silent one added as my eyes examined his face closely. He was bald and scary-looking, like a punk rocker out for revenge, only no Mohawk haircut.

"We're here," the driver, Orange Hooded Jacket, announced.

They led me out from the car, and walked behind them up to a house that had no neighbors within sight. It looked abandoned and isolated out there in the middle of nowhere. I followed and entered the house, glancing around at the minimalist furniture and dim lights. Then, detecting someone staring at me, my eyes landed on a man.

"Evan," Skinny Guy said. "As you commanded."

"Please sit down, Jack."

Evan sat in an armchair. Wow, how good-looking was he, and how odd his eyes appeared.

"What's going on? Who are you?"

"I'm Evan. Jack, nice to meet you. Can you do me a favour?" He looked at me intently.

"A favour?"

"Yes. Listen to me." Evan dismissed the witches. The front door slammed shut. What could this guy—this total stranger—possibly want from me? "I will tell you," he said in a calm voice. "Don't interrupt me."

I wanted to slap him.

"I am a vampire—a vrykolaka, to be precise. A long time ago, Hunter, your best friend turned into a vampire, by me. I am his Maker. You don't remember him because we have erased your memory. The spell takes four years to depart completely from one's body. If you do what is requested, we will reverse the spell sooner than that. I need you to do something vital. Precisely, as commanded.

"Hunter can no longer stay where he is, but he does not want to leave. This has been told to him time and time again, but he is not listening to my orders. He has explained that he likes Saint-Tropez. He has made many friends, such as you, whom he refuses to convert into a vampire. He likes you too much, apparently, but he must leave because some people have become suspicious of him. Hunter has been there for far too many years, and he is putting our kind in jeopardy.

"I had no choice but to take you from him, to scare him, intimidate him, make him understand the severity of the situation. Your job is to go back and tell him you know who he is and tell him that he must leave and is to be sent to another place in the world."

Evan paused, and he looked serious. He'd spoken in an even tone while following him and understanding the crazy words escaping his lips infuriated me further. From what was being said, my best friend was a vampire, and my job was to go tell him to come back here.

"What exactly do you want me to do about all this?"

How could my involvement change a vampire's mind, and did this even interest me in the slightest?

"I need you to do your best to make him leave Saint-Tropez."

"I don't even remember his face or my relationship with him."

"You don't need to. You just need to explain to Hunter all that has been explained to you, and your memory will be given back to you."

"And if I refuse?" The dreaded question hovered over me.

His eyes instantly darkened, and anger filtered out from them like daggers.

"Then, Jack, you will not get your memory back."

"You said it would come back in four years."

"Do you really want to wait that long, Jack?"

I couldn't breathe, feeling sick to my stomach, my calm demeanor disappearing.

"You will feel better once you comply," Evan stated, looking down at his shoes. I stared at him." "Yes, reading your mind is part of my many skills."

I needed air. How could this be happening? Vampires? Witches? My best friend was a vampire?

"Go get some fresh air. I'll be right here when you get back."

I stepped outside, and my first instinct was to run, to run so far and get the fuck away from these freaks of nature.

Who was Hunter? My giving a fuck about vampires and their petty problems was not my business at all. Ever. They were all dead, anyway.

They were blackmailing me, and my instincts told me to not help them. The only problem was that Evan had me exactly where he wanted me.

Four years was a long time. Perhaps a bargain, but with what? My life? That was exactly what they wanted, but their problems did not interest me in the slightest. Getting the fuck out of there was my only concern.

Fuck this shit. Four years was not that long a time.

I didn't know what was waiting for me, anyway. Hunter? He didn't sound like someone worth helping. He was a vampire, after all. Who in their right mind would believe any of this?

True or not, being on my own for the next few years, without a memory would be a challenge, but not as much as meeting up with vampire friends. The whole thing sounded ludicrous.

At least the one thing my memory grasped was my musical ability. It wouldn't be hard to find a job, a guitar, and a bar to sing in.

I knew Evan wouldn't come after me, because his plan really sucked, and what kind of vampire couldn't control his own kind?

Chapter Fifteen
You're kidding me, right?
Hunter: 2009

As we flew in the sky, knowing how desperate and alone Maria felt, was a familiar emotion for me.

I did feel guilty for transforming her. I'd struggled with the guilt for so long, but losing her would have killed me. She had become my best friend, the only woman my mind and soul wanted to talk to and be heard by and understood for all my flaws and insecurities, and man, were there many.

I glanced back at her and yelled through the wind, "Are you all right?"

"Yes," she shouted back. "Do you ever get tired?"

"Never."

Her hair was swept back by the wind, and her body flowed through the air like an acrobat's. That may have sounded fucked-up coming from me—I was the least romantic guy out there—but I'd never flown through the sky with another woman before, and to me, Maria was not a typical woman.

I thought she'd never come with me, but sensing her terror, she took my hand.

"You want to take a break?" I asked, slowing down beside her.

"P-please." Her lips trembled.

"Sure, take my hand. I'll land first and catch you."

I could tell she felt uncomfortable, but she nodded.

There was a clearing between some bushes down below, and my hand grabbed a hold of her hand, steering her that way.

My arms ready to catch Maria as I landed, she somehow turned the other way, and my balance was lost. She landed right on my chest. For a split second, the wind had knocked me out of breath, and she immediately jumped off me.

"Are you all right?"

I took a deep breath, and it took me a few seconds to reply. "Of course." Still laying quietly on the ground.

I didn't know why, but "Born to Run" started to play in my head, and standing up I shouted the lyrics to the song echoed in the night sky as the chorus sounded loudly.

"Are you fuckin' nuts?" Maria yelled.

I sang louder this time and played air guitar. "Yeah, nuts, nuts," I replied to her surprised face, and continued to sing.

Then she burst out in laughter—uncontrollable laughter. She couldn't stop. It was infectious, and of course, we were both cracking up hysterically.

"Hunter, you're crazy," she said in that comforting voice of hers, but then her voice suddenly changed. "This is horrible. What on earth is going to happen to me?"

"I'll help you, Maria." My voice filled with compassion, settling down from the laughter at her seriousness.

"Help me find Jack," she whispered.

Jack. It was always about Jack. He was right here even when he wasn't. Why couldn't she forget about him? The same reasons he was unforgettable—true, honest, and the love of her life. Bull. Shit. Why could I not be the one love of her life if she'd let me. But who was I kidding? I was an asshole.

"I'll help you do anything you want." My loyalty, above all, to her and her needs. I could not convince her to love me. My pride and ego would not let me. Knowing that her eyes and emotions could not lie, my agreement to do this was only for her peace of mind. "I love you." It was already out of my mouth before I could take it back, looking deep into her eyes for some kind of response.

"I love Jack. You know that." She sighed and looked away.

No matter how many times she said it, it appeared as if she was trying to convince herself, not me. Feeling the bile slowly creep up at the idea of losing her again, my mind started to think…. Me, Mr. Tough Guy…I was a jealous man.

"We're going to go see Evan." This appeared to be the only solution; I knew how Evan wanted me to get the fuck out of St-Tropez for years, perhaps he could help me. It didn't look like I'd ever go back to St-Tropez anyway. Avoiding his calls for years, refusing to leave Saint-Tropez, refusing to change my life once again and just sending him blood didn't put me on his good side. Now was a perfect time to abide by his fucking rules. Evan would help us find a new place to live. He probably wouldn't be able to do jack squat about Jack—no pun intended—but Maria didn't need to know that.

"Who is Evan?"

"He's my master, maker, whatever the fuck you want to call him." My reply was curt and irritable, for reporting to someone was not my forte. "He'll help you." Not wanting to get into too much detail, my affirmation should have been enough to calm Maria down.

By her reply, and guessing she didn't want to hear anymore either, she said. "Let's go," with hope in her eyes.

Maria took off like an airplane. She had no idea where she was headed, but determined to get there. She followed close behind.

"I know what it's like to leave everyone behind." My statement hoping to comfort her.

"I've known how that feels for years, Hunter," she shouted back. "Only there were never any choices in my life. Everyone either left me or died."

"I guess you are a perfect vampire, then. No one will ever come looking for you." Even if it would hurt her feelings, it was the fucking truth.

"I guess it's true," she said after a while. She must have been thinking the same thing, or she was thinking about Jack. Either way, she was better off with no one to worry about answering to. And that actually made my life a little easier. Making up fake deaths was deplorable; it was one of my pet peeves as a vampire.

Who knew what had happened to Jack? Could his disappearance somehow have been part of my responsibility? Nothing made sense.

I looked up at the moon to try to discern how long we had till sunrise, and then glancing at my watch, it was four o'clock, and given the time of year it was—May—we had one hour to find a place to sleep. We flew silently for a while. Trying to gauge where we were, and determining we were in Spain, my sense of geography impeccable, I decided to slow down.

From the last message on my answering machine, I knew Evan was in a remote village off the coast of

France, but because of my strong sense of smell, the exact location was easy to detect. We were connected for life, just as Maria was now connected to me. Preferring the word maker to master because master sounded like a slave owner, my maker Evan always knew my precise location. What was admirable about Evan was that he never came at me like a bullet. He gave me my space. He called me a "a crazy motherfucker."

Looking down the land seemed familiar at the realization of where we would land.

"We have to land and rest."

"Okay."

"Do you see that open space between the trees?"

"Yes," she said, looking down and scanning the area.

"That's the spot." My flying lowered me toward the ground as my feet touched the ground. Looking up to see where Maria was, but she had landed feet first close by.

"Smooth landing." I was astounded at how naturally she'd done it.

"Thanks." She laughed. "I've practiced a few times. The first time almost killing myself."

"Me too," I said, chuckling to myself.

"Where are we headed?" she asked, looking around.

"Come. There's this great place where we can stay. It's a bed-and-breakfast not too far."

"You're kidding me, right?" She looked at me perplexed.

"What's wrong?"

"Bed-and-breakfast? How in the hell could you possibly know where we are?"

"I used to live around here," my reply was nonchalant. "Before Saint-Tropez. Just follow me." I headed east. "My ex-girlfriend owned a bed-and-breakfast."

"Aren't you full of surprises," Maria mused as she tried to keep her balance while walking. Slowing down then stopping to give Maria a break, it hit me that she must have been dizzy. I'd been there. Suddenly it hit me.

"We can't go there."

"What is it?"

"My ex-girlfriend will see that my skin looks the same. What the fuck! Should have thought of that already!?"

"How about we go to another hotel close by?" Maria suggested.

"Of course. And if anyone recognizes me, I'll pretend to be someone else. We need to walk faster. The sun will rise in fifteen minutes." Glancing up at the sky; it was quickly turning pink, hence our limited time. "We have to buy sunglasses." We couldn't walk around in daylight without them.

"We'll go to the closest hotel and use a different name for you."

"I've always gone by the name of Hunter. It's only my last name that I've changed every twenty years or so. This is going to be fun. Let me see…how about Kirk—like Kirk Douglas."

Maria burst out laughing. "Hunter, you're so funny." And she stopped dead in her tracks, holding her stomach and laughing even harder. "Kirk. Now that's hilarious!"

"Okay, forget it. You pick a name." I felt stupid at her reaction.

"No." She giggled a little more. "Kirk it is. It's fine. It doesn't suit you at all, but it'll do."

"And why doesn't it suit me?" I felt myself getting angry.

"Kirk is such a mature, distinguished name, and sorry, Hunter, but you are definitely not that." She laughed again, having a grand old time over my new name. "You're more infantile than mature," she added. Nice afterthought.

"You should see your hair right now. You look like a train wreck."

Maria immediately patted her hair down. "Fuck you."

"Now we're talking. Love it when a lady curses."

"Curses?" She glared at me as if my words were from another planet.

"I'm from the South. We curse."

"I know, Hunter. Do you think I'm stupid?"

"Now why would you say that?"

"Because you are a natural prick and an asshole."

"Why are you referring to my body parts, m'lady?" My smirk plastered on my face.

"You are impossible! Are we almost there?"

During our exchange, my eyes were on all of her body parts. She was heaving and pissed now, and my libido was invigorated. Okay, maybe slightly pissed too, but I'd quickly gotten over it.

I imagined her naked, posing for me as my paintbrush encompassed her beauty on canvas. For once, my mind wasn't in the gutter.

"Snap out of it," she shouted. "Stop looking at me that way." She snapped her fingers in my face.

"I was imagining you naked," my mouth blurted out, and then regretted it.

"Imagine this, Hunter…you will not see me naked

again," she announced for all the forest animals to hear. "Focus on finding that hotel." She huffed and puffed like a bad wolf, and then she did the darnedest thing—she took out a pink hairbrush from a small purse that was hooked to her belt, and brushed her long, tangled hair.

"There it is." The little hotel named Carmela's Inn came into view. "Let's walk faster…the sun is almost up."

In a few seconds, we were at the front door, and Maria had just finished detangling her knots.

I opened the exquisite Spanish doors.

"Ladies first." My smile plastered on my face to let Maria pass me, and she did—a little too closely. She wanted me, just knew it.

"*Buenos dias*," a young girl said from behind a tiny counter. There were eight key slots behind her.

"*Buenos dias*." My Spanish flowed fluently, asking her for a room in the basement, as we were tired and would likely sleep all day and night. Not wanting us to be disturbed, also telling her not to clean our room. I noticed her crooked name tag—*Diana*—and addressed her by her name. Acting natural and flirtatious, my actions needed to seem normal, not suspicious in this small, so-called inn, so continuing in my perfect Spanish I emphasized that we would like to leave Sunday evening. She told me we had to pay for Sunday if we didn't respect the checkout time.

"Diana, I'll pay you whatever you ask me to, just please do not disturb us." She asked me if anything else was needed; winking at her and smirking that everything I needed was right here, placing my hand in Maria's.

Maria didn't understand Spanish, so she was stuck with a ridiculous smile on her face, and as soon as the name Kirk escaped my mouth, Maria let out a sigh—to keep from laughing,—and looked away.

"So you speak Spanish too," Maria commented and then looked at me. "You really are full of surprises, Hunter."

"You don't know the half of it, ma'am," my reply full of sexual innuendoes as we walked down the stairs. Maria pulled her hand out of mine. This hallway felt like we were walking into a cellar. There were two rooms on this floor, glancing down at the number on the key and searched for room number five. I unlocked the door and stepped inside. No windows. Perfect.

Maria switched on the light. The room was quaint, with its distinct, musty, mildew smell so common to hotel rooms, at least those on my budget.

"I like the furniture," she said, glancing around and throwing her purse on the dresser. "I'm ready to sleep."

I switched off the lights, and we collapsed from exhaustion onto the bed.

Chapter Sixteen
Close enough to love

Twenty-four hours later my eyes opened and turned to my right to gaze at Maria. Her face was relaxed and ethereal. Of course, the need to touch her was my first instinct as my hands traced her succulent lips and my head leaned in closer, when she swatted my hand away as if it were a fly.

"What the fuck?" She bolted upright like a bat out of hell. Loving this analogy and never being taught how to transform into a bat yet because Evan had said that a vampire had to be over two hundred years old before he could be able to undergo a metamorphosis.

"Don't touch me!" She rubbed her eyes. "I need a shower," she added, ignoring my advances. My hands were still outstretched trying to reach out to her.

"Go," I mumbled, frustrated. "And leave me some hot water."

"I can't promise you that," Maria said in a sleepy voice as she removed her clothes in front of me.

"You're obviously not a shy girl,"—keenly observing every movement—"Are you trying to drive me crazy? My woody is waking up." Fuck, was it ever.

"In that case maybe using up all the hot water would be a good idea!" She walked into the bathroom, still wearing her panties and bra, and shut the door.

I heard the shower, and just the thought of Maria's naked body made me want to explode all over the green one-hundred-year-old quilt.

I got up and undressed. My boner was talking to me now. Go and get her, it said. It had a mind of its own.

I checked the bathroom door to see if it was locked, but it was ajar; it was such an old bathroom, the door had popped open.

"There's hardly any hot water to begin with," she cried being two feet away now. She saw me then, in all my glory, and smirked. "Get the fuck out of here, Hunter!"

"I want you." Pushing my hair out of my face, and half-sick with lust, my hand pushed open the grungy curtain and stepped into the shower tub.

"No!" she shouted. "I'm serious." She turned off the faucet, still holding the bar of soap.

I grabbed it out of her hand. "Don't move." Not waiting for a reply, the bar of soap and my hand touched her skin.

She stared at me. "Don't you understand the word 'no'?"

I shook my head. "Not when it comes to you."

Maria let me wash her. I rubbed her sleek skin clean all over—up and down her back and breasts. Her body reacted. Her eyelids grew heavy, and we kissed hard on the mouth. My hands reached down to spread open her legs and bent to slip my cock into her slippery pussy. The need to be inside her was intense.

That was when she decided to scream, "No," and pushed me back. She was strong, and almost losing my balance from being so turned on, my legs stumbled out of the tub as she shrieked, "Get out!"

I knew that my instincts were uncontrollable. "Vampire" equaled "animal" when it came to sex.

I lay on the bed with my erection in full swing.

I heard the shower turn back on, and a few minutes later, she stood in front of me with a towel wrapped around her body and another around her hair. She sat on the edge of the bed. By then my boner had gone down.

"Hunter," she started, "I don't know what's going on with my body and mind. It's like they aren't communicating."

"You're a vampire now. You act more on instinct than on logic." Getting up and looking down, avoiding her gaze, my hand turned the old knob, while my cock was ready to burst. "Don't come into the bathroom!" My shout was loud, shutting the door and jumping into the shower to whack off. Man, was this a shitty situation; being this pissed and horny was not a good combination for me.

Even though my hard-on had softened, the moment Maria's nakedness popped into my mind a few minutes before, here in this same shower, my hard-on stood firm and erect.

Ah, relief.

Maria wasn't in the room.

Where could she have gone? She couldn't have gotten too far. Wherever she'd gone, it must be around here. She doesn't know her surroundings.

I quickly dressed and hurried outside. Sure enough, there she was, sitting on a park bench in front of the inn.

She looked so lonely; fuckin' hated myself for doing this to her, Yet, at the same time, knowing it was the only thing left for me to do. Losing her forever was out of the question. Even if she was never mine.

Chapter Seventeen
I'm becoming complicated in you
Maria: 2009

I was losing control of myself. Focusing on Jack; his sweetness, yet the way he smelled had slowly escaped my memory. Forgetting so much left me restless.

I wanted Hunter. Why? Thinking of Jack and wanting to run to find him, was a useless thought. Pointless. Oh, where could he be?

I felt so weak and realized, that food would be what my body needed right now, sitting in front of the inn.

I craved a cigarette, walking back inside to the front desk—if it could be called that—and in English with gestures, asked the same young girl who checked us in the day before, Diana, if she had a cigarette. She nodded, said "si," and gave me one from her pack tucked in a corner. As she gave me a worn-out matchbook, she gestured for me to go outside to smoke.

"Gracias." She smiled at my Spanish as I returned to the bench.

Feeling the sunlight on my face and tanning were long gone pleasures from my mortal life. How ridiculous was that? As much as sun tanning was never my thing, at least there was a choice involved.

Now there were no choices. There were simply rules to follow.

"There you are." Hunter's approaching footsteps shook me from my thoughts. "I'm sorry, Maria," he muttered as he sat next to me.

Wow. Hunter apologizing.

"It's okay. I'm sort of out of my skin right now," I said exhaling the smoke.

"Pass me a puff?" His hand extended, waiting. "Where did you get the cigarette from?"

I pointed to the girl at the front desk. "Diana."

Hunter inhaled two quick puffs, and reluctantly passed the cigarette back to me.

"I miss Jack so much. The memory of his kisses are fading, the way he tasted, smelt, all of it." I crossed my legs, confessing to Hunter, who sat silent and extended his hand for another drag. "I don't know what's happening to me. I'm losing control of my emotions, my logic. Fuck, we almost fucked." My tone must have sounded full of disgust because he glanced at me, blowing out his smoke, and his eyes flashed with anger.

"Maria, you will lose most of your self-control. I'm more impulsive, and reacting immediately to what you want is normal. Get used to it. My instinct has to fight every second to not reach over and kiss you, but I'll respect that you don't want me, *for now*."

But he's misinterpreting me; my instinct was to be with him; wanting him to fuck me in the shower, but letting go of Jack was the issue.

So it was true—I was losing my self-control.

"I'm so hungry," I blurted out, changing the topic and waiting for the remainder of the cigarette.

He looked at me intensely. "Don't you want to know everything?"

"Yes." My heart fluttered as his eyes darkened and his whole body slumped a little lower on the bench, and waited for an explanation of something—anything. "I remember everything you said to me about the powers: hearing, sensing, touching, seeing, tasting, lifting, singing, painting, and writing. Could it be that the power of sensing was already inside of me? My senses told me it was you when you found me."

"Really?"

"Yes."

"That could be because I'm your maker. Or not." Hunter smiled. Wow. He did have a great smile.

Don't get sidetracked.

He continued. "People think I'm psychic, you know. Jack used to want me to meet a girl he liked so he could hear my analysis. He'd say, 'So what about her?' and we would laugh. 'No, she's a psycho,' or any other derogatory term that popped into my head. When Jack met you, he asked me what about you. 'She's the one.' That's not being psychic; that is knowing an amazing woman when she presents herself. You're special to me. It's taken me twenty years to finally tell you."

Was he referring to himself when he said, 'She's the one'? The one for whom? Hunter's gaze flickered across my face, looking for something, but my expression was blank purposely. "Evan told me to never fall in love. That was his number one rule, and now I'm fucked because I've broken that rule." Hunter appeared preoccupied.

"C'mon, Hunter."

"I speak the truth, if it's one thing that is right about me. It seems I'm always fuckin' up when it comes to you."

"I hate you."

"That's why I'm trippin'. Listen."

"I'm waiting for you. You, you set my desire. I trip

through your wires."

Harmonica.

"Angel or devil."

I thought of that night twenty years ago, when we had met, and Jack was performing at Bar La Tulipe and the same CD was playing, only back then it was an album. I thought of Jack and the song he'd written for me, and felt a deep sadness at how I'd never have that again.

I peeked at Hunter, who was concentrating on some distant star, far away. He was contemplative. Was he in love with me that much? It was obvious and so easy for me to jump into, but these conflicting emotions stopped me. One second it was hate, the other desire. The song ended.

"You see?"

"I see." He got up and extended his hand as if we were going to a ball. Giggling escaped me like a young school girl.

"Shall we eat?" he asked, changing the subject.

"I'm starving."

"You run like a river," Bono sang on.

I took Hunter's hand and followed him. Hopeless.

Jack was a figment of my imagination now, a part of my human life that was forever long gone.

Quick as lightning, we went back to the dreary basement and got my purse, paid the front desk, and walked into the forest, where no human eye was upon us as we sped off into the night, running like the river.

Hunter killed a small rabbit by breaking its neck in one fierce motion. He opened his mouth and sank his teeth deep to puncture it, then he held it close to my mouth.

"Drink." With a vicious need to feed, my mouth sucked and drank till there was no blood left.

"Finished?" he asked, grinning at my new thirst for blood.

"How about you?"

"I'll be right back. Listen…another rabbit." He ran fast as I concentrated and listened to the sound of the rabbit. My sense of hearing was so different now.

There was rumbling nearby, and a few minutes later, he was back.

"Ready," he said, after wiping the blood dripping from his mouth.

"How do you feel now?"

"Revived," It was true and honest. It was like drinking the best wine without getting drunk. It was beyond the mundane description of delicious. "It's hard to describe the taste."

I was a vrykolaka vampire, and was transforming into someone never imaginable in my mind. Yet, this was happening. How life can change so quickly, so astronomically.

"I still hate you, you know." I sneered, kicking the dark grass at our feet.

"I know," Hunter sneered back. "Hate is the opposite of love, but sometimes it is equivalent."

"I had named your entourage the Gang of Cat's Eyes." And for no apparent reason, my giggling started again.

Avoidance and giggling to ease my nerves; even a vampire could get nervous.

Hunter laughed. "Good one. You're a genius!"

"Let's go." This need in me to want to fly took over.

It was such an exhilarating experience.

"Getting used to this, huh?" He threw his hair back, then leaned down toward me. "You first, beautiful."

We flew side by side. He guided while remaining close by. We made it to Evan's house within a few hours. We didn't stop for a break. My energy was full and this discovery of maneuvering my body in ways that surprised me kept me on high alert. Feeling Hunter's gaze penetrate through me, it was true we had a magnetism, an electricity between us that was so alive, yet so fearful at the same time. For now, ignoring it instead of dealing with it would have to work for me.

In all of this craziness, it hit me hard how in this moment, this feeling of being invincible—the most free I'd ever felt in my entire life—was something I'd never felt as a human.

Chapter Eighteen
Evan is what Evan does

Evan was a specimen; a vampire like him came around once every couple of hundred years. Not knowing what to expect, his masculinity did not surprise me at all.

He greeted me like a gentleman. Under his scrutiny, being transported back a few centuries, was an experience out of a historical novel.

"Welcome, Maria." His dark eyes gleamed. "You are one of us now, so you must embrace it. Stop fighting it."

For once, my being tongue-tied surprised even myself.

I nodded, trying not to stare. "Thank you, sir," my murmuring voice hardly audible. *Did sir just come out of my mouth*? Instead of shrieking, *"Are you crazy?"* But all that was left for me to do was fall under his hypnotic gaze placing me in a trance.

Hunter stood tall next to me; feeling his strong presence next to me, I turned to him for some kind of assistance. *Throw me a rope, Hunter. Please, say something.*

He spoke softly. "Evan, we have a favour to ask you."

"Yes," Evan said clearly. "Jack was here."

"What?" My voice as high pitched as I'd ever heard it.

"Oh, are you his mistress?" *Mistress?* What era was he from? "Excuse me. His lover. Is that better?" Evan lifted one eyebrow, waiting for my approval.

I turned toward Hunter. "How does he do that?"

"He reads minds. He read mine. My next question was Jack's whereabouts."

I tried not to think of anything. Fuck. He could read my mind.

"You're good. You can block me off," Evan said with a grin. He sighed. "Well, if you must know, your Jack was useless. He ran away, and my intention to pursue him fell through. In truth, he did not want anything to do with me."

"Can you please explain?" My question high pitched and my emotions nervously waiting for a reply. After waiting five years for answers, the world around me was spinning.

"Do you need to sit, my dear?"

"I'm fine." *Block him off.*

"What do you mean, Evan?" Hunter asked, holding onto my arm for my support.

"I kidnapped Jack five years ago," Evan replied.

"Why?" My incredulous face and voice shook with shock. This was the furthest thing from my mind. Kidnapped?

"I tried to reach you, Hunter, for years, but you never returned my phone calls. There are so many people to keep track of. Kidnapping Jack to get him to go back and tell you that you had to depart from Saint-Tropez in exchange for his memory seemed like an ingenious idea at the time. A simple plan—I'd say it was quite brilliant, in fact. Jack's memory for Hunter's departure. But Jack ran off instead. And apparently nothing could make you leave." He looked at me as if my existence was to blame. "Now it's clear why… He's worked his manly charms—or is it say, *devilish* charms—on you?" Then he winked at Hunter.

"Did you know about this?" Looking at Hunter, confused and wondering if Hunter could have known about this?

"I don't know what Evan is talking about!" Hunter was mad as hell. He looked at Evan, "Why did you wait so long to tell me?"

"Hunter, my dear boy, you avoided my calls like they were the plague. You left me with no choice. Did you not heed my warning about love?" Evan smirked.

Out of nowhere, a woman walked into the room and came toward me with a tray of blood-filled martini glasses.

"Drink, Hunter?" She squealed and peered at me, her awful makeup and scanty attire hard to avoid.

"Do you like what you see, love?" She gestured to her body with her free hand and grabbed her breasts. "There's more." She licked her lips.

I smelled her reek and wanted to barf. She was the most disgusting creature I'd ever seen.

I tried to erase my thoughts. Too late.

"Gaby, could you leave us, honey?" Evan said, and looked at me with a grin.

"I had no idea Evan kidnapped Jack," Hunter whispered to me. "That's the absolute worst fuckin' plan, if you ask me! Why didn't you tell me?" he shouted at Evan.

"You could have returned my calls."

Hunter moved toward him.

"You know my strength as opposed to yours. So

don't try anything you will soon regret. I'm your maker," he reiterated angrily.

"Hunter, it's okay," Laying my hands on him and grabbing a hold of his shoulder to calm him down. It was apparent Hunter didn't know. He wasn't that much of a prick. He did truly love Jack.

"Where's he now?" My question put forth eagerly while trying to remain calm and not think of anything.

"Who the fuck knows? I erased his memory four or five years ago. He's probably got it back by now, or he's slowly getting it back."

"It was five years ago!"

"Well, he should be getting it back soon, m'lady. Four years is the earliest and five is the latest. Sometimes the witches are off by a few months."

I felt nauseated, and then blacked out.

Cold water hit my face, and I heard voices from far away.

"What the fuck were you thinking, Evan?" Hunter yelled. "Jack was my best friend."

"That was the problem. You were too attached. There had to be a way to get rid of him, only Ed told me you were in love with Maria."

"Ed told you?"

"Yes, last year. He knew not to tell you or he would be easily staked by me."

"How could Ed have known?"

"He said, word for word, that you were like a puppy dog around Maria."

"Now what?"

"Now you and your girlfriend find a new place to roam," Evan said. "How about Italy?"

"I hate Italians. You know that!" Hunter roared.

I hadn't opened my eyes yet, but listening and thinking of Jack.

"Your girlfriend is awake," Evan said. "She wants to find him. Get those thoughts out of her mind. She has to forget her past. She is one of us now."

I opened my eyes.

"Are you okay, Maria?" Hunter asked, his dark eyes full of concern.

"Yes. It's just too much to handle. Fresh air was what my body and mind need."

"Watch her closely. That's what her boyfriend Jack said when he ran away, but honestly he was of no use to me."

Hunter helped me get up and held me by the waist for support. We were walking toward the door as Evan spoke his last words. Hunter led me outside.

Suddenly there was this need in me that arose out of nowhere. "Hunter, can you get me a piece of paper and a pen, please?"

He left and was back in a flash as my hands grabbed the pen and paper out of his hand, sat on the lush, green grass, and wrote. Not sure what was pouring out of me, but soon enough, the page was filled with my handwriting.

"It's a poem." Hunter had been watching me keenly, and at the word poem he widened his eyes.

"So it seems you have the power of writing," he said with a twinkle in his eyes. "Don't you love it when we artists stick together?" he said jokingly. Then he looked at me with serious eyes. "Read it, Maria."

"The title is '*Another Sunrise*.'"

"I saw the sunrise today,

and then went back to bed
to try to catch some beauty sleep.
But thoughts of you and your reckless way
trapped inside my head
of talking to me without caring,
of liking me when not wanting to,
of trusting me when your better judgment dictates otherwise
But you do,
and waiting for you till you do it again.
To see you over a fence
Or in a faraway field
where carriages used to roam
and sunflowers still grow higher than us,
where we can sit and share an insipid story
or pretend to strum a guitar
and feel the sun's Mediterranean rays through our clothes,
I want to stay there indefinitely, from dawn till dusk.
You have a natural way of sliding under my skin
without touching me,
without wooing me.
If you try a little harder,
I'll step into your circle without a sound.
The illusion is much more intriguing
than my skin under yours,
or so believing this farce
to get through another sunrise
with no one to share it with.
Don't reply to my stream-of-consciousness prose
that is never edited.
I want you to open your eyes
and read me like a book.

Flip any page
and see if you were always right
about my thoughts.
You'd be surprised at how smart you are."

I exhaled.

Hunter stared out into space.

"Well?" My eyes looking into his, feeling high from the words that just poured out of me.

"You are a writer now. Your poem is beautiful, just like you. You know, when I was a mortal and a writer, my favourite book would be read over and over again."

"Which one?"

"The Great Gatsby."

"I loved it too." How could one not?

Suddenly he said, "I was such a fuckin' prick in my human life."

"You haven't changed all that much." My joke made me smile.

He smirked and crossed his arms over his chest, looking smug. "You know you like it. I'm a badass."

I giggled. "I always hated badasses."

"I love it when you hate me." Hunter pulled his hair back and grinned. "Hate me or love me, at least you feel something passionate for me."

"Your brain is really screwed-up!"

"You don't know the half of it." He grinned again.

"Do tell…" Yes, my desire to know more about Hunter and to probe him, couldn't be denied.

"I reckon you're interested." He turned to me. We were sitting on the grass as if we were kids in a playground.

"I want to know." My face turned serious.

And he didn't stop talking most of the night as my eyes pretty much focused on him and paid close attention to his words for the very first time.

We got up and didn't even say good-bye to Evan and Gaby.

"Fuck them. Let's go," Hunter said, and waved them off.

I'd finally found out the truth about Jack. And what was I doing? Listening to Hunter's stories. He told me about his ma and pa, about the night he died, and how he became a vrykolaka. He told me about his loneliness, and my sympathy for him grew, his stories were fascinating as my ears and heart needed to hear more and more, it was evident that my mind was on Hunter and his life.

I glimpsed into Hunter's world and realized how faraway Jack truly was from me.

Part Five

Jack's back

Chapter Nineteen
Streets and names with undeniable truths
2009

It was just another Saturday night in *le petit village* LeBlanc, near Montmartre. Singing at my regular bar, where everyone knew me, was my normal routine. Well, they'd actually known me ever since I'd stumbled into this village.

At first, everyone found me fascinating.

"He has amnesia. He doesn't know where he used to live. He is so nice, and he is a great musician." People spoke about me as if my presence meant nothing. Getting used to the small-town friendliness and outspokenness, I'd never left, enjoying the tranquility and the solitude of this village.

I tried to forget about the vampire and his story knowing my memory would come back this year, but when? The only memories that were clear were of my childhood, and not the good ones. There were these vivid dreams of chasing a redheaded girl. Not being able to ever see her face, though, it was always the same vision: only her long hair and slim back.

You could say I'd adjusted pretty well, considering all the shit that happened to me. Although not knowing what had happened to me preoccupied me, eventually, it didn't matter anymore.

Tonight there were some new songs on my set list. While writing them it felt like familiar lyrics. Could it have been a memory? They reminded me of a beach. What the fuck? How corny was that?

I was waiting for Denise. She was quite the girlfriend. She loved to cook French dishes. She said Julia Child was her favourite French cook even though she was American. Denise was infatuated with anything American. The culture and the name brands were her obsessions. She loved me and I had strong feelings for her, but not so sure if it was love. There was something missing…I didn't quite know what that something was.

When she'd said she was in love with me, I'd smiled at her. Maybe she particularly liked the fact that there was no past in my memory. It was probably a girl's wet dream to have a boyfriend with no baggage, no ex-girlfriends to bitch about or compare them to. At times my restlessness would eat me up inside which was probably understandable with no recollection of anything substantial. But it was this hollow feeling inside that bugged me the most and kept me up at night.

I did feel comfortable here, and the people were so hospitable. They loved to hear my music. I'd made so many friends; Daniel, Eric, and Robert were my closest ones. They were the local musicians, and we jammed and talked about music till all hours of the night. Although my memory of people was nonexistent, my memory of songs was alive and well, the memories of melodies, lyrics, frets, and chords were always constant.

I looked around the bar for Denise. She would be here any minute. My glance fell to the entrance and paused. *Wow.* There was the most striking-looking couple I've ever seen at these neck of the woods. They looked like movie stars. He was a fuckin' giant, and she was a goddess. It was hard not to stare. They quickly scanned the bar and found two empty seats. My glance fell to the crowd, as they gawked as well, while the couple walked toward their table.

"Hey, check out the redhead," Daniel said, sitting next to me, a twinkle in his blue eyes. "I would love that ass in my face." Looking at him and smirking, for although he was thirty-eight years old, he looked twenty-five, and he was a horndog. He was used to women throwing themselves at him. After all, he was the star guitar player at the bar—besides me. My only talent was my voice; that was my advantage.

"I saw her." How could she be missed?

"She's fuckin' hot." He stared right at them.

"Stop gawking. Her boyfriend looks like he could kill you in one sweep."

"Fuck that." Daniel grinned. "Look at these,"—and he showed me his wimpy muscles.

I laughed. "Yeah, right." My glance peeking back at them without any sort of self-control.

She examined the place now, no longer engrossed in a heavy conversation. Our gazes met, and that was when inside me something froze.

She stared at me as if she recognized me.

"She knows me," my voice murmured and my eyes widened at her reaction.

"What the fuck?" Daniel cried, swinging his head at me. "Do you remember them?"

My words rushing out as she turned to her boyfriend, and he then looked straight at me. My head swerved, glancing from one to the other, clueless as to who they were.

They both definitely knew me. Daniel was talking to me, but my senses were one hundred percent focused on the couple. Everything else just evaporated, voices, sounds, music, my eyes were like magnets stuck on both as she got up and walked toward me, her eyes never leaving mine. Actually, it was more of a run.

"Jack," she said, breathless, inches from my face.

I stood, surprised. "How do you know me?" My whole being mesmerized by her mouth speaking my name with familiarity.

"It's me. Maria," she said excitedly as her boyfriend suddenly appeared next to her.

"Jack!" he hollered, and slapped my back. "Oh my God! We thought we'd never find you." His dark eyes looked from Maria to me, and his excited tone indicated they knew me well.

"Jack, do you remember me? Has your memory returned? Why didn't you come back to me?" Questions poured out of Maria's mouth.

"How do we know each other?" I was sure confusion displayed clearly on my face. "Who are you?" My glance directed at Maria.

"He doesn't remember," the giant said. "Wait, don't tell him anything yet." He pulled Maria to the side and said something in her ear. She nodded, but her eyes looked hurt and sad. They whispered to each other and seemed to be arguing about something.

Daniel turned to me and asked, "You okay?"

"Yeah, fine, fine, just want answers." Finally, these two people could answer my questions. My need to know overwhelmed me and with two long strides, not waiting for them, we all faced each other.

"Maria, right?" I tried hard to place her face. But my mind was a total blank. There was no memory of her, yet I couldn't shake this feeling like my heart was going to pound right out of my chest. “Can we talk?” She glanced at the giant. “Alone.” My intention clear that it was her I needed to talk to.

“Hunter, I’ll be back,” she said to him.

At the mention of the name Hunter, my stomach turned. Fuck.

Hunter, Maria… Those were the names the vampire Evan had mentioned. What the fuck? It didn’t hit me earlier. This Hunter was a vampire. He was the reason I’d lost my memory. And my life. Turning to him. “Hunter”—I swallowed as my mouth became parched—“You’re the fuckin’ prick that head vampire wanted me to bring to him!” My voice loud now, my anger brewing, not giving a shit who heard me.

“Evan.” Hunter confirmed the name. “Yes.”

I grabbed Maria’s hand and said to Hunter, “Stay here.” He didn’t object or move. Daniel, who had been silently observing the whole time, made room at the bar for Hunter.

As soon as we got outside, my anger flared.

“What the fuck is going on?” My demand to know echoed in every word.

“Jack, oh Jack, I can’t believe it! Never thought I’d see you again.” She was about to throw her arms around me when my legs stepped back at her approach.

“I don’t remember you,” my voice flat and out of emotion.

“It was my birthday party. You threw me a surprise party. You said you were going to get ice, and never came back,” she hurriedly explained. “We loved each other, Jack. We have been in love since that first day we met on the beach at Saint-Tropez.” Maria searched my eyes for a trace of recognition. She was out of breath but so goddamn beautiful. Her words registered but my mind didn't.

"I don't remember you," I repeated, and looked at her closely. "Is Hunter your boyfriend?"

"No!" she shouted. "You know Hunter. He's an asshole."

"No, don't remember him either. He seems pretty scary to me." My cold reply and my continued hostility over took me.

"I still love you," she said, sounding desperate.

If she still loved me, why was she with him?

"I don't remember loving you," my voice low, my suspicion high. "Although, looking at you, there are some feelings that are unrecognizable." I rubbed my head, trying to think clearly, but everything seemed hazy, confusing.

"Tell me everything that has happened to you. Don't leave anything out," Maria urged me. People were coming in and out of the bar, so we slowly moved to the side of the building, away from listeners.

"The first memory I have is of waking up in some place and being taken to that vampire by so-called witches. I've never repeated that story to anyone. People would have thought it was nuts. Not sure what to believe, myself. The vampire told me he wanted me to bring Hunter, my best friend, apparently, to him. Getting the fuck away as soon as possible was the only thing on my mind at the time. When the chance presented itself my instincts told me to run. Not wanting want any part in his hair-brained scheme, not wanting any part of it at all! Evan told me my memory would come back in four years. I'm still waiting." It was frustrating to say it but felt relieved to finally be speaking the truth. I'd wanted to tell my story to someone for so long, but too scared no one would believe me. Looking her straight in the eye, I said, "I don't know who you are anymore."

"So you've been here, in this town, this whole time?" she asked, looking perplexed.

"Yes," I answered simply, examining her. She had lovely brown eyes, a button nose, and full lips. Her slender frame suddenly slumped, and then wondered what was the matter, but then feeling a hand from behind entwine my waist, it was clear. Ah, Denise. Thus, the slump.

"*Bonsoir, bébé,*" Denise said, oblivious to the intense conversation with my apparent long-lost love, Maria. Denise was in her own world.

I glanced at Maria, and she looked as if she would attack Denise any minute.

"Are you going to introduce me to your friend, *mon amour*?" Denise asked, glancing up and down Maria's body. My eyes followed her gaze, admitting to myself how glamorous and exotic Maria looked. Her black dress and boots hugged her body like a glove. Maria's eyes met mine smiling.

She saw my expression. Desire could not be easily hidden. Denise glared at Maria, waiting for something.

"Denise, Maria. Maria, Denise." Maria nodded, and Denise eyed her closely. Denise had that natural French look—no makeup, classic features, and attitude. She wore a frilly blouse and jeans.

"Listen, Denise, I'll be inside in a few minutes. I'm just catching up with an old friend." Kissing her cheek, I said, "See you inside."

"Okay." Denise turned and walked away, but as soon as she reached the entrance to the bar, she turned around again and gave me a puzzled expression, as if to say, *what old friend? You have no memory.*

"That's your girlfriend," Maria stated, jealousy in her voice.

"Yeah, My life here is pretty settled. No matter what happened in the past between us, there's nothing left of it, especially, without a memory." Rubbing my eyes, trying to be logical wasn't working. "I don't know what you want from me."

"I want you to remember me!" Maria cried. "I love you, Jack."

"I don't know you anymore." Not remembering my own feelings was upsetting me. "Listen, I'm doing fine. Better to not remember people who fucked up my life!" Shouting a bit loudly only because being sick and tired of not knowing my past was getting the better of me. "I can't do this, have to go now. I'm on soon." I turned, walking away angrily, leaving her to stand there alone, and giving her no chance to say anything else, felt fine by me.

I didn't know what else to do, feeling that nothing would come together again.

Walking back inside, my glance fell on Hunter, who was sitting at the bar, waiting and looking impatient as he stared at the door.

I walked straight onto the stage, feeling upset, nervous, shaken up, and distraught. Daniel was tuning his guitar, and stood next to him. He peeked up at me with concern on his face.

"Are you okay, man?"

I nodded, speechless. What the fuck was there left to say?

I picked up my guitar and winked at Daniel.

Glancing around the room, at that moment, Maria walked in, looking mortified. She went straight to Hunter and spoke into his ear. He looked at me, said something to Maria, and tried to rub her back, but she pushed his arm away.

"*Bonsoir*," my voice a bit shaky into the mike, adjusting its height.

The small audience clapped, but my eyes were pinned on the couple. They seemed to be together, but I wasn't so sure anymore. The way she pushed his hand away told me she wasn't with him but the look in his eyes was completely different. The simple gesture spoke a million words to me, should this even bother me? He—Hunter—used to be my best friend, and she used to be the love of my life. And now they could be together, obviously something was going on…

I strummed my guitar, taking in a deep breath, and sang my new song, forgetting my thoughts for a while, or at least trying to.

That was when all hell broke loose.

"You're a fuckin' prick!" Maria yelled at Hunter. "I hate you!"

He yelled back, "I hate you too!" and smashed his hands on the bar.

I stopped singing, and Maria was hysterical now, swinging her arms about, red in the face with anger.

"I know that song! That's my song!" she shouted to Hunter. Then she looked at me and bellowed, "How could you *not* remember me?"

I instantly felt Denise's stare on me. Knowing she was sitting with the same clique of friends she sat with every night, my gut had completely blocked her out of my sight. She glanced from me to Maria, understanding now who Maria was. Heck, everyone probably realized who she was. My fingers stopped playing, staring at the spectacle that was apparently my fault. The audience looked at me, then back at Maria and Hunter. They seemed to be enjoying themselves, while my insides were falling apart.

"I'm leaving and never coming back!" Maria hollered, making sure everyone heard her, especially me. Hunter tried to calm her by whispering something in her ear, but she pushed him away again.

"You've ruined my life!" she yelled, and walked out of the bar.

I thought of going after her, but my pity wasn't a strong enough emotion to guide me. I was devoid of any emotions. Hunter walked over to me and said, "I'm sorry, Jack. You were like a brother to me."

I eyeballed him and didn't know what to say. And just like that, he was gone too, following in Maria's footsteps. They were both out of my life.

I stared at the perplexed audience. It was not a good time to be tongue-tied. Denise stood up to walked toward me, but I gestured for her to sit right back down.

"Excuse me." My voice sounded nervous as my legs took me straight outside in a mad rush.

I had waited years for answers, and now was my chance to get them. Glancing to the right then the left, they were nowhere in sight. My multitude of questions should have popped into my head like a jack-in-the-box.

"Maria! Hunter!" The tone of my voice, desperate and loud. No reply.

I'd fucked up.

Shouting their names even louder and walking down the street, my guts were being ripped open by all these unanswered questions on the tip of my tongue; full of desperation, wanting, *needing* to hear their voices and answers.

Continuing my aimless wandering up and down the streets, around the back of the bar, then back to the front entrance, the realization that they were gone shook me back to reality where the only thing left for me to do was finish my gig.

Deep down, there was a truth that was undeniable.

The truth of loving a girl with no recollection of loving her. She'd seemed so upset. We must have loved each other. Feeling lost and sick to my stomach; this lack of emotions; this frustration; this unwarranted jealousy; was killing me slowly inside. Wanting so badly to remember, I shut my eyes tight and tried desperately to revive my memory. Nothing. Blackness.

I walked back into the bar and went straight to Denise. Kissing Denise erased the questions from her eyes as her familiarity comforted me. She was here. I remembered her.

"Don't worry. Everything is okay." My whisper in her ear made her smile. "I'll explain later. Show must go on."

"*Je t'aime*," she whispered back.

"*Moi aussi*." My reassurance meant for both her and me to hear, to root myself into this new life of mine and far away from Maria and Hunter as possible.

Epilogue
Maria

Sometimes you have to draw your own stars in the sky.

"Maybe he got his memory back." My frustration overcame my emotions once again. A few months had passed since the encounter with Jack.

"And what will you do?" Hunter's voice reached me from across the room full of anger and defeat. He started to pace back and forth, my staring at the ceiling while on the bed and cursing my life was aggravating him, as was my constant preoccupation with the past and with Jack.

"I don't know. Talk to him. Explain everything."

"Maria, do you think he will take you back with open arms?" Hunter asked, looking at me nonsensically. "Did you forget you're a fucking vampire now?"

"I have to try…I can't live like this." This feeling of no closure with Jack was killing me. We heard Jack calling our name that night, but didn't turn back. As much as the need to go back burned me up inside, Hunter said it was best this way. He was fucking right, but this need to see Jack now that his memory probably had returned; and how we met and fell in love, haunted me day and night.

"Why can't you let him go?" Hunter approached me and stood before me tall and beautiful with that look in his eyes that made me weak. My promises of not giving in to Hunter were futile…I turned away.

"It's n0ot you…it's me." My insides felt as though ripped to shreds again. "I have to know one last time if Jack got his memory back."

"Maria." Hunter lifted my face with his fingertips and his voice softened, but his eyes remained distant. "Do it, or else you will never have peace. Go." He broke my heart the way he spoke to me…so desolate. There was pain in his eyes, still I refused to acknowledge my feelings for him. All that consumed my thoughts were seeing Jack. Ever since leaving him at the bar, the past kept haunting me.

"Please, Hunter. It's something I need to do."

"I will go with you then," he said, changing his tone. "I can't leave you alone in this." He touched the top of my head to comfort me and my heart melted at his sweet gesture. Feeling that Hunter would do anything for me, gave me some kind of happiness, security. Relying on him had become like second nature for me. This alone scared me and comforted me simultaneously.

"Okay."

We left England for France and arrived at the small village within a couple of days. Hunter was quiet the whole time. It was night-time when we arrived. We walked up the pathway to the same bar and I was about to tell Hunter something, anything but this harsh silence, but no words came out. He pushed open the bar and let me walk ahead of him.

"Might as well go to the bar," Hunter said. "I need a few drinks."

As we headed for the bar, all eyes turned to us and then to the back of the room where Jack sat sipping a beer. His eyes met mine and he sputtered the beer all over the place. He quickly got up and excused himself as we sat on a stool at the bar. Waiting for that magical feeling to possess me, but nothing came. In my daydreams, my emotions would lead me to run to him, embrace him in front of a large crowd and profess my undying love, but my legs were motionless, as my heart didn't pound at all, or my intense love didn't overtake me, following Hunter to the bar. Hunter didn't look at me at all. He sat down and ordered two Scotch doubles. By the time he placed the orders, Jack was in front of me.

"Maria," Jack said breathlessly. "Finally." He did not acknowledge Hunter's presence.

"You came back." He took my hand and led me outside, while I still waited for that *feeling* to materialize. His warm hand against my cold one didn't make him flinch. Instead, he squeezed it harder. We walked behind the large trashcans and exit door, where there was a small light hitting the cement wall. It was quiet, in the distance the sound of a jackrabbit intensified my senses, but my eyes were on Jack, concentrating. No one could hear us back here. Jack faced me, letting go my hand. "I have a lot to say to you."

"Oh, Jack." My body suddenly filled with sadness, not joy.

"I don't want you to talk, Maria. You need to listen. First, I'm sorry for not remembering you. That expression of pain on your face is still in my thoughts. Remembering everything now, has made me sick over the whole thing. But, before I tell you anything more, know that I loved you and still love you." He ran his hands through his hair and my insides knotted. A simple action like that would have made me swoon as a mortal.

Taking a step back, for some strange reason I knew things were shifting now. The truth.

"Things are different now, Jack." *Where did that come from*? Didn't I want him to love me? My thoughts suddenly turned to Hunter alone in the bar drinking Scotch.

"I know, you're a vampire now," he said, and took my hand again. "But…Maria, I can never be with you." He swallowed. "Denise and I are going to have a baby." The words relieved me and hurt me at the same time.

"Why did you have to disappear?"

"I didn't do it on purpose, Maria…you'll always have a special place in my heart. I'll always love you but you know that having a child is something that would forever come between us and when Denise told me she was pregnant, I swear it was the happiest moment of my life. Sorry."

"Don't be sorry. I will always love you too, but not in the way I loved you. My feelings have changed since my transformation. I think I've changed too much." My confession led me to tell him everything that had happened between Hunter and me. I felt I owed him that much. He listened and didn't judge at all. He kept his emotions under check and after our talk, we both took some deep breaths.

"I have one last request."

"What?"

"A last kiss before we part."

Before I could respond, he pulled me close to him and kissed me hard on the lips. Not feeling that connection between us that once used to make my heart pound and my blood boil, felt odd. The attraction was no longer there; it felt as if Jack were a stranger. As familiar as his lips once were, now they felt strange and uncomfortable. Hearing a rumble behind us, we turned and Hunter suddenly appeared with a dead expression on his face.

"I will make the choice easy for you, Maria. You will never see me again." He looked directly at me, and ignored Jack.

"Hunter!" The sound of his name echoed loud, as he startled me and wondered how long he had been observing us.

"It's okay, Maria. Your love for Jack has been between us all along. Good bye." Hunter flew away quickly, coldly and angrily, hiding all feelings like a vampire could. *That was his good-bye?* Wanting to smack him; hit him, anything but this, my inner voice was shouting *no, come back* because the thought of losing Hunter forever had never even crossed my mind. Jack's eyes firmly held mine.

"Go after him," Jack said, and watched me closely.

The realization that Hunter was gone, made me shout loudly.

"Hunter, wait!" I cried out into the dark. The only thing rustling was the wind, the quiet of the night drawing me toward it and the world crashing down upon me. Hunter.

"Jack, good luck. My love for you has changed."

"Go after him," Jack said. "I could see it in your eyes all along." Jack's eyes glistened with tears and a smidgen of understanding. "Good-bye, Maria."

"Good-bye, Jack."

Flying fast up into the sky, full of adrenaline, my voice was shouting Hunter's name over and over as my body took me back toward the direction we arrived. In my frenzy, a tree in front of me quickly appeared, and swaying to the right to avoid it I caught sight of his silhouette in the far distance and sped faster. "Wait! Hunter! Stop!"

Hunter turned his head at my voice and as soon as he saw me he shouted, "I think we've said all we had to say!"

"Well, there's more, much more!" My voice turned angry without my intention.

"More what?"

"More to say!" Feeling scared that he would not listen to me, he suddenly grabbed my hand and led me to a tree.

"Say what you want to say, then. You were kissing Jack. This is hard enough for me as it is." Knowing him well enough to know he was trying to remain composed, as his anger seethed through, gave me the push to tell him all.

"Hunter…you have no idea what you mean to me…until the thought of losing you forever hit me." I admitted quietly, trying to choose the right words. "And, that kiss meant absolutely nothing. It was our final good-bye."

He still seemed confused. "What are you saying?" His eyes narrowed.

"I can't lose you. You are the only one who understands me…I am not the same person."

"Go on," he said, leaning back against the tree trunk, his eyes suddenly warming up to mine. "But first tell me one thing…do you love Jack?"

"Well,"—my nerves were getting the better of me and I began fidgeting—"It's not that simple. He is with someone; he'll finally have a baby. Something you know, I never wanted. He has a new life now. So do I, with you. So much has changed." He examined my face closely. "I didn't have that *feeling*."

"Which feeling?" he asked, smirking.

"Remember when you read my palm when we first met?" My memory of meeting Hunter suddenly flashed back to me.

"Yes."

"Remember you said that in my forties my life would change…and that you had the same reading…well, it's you. It's always been you. You know my loneliness and you embrace it. You don't question it or try to make it right. You understand parts of me that even confuse me."

"You still haven't answered my question. Do you still love Jack?" His eyes were dark and scary. The fear in his eyes at this question consumed him.

"No, Hunter. No, it's over between us." My confession immediately relieved the tension in his face. He took a step closer, but I felt him holding back, unsure yet hopeful.

"Maria, are you telling me that—"

"Yes, Hunter! I'm telling you that my life is with you now. I've been fighting with my own feelings over you, not wanting to admit the truth."

He leaned further into the branches, his eyes suddenly turning tender. "Say it, Maria, just say it…"

Taking a deep breath, I let out the words that were holding me back, "Hunter, I love you."

He grabbed me and kissed me hard on my mouth, then my cheeks, my forehead, my hair…my insides went all jiggly like a schoolgirl. Looking up at him the air around him somehow changed, then suddenly out of nowhere a light appeared over his left shoulder and shined down on him.

My eyes widened…Hunter smirked and said in a quiet voice. "Do you see it now?" He smirked. "Do you see what I've been seeing from the first moment we met?"

"Yes." The light connected us.

"I see it too," he said, kissing the top of my head.

Lifting my chin and touching his face, my truth was finally coming out, "You've reached parts of me that no one has ever dared to reach." My hand caressed his cheek, and I finally let myself go, removing all the walls around me, and letting the light shine down upon both of us.

"Oh, Maria, you are so worth the wait," he said as his lips hungrily crushed mine, and Jack's love became my past; my human life that was let go. Hunter pulled away from me and looked deeply into my eyes. His eyes were dark yet seemed almost golden as the moonlight shone down and reflected a painting I'd seen long ago.

We stumbled out of that tree and Hunter led the way.

"I hope you like the rain," he hollered.

"Why?"

"We're heading back to London, England, m'lady," he joked as my giggles left me feeling free and content.

Hunter made me feel that anything could happen. Anything was possible. There was this freedom at finally opening up and saying goodbye to my past with Jack.

"Don't we have to tell Evan?"

"Fuck, Evan! We're on our own, baby, just you and me." He laughed. "Sooner or later we will contact him…we'll make him sweat for a while. Plus, my…what did you call them again? Gang of…"

"Cat's eyes."

"Yes, they can't live without me much longer. It's

already been a few months and for sure they are preparing the big move. I've told them many times to not get attached to possessions. It should be a fresh start anywhere we go…and after that…years and years of fresh starts."

"I love the sound of that."

"I love the sound of your honesty." He smiled.

Finally, accepting my entire existence felt safe for once.

Along with that acceptance, opening up to Hunter, to the night, and to the exciting new future ahead of us made me feel how everything would weave itself into this love. Hunter knew that once he had my body, it came with a soul united. He can deconstruct my soul, he can track me down, he can find me anywhere and the only place I *want* to be found is next to him with his arms wrapped around my waist firmly, tightly, living all our lifetimes in this one.

A word about the author…

Christina Strigas is an author and poet. She has written five novels, four poetry books, and one self-help book based on her popular quotes on Twitter. She writes romantic love poetry in a stream of consciousness narrative. Her novels vary from paranormal fiction to erotica and romance. She holds a BA in English Literature and a Teaching Degree. She teaches English and French in an elementary school and is a part-time Course Lecturer at McGill University. http://christinastrigas.com/

Thank you for purchasing
this publication of The Wild Rose Press, Inc.

For questions or more information
contact us at
info@thewildrosepress.com.

The Wild Rose Press, Inc.
www.thewildrosepress.com

www.ingramcontent.com/pod-product-compliance
Lightning Source LLC
Chambersburg PA
CBHW060532260626
47161CB00003B/866

* 9 7 8 1 5 0 9 2 3 8 9 4 1 *